Carnal Hunger...

The big male was suddenly in front of her. His feet were spread and his huge arms hung loosely at his sides.

Fear gripped Zia and held her rigid. The creature grabbed her and, swinging her over his shoulder, ran toward the rocks.

Zia kicked, screamed, struck at him awkwardly with her fists. He only snarled in annoyance and held her tighter. When they reached the clearing beyond the rocks, he threw her to the ground.

Suddenly he was tearing at her clothes, ripping and clawing the fabric away with incredible strength.

It can't be, she thought wildly. No, really, it can't be. But with horror she realized that it was plain enough what the beast meant to do—and there was no one to stop it....

THE BEAST

by

Walter J. Sheldon

FAWCETT GOLD MEDAL • NEW YORK

THE BEAST

© 1980 Walter J. Sheldon

Published by Fawcett Gold Medal Books, a unit of CBS Publications, the Consumer Publishing Division of CBS Inc.

ISBN: 0-449-14327-9

Printed in the United States of America

First Fawcett Gold Medal printing: March 1980

10 9 8 7 6 5 4 3 2 1

Chapter One

The engine had cut out completely now; there was only a sighing of air along the fuselage, and a harsh whistling from the tiny crack in the door fitting that Fred Garvey had never been able to caulk properly. The long snowbank in the narrow canyon was rising toward him.

My God, thought Fred Garvey, I believe I am going to die. I've had it, I've bought the farm. This is it.

It, man—*it*.

The mountain on his right towered several thousand feet above him. Its sharp slope plunged down toward the valley at an almost vertical angle, and a thick skirt of snow stopped abruptly at the edge of a clifflike formation that was the canyon wall. The snowbank he hoped to land upon stretched along the floor of the depression just under the cliff.

This is it.

Fred wondered why he did not fall apart now. He wondered why he sat here in the old Cessna 180, gliding earthward, still working wheel, flaps, and trim tabs with conditioned reflexes, while all his emotions were coagulated into a jellylike mass in his gut. As inevitable as death seemed, he still did not accept the idea of it. Other pilots crashed and died, but not old Fred Garvey. There had to be a miracle around somewhere, ready to drop into his lap in the next few seconds and save him. There always had been before.

His own fault, of course, that this was happening.

After depositing his passenger—a mining speculator he'd flown across the border and put into the bush of British Columbia—he'd refueled at the boondock strip just north of God-knew-where, and he'd filled up out of those rusting fifty-gallon drums they'd had on hand. Then he'd taken off on a route for home directly across the mountains, deciding to eyeball it instead of laying out a compass course and flying legs from checkpoint to checkpoint. The old ten-thousand-hour disease of overconfidence. It had brought down other pilots, and he knew it, dammit; he knew it all along.

To make it all worse, no one would know where he'd crashed—at least not for a long time. Strictly speaking, he should have gone through customs, but his passenger hadn't wanted that—business secrecy or something—and since there was a bonus, and since Fred had flown in and out illegally before with no great consequences, he'd simply taken off and headed for his destination.

And it had been such a fine day ... a big cold clear sky with all the sharp white mountaintops reaching into it. A day for old-style, seat-of-the-pants flying with all its delights. Point the bird where you wanted to go and let her take herself there.

Knowing that he could easily avoid the higher summits so clearly visible today, Fred had cruised at 7,500 feet, in and out among the peaks, making an indicated airspeed of around 130 knots, and consuming, as he knew from experience, a little over eleven gallons of fuel an hour. Until a few minutes ago, the airplane had handled fine, just fine. It was one of the early 180s, now more than twenty years old, and he'd bought it at a bargain price, even if he had gone into hock to do so. It was the perfect airplane for the bush. It carried four, and plenty of baggage. It was a high-wing tail-dragger you could plop down damn near anywhere, and it had a rate of climb that would almost pass a rocket. Fred Garvey loved the airplane more than any other object on the face of the earth. It hurt him to think of losing it now almost as much as it hurt him to think of losing himself.

When he'd first heard the engine stutter he'd looked around immediately for a place to put her down. He saw that a glide wouldn't take him out of the mountains. This country along the Canadian border and Washington State—the Kayatuk Wilderness, they called it—was some of the loneliest to be found this side of Alaska. Its murderous year-round weather had discouraged thorough exploration since the first trappers had come west a century and a half ago. And so, for a landing, he'd picked the least bad of a number of very bad places: a long, sloping snowbank in a high, hemmed-in canyon a few miles long and maybe half a mile wide. It was a place that quite possibly had never been trod upon by human feet before, and the hell of it was that it might never be trod upon by human feet again.

And now that he was only a hundred feet or so above the ground, the swirling clouds were closing in; he could no longer see the tops of the peaks that loomed far above him on all sides. It wasn't enough that he had to crash; now the whole sky wanted to fall down on him and hide him forever. There would come a day when hardly anybody would remember that Fred Garvey had ever existed, so what had it all amounted to?

Jesus!

Fred Garvey...a quietly cheerful little guy with a rolling, banty walk..."Cricket," they called him as a kid...flew L's in Vietnam...then came back to the country of big mountains and tall evergreens and the world's lousiest weather, which you learned to put up with for the sake of the rest of it. All the space you could want; plenty of elbow room. He'd bought his airplane and hung out his shingle. Garvey's Air Service. Fly you anywhere, God willin' and the cricks didn't rise. Sometimes God not so willin' and the cricks up to your ass. Out to the San Juans between

7

Vancouver Island and the mainland. Up into the bush of British Columbia. Across the Cascades to the plains of eastern Washington, where there was sagebrush and four distinct seasons. There was always some damn fool who wanted a ride to some damn place nobody ever heard of. So he flew them where they wanted to go and he made a living. Enough to keep himself and Eleanor and Denny from starving. Mainly, though, it was what he'd dreamed of doing all those years before the money he saved in Nam made it a reality.

What a hell of a time for everything to come to an end, thought Fred Garvey—just when things were going so well; right in the middle of the dream-come-true....

He was almost at the long, sloping snowbank now. He was close enough to see that it wasn't the kindly virgin snow it had seemed to be, but a rough-surfaced stretch dotted with rocks and scrub timber. He tried to judge the exact distance between the airplane and the snowbank. He pulled back and flared out at what he hoped was exactly the right moment. The airplane hung, as though floating. "Do it, baby!" muttered Fred Garvey.

There were crashing sounds so tremendous his ears couldn't absorb them. The world went into a series of blurred somersaults. He was wrenched away from all normal perception of time, distance, and being. A kaleidoscope spun within his skull. The taste in his mouth was queerly like that of green seawater. And then all of this fused together into the deepest blackness he had ever known....

He was trudging across crusted snow, his feet sinking with a crunching sound at each step. Snow, ice, and gray rock towered above him in dizzying perspective. He was in a field of strewn jagged-edged boulders.

Hell could have a landscape like this.

How long had he been stumbling forward? No

idea. The memory of each instant seemed to dissolve as the next one came along. There was a drug that did that. Hyoscine. He'd popped a little in Vietnam. That had probably been the least of his sins, which included breaking most of the Commandments and bending the rest. So naturally he'd probably end up in Hell, if Hell this was—

As in a dream, the scene changed abruptly. Walls of dark rock were hemming him in. He was in a cave—a shallow, squeezed-together cave with an irregular rocky ceiling high enough for him to stand erect. Outside the cave, gusting winds and torn pennants of sleet and snow were ripping in different directions. Now he remembered being in the storm outside and hurrying forward, looking for shelter.

It was dry in the cave. Not warm, but at least dry. He lowered himself to its floor, put his back against the wall, and drew the collar of his leather flying jacket up around his neck. Shivering, he curled himself into a fetal ball.

There was a gray light outside when Fred Garvey awoke; he had no idea how much later. His mind was still slipping in and out of gear. He felt a pain in his chest, and the pain sharpened when he poked it with his finger. Broken rib, no doubt. He was thirsty and hungry and dizzy and weak, and it took all the willpower he could rake out of the muck of his subconsciousness to make himself rise.

There was a small pile of something against the wall at the back of the cave. It seemed to be some kind of rubble until he blinked at it. Then he saw that it was a skeleton, its bones jumbled out of order. He went toward it with swaying steps and bent over it to examine it more closely. His eyes were drawn to the skull.

What a brute the owner of this skull must have been! He had never seen such immense fangs or such a long, heavy brow. Or such a queer braincase. There was a ridge along the top of the skull like those things

9

on Roman helmets. Grizzly? Probably. That was the only huge animal he knew of that might be in these parts. Though somehow it wasn't quite what he'd thought a grizzly skull would be like.

Anyway, this was no time to be reflecting upon the wonders of nature. The first thing was to find out where he was, and the second would be to get the hell away from there.

He stepped toward the gray light at the mouth of the cave. Resting one hand upon the rock, he looked out into the canyon—a large, irregular depression like a wide gouge in the mountain landscape. Its floor was strewn with rock and glacial moraine. He could not see through the swirling sleet to the other end of the canyon. He presumed the wreckage of his plane was somewhere down there. If he'd had his senses about him he never would have left it. That was always wisest, although plenty of airplanes had gone down in these mountains never to be found again.

The thing to do now was work his way downslope and find some lower land where there might be a road or a trail that would lead him to people. That might take days—even weeks. He wasn't sure what he'd do for food. Food? He reached into the pocket of his flying jacket. Package of Life Savers, half gone. He thumbed one loose and slipped it into his mouth. He remembered an old box of dried rations in the plane, enough for one meal. He'd stowed it away against the time when he might be lost, not really thinking that time would ever come. He'd definitely have to make his way back to the plane now.

He stepped out of the cave.

Some kind of motion to his left, maybe a hundred yards off, caught his eye. He turned his head. Through the gray, swirling weather he saw a creature walking slowly across his line of vision. The canyon wall was pocked with caves. Garvey saw more creatures near the caves, squatting or leaning on the rocks. Creatures of some awfully damned big

10

kind. Grizzly, maybe. No, not exactly. Something about them wasn't bear.

Slowly his mind put together the elements of what he was seeing. A moment later Fred Garvey, still staring, said in a whisper, "Good suffering Christ!"

He drew back quickly into the shadow of the cave. He continued to stare. The creature had stopped walking now. It had slithered up to a second creature, who had begun to pick at its back, grooming.

Fred had heard of bigfoot or sasquatch, he'd heard of it and shrugged it off. Like those Montagnard evil spirits in Vietnam. But here these sonsabitches were, right in front of his eyes, and he'd damned well better believe it.

He continued watching, stunned in his astonishment. Were the damned things dangerous? He'd better assume that. They looked fierce enough, if they did seem a bit sluggish. From this distance he had only an impression, not a clear delineation, of apelike features: massive projecting jaws, flattish noses, thick overhanging brows. They all had fur that could have been bear-color: black, reddish, brown, one tawny-yellow one. They didn't walk like apes. They stood fully erect and their arms didn't knuckle-drag on the ground. They were surely bigfeet, or whatever the hell the plural was—they *had* to be! If Fred Garvey hadn't been so wrapped up in the problems of his own survival he would have paused to take in the wonder of what he was seeing. But he had to get out of the cave and back to his plane. But if he stepped out they might spot him and attack.

He nervously ate another Life Saver and backed farther into the cave to give himself time to think. He turned and looked at the skeletal remains at the rear wall again. No telling how they got there, and fat lot of good it would do him to know anyway. But there must be people who'd *want* to know all about these creatures; no real trace of bigfoot had ever been found, and maybe there was some money in it if

11

somebody came up with some. The skeleton he was staring at would be that. He could hardly lug it out with him, however. Even the skull would be too much. How about a tooth, then? Some professor in China had reconstructed Pekin Man from a single tooth. Something like that. Okay, a tooth.

He found his jackknife in his trouser pocket. He bent down—feeling another twinge in his ribs—and began to pry at one of the molars in that grinning, lopsided skull. Somehow, when it got darker, he'd slip away from the cave without being seen by those creatures (Please, God, don't let the sonsabitches see me; just do this for me and I'll really behave from now on; yeah, I know, I made that promise before, but this time I really mean it), and then, when he finally got back he maybe could realize some money out of it and this whole stupid, fucking crash wouldn't be a total loss after all.

In the wet coolness, and in the invigorating sting of the sleet outside the cave, Self picked at the fur of Big Male's back. Those of her kind did not possess the concept of true naming, yet they did label each other in a dim way. She thought of herself as Self.

And in the group there was Old One, whose coat was turning silver, and Giver-of-Milk, at whose breasts she had once suckled, and Young One, who wasn't very tall yet and played foolishly all the time, and Broken Foot, who had once injured himself in a fall, and Yellow Fur and Skinny One and others she couldn't keep in her head all at once. Self had seen fifteen Times of Snow. She couldn't count them; her mind went up to three and after that anything was Many. Periodically, at a certain time of the moon, she showed blood and was therefore no longer a young one. She also tingled when males came near her, and sometimes just at the thought of them. Her vagina itched with desire. It hadn't happened yet, though. Big Male—the one she wanted most—already had a mate. Skinny One. And on the few occasions when there might have been an opportunity for Big Male to lay her down, straddle her, and penetrate her, Skinny One had managed to show up and interfere.

That would probably happen again this time, even if she managed to entice Big Male away from the caves and into the rocks. Just the same, she thought she ought to make the overture of grooming him. It had to happen sometime, and now was as likely a time as any.

Big Male belched sleepily and his stomach rumbled as Self's fingers scratched deep in his fur, probing for snarls or knots or fleas. He tended to be surly sometimes, but grooming usually put him into a better mood. If Self didn't manage to lure him behind the rocks today she might be able to get to him during one of the long sleeps in the Time of Snow, which was again approaching. Soon the Ones would be spending longer and longer periods in the caves, their metabolism slowed to a torpor, with only a few of them emerging now and then to forage for food at great distances from the Place of Safety—and that only when there was exceptional hunger. It was the way of the Ones for those who foraged to bring back whatever food they did not themselves consume and add it to the stores. Higher up the mountain, in rock crannies and ice caves, were the frozen carcasses of deer, coyote, rabbits, marmots, salmon, trout—a host of creatures. The wolverines were the only other animals who stored food in this manner, and they sometimes got into these supplies, but, as often as not, the wolverines themselves were caught and killed and cached away. When there was no meat there was always such fodder as bark or juniper buds, and in the warmer season berries and fruit from the lower forest land.

Big Male turned and regarded Self more closely with his deep-set, bloodshot eyes. She stretched her lips over her teeth. She made a soft, high-pitched

13

murmuring sound. Big Male grunted.

Self now backed away from Big Male, turned, took a couple of steps toward the rocks, then looked at him again. He stared back darkly for a moment, then stepped after her. She continued toward the rocks. There was one nest of boulders a short distance from the caves that was Self's favorite. She led the way there. Big Male came along behind her, sniffing and scowling, examining the ground along his path and pretending he'd been headed this way in the first place.

Self's pubic region was beginning to tingle in anticipation now. She wanted Big Male very much in this moment, but, oddly, she did not care a great deal for him in other moments. He was grouchy and stolid and lacked a sense of play. He was, however, the dominant male of the troop. He had long ago taken over from Old One, who now spent most of his time wandering about aimlessly and complaining about things in general with little growls. Self could remember, many snows ago, when Old One had had more vigor and, indeed, more expressiveness. He told the others of the many things he had seen and done. He communicated with a wide variety of vocal sounds, articulated as much as possible within the physical limitations of his huge jaw and his palate with its now-vestigial trace of a simian shelf. To these sounds he added broad gestures and facial expressions. Thus he told tales, and thus he was understood, slowly and imperfectly by some, more quickly by others. Self was always very quick to grasp his meaning. Big Male was usually quite dense about it.

"The Pink Skins," Old One would say, garrulously passing along his wisdom, if that was what it was. "You must take care when you see the Pink Skins."

There was a gesture that meant the Pink Skins: the hands came down a few inches apart in parallel lines to show the shape of these creatures, and this was accompanied by a trilling sound that reminded one of

14

their noisy vocal habits. The Pink Skins, as everyone knew, dwelt in profusion at lower altitudes. They lived in square-cornered caves they apparently made themselves. They also knew how to construct hard rivers across the land, and they rode upon these in wheeled creatures that had no animal smell—no telling where such things came from.

"The Pink Skins with their firesticks," Old One would say, making the gesture for "stick," and then for holding it to the shoulder, as the Pink Skins did when using it. "It is the greatest of all dangers. It can kill at a distance. As far as from here to that rock you can barely see. Beware of the firesticks of the Pink Skins. Take cover when you see them."

Old One would shuffle off to one side and sometimes pause to urinate or pass wind.

"But without the firesticks," he would continue, "the Pink Skins are weak. They cannot run fast, they cannot lift heavy rocks, and they cannot kill with their hands, twisting the neck, as we do. When they have no firesticks, the Pink Skins need not be feared."

Self wasn't sure how much of Old One's ramblings were true. She had never seen a Pink Skin, but then she had not yet foraged. Someday soon she would go out and search for food on an extended trip, as all the Ones did from time to time. That was the way of the Ones.

"Sometimes the Pink Skins have much hair, sometimes not," Old One had said. "They are covered with fur of many colors—it is not hairy like fur. Once, indeed, I even saw a Pink Skin whose skin was black!"

Now and then Old One's tales were truly hard to believe.

Well, thought Self, she didn't have to think about Old One and his curious statements now. That was one thing to be said for Big Male. He seldom burdened your brain with more than a few grunts or

15

squeals to express his passing moods.

He was crooning softly now as he came along behind Self. That meant that he wanted her.

In the hollow crevice among the jumble of rocks, Self lay upon her back, spread her legs, and extended her arms toward Big Male. That was another strange thing Old One had once said. He'd seen two of the Pink Skins copulating in the woods, and he said that they'd done it face to face with the female on the bottom. Only the Ones and the Pink Skins, among all creatures, did it that way.

Big Male's flattish nose twitched in a rubbery way. Saliva drooled from one corner of his mouth. He lowered his eight hundred pounds of weight atop Self, and she wished that he would do it more gently. He began to thrust and squirm with his hips, trying to force them into the fork of her opened legs. His penis, now erect, was short, considering his size, and he had difficulty finding her aperture with it. She reached down, grabbed it, and slipped it into place. He shoved his pelvis forward wildly and missed. She put it into the slot once more. He gave a mighty thrust this time, and entered.

Self let out a cry that was half pain, half pleasure. She hadn't expected it to hurt this much. Big Male kept working back and forth, rhythmically. The sounds he was making were breathy moans, one to each thrust.

To Self's surprise and disappointment, it was over with very quickly. It seemed to her that Big Male had pushed back and forth only a few times before he gave out a shuddering groan much louder than the rest and then held himself jammed against her while she felt his warm sperm spurt into her vagina and dribble out, mingling with her own fluid and sliding down along the crack of her buttocks, where it felt wet and cold. The great explosion of pleasure her Giver-of-Milk had sometimes mentioned had not manifested itself. Maybe Giver-of-Milk was wrong; maybe there was no such explosion. She wanted to go on and on—reach for that explosion—and she began working herself back and forth on the nubbin of Big Male's penis, still murmuring in pain and pleasure. Big Male's penis was getting soft. He growled and tried to withdraw it. She grabbed him by the hips to pull him back. He withdrew forcefully, then reached out and cuffed her on the side of the head.

She yammered at Big Male—hostile, cursing sounds. He cuffed her again, a little harder. She bit at his hand, but he moved it back too quickly for her teeth to catch.

Big Male rose away from her. He grunted, turned, and stepped out of the nest of rocks. Self stayed in place, breathing hard, making soft, whimpering sounds to herself. The whole experience had not been at all what she'd expected. Why, then, did she wish to do it again and wish that Big Male would come back to her? The tingle in her loins had turned into an awful hunger. She reached down, inserted two fingers in her vulva, and began to work them up and down upon her clitoris, hoping she could find the great explosion of pleasure this way. Giver-of-Milk had cuffed her before for trying this, but Giver-of-Milk wasn't here now, and, anyway, she, Self, was long past the time of obedience.

Fred Garvey lurched along the scrabbled turf of a lower valley, stumbling, staggering from side to side, lifting his head now and then to stare into the distance, hoping he'd find something toward which he could direct his steps. There was nothing but more distance, all of it essentially the same as that he'd already covered.

There was little awareness left in him now. He was driven only by an urge to keep moving downslope, the way water ran. A while ago he'd been following a stream; now he seemed to have lost it. At the moment he did not know in what compass direction he was traveling, although earlier this day (or had it been the day before?) the sun had appeared for a while and he'd tried to take rough bearings. There was a thick buzzing in his head that kept him from thinking clearly. It fogged the memories that tried to float through his mind.

It had become darker toward nightfall when he'd been in the cave—he remembered that now. He had slipped out of the cave cautiously and fearfully, glancing constantly toward the cliff face where he'd seen the creatures. He hadn't seen them, and that meant, thank God, that they hadn't seen him. After he'd made his way down the gorge, the moon had begun to shine through a break in the clouds, and he'd been able to discern some of the vague shapes of his surroundings. He had not found his plane, which, he was sure, was still somewhere in the canyon. He had trudged along a swift-running, narrow stream in the center of the canyon. Suddenly the stream had entered a tunnel in the cliff face at the lower end of the canyon. In the tunnel he'd found a precarious shelflike passageway beside the stream. When the passageway became too narrow for him to negotiate it safely in the darkness, he had wedged himself into a wide crack and slept, huddling upon himself to keep warm.

There had been light, in the morning, from the other end of the tunnel. He'd made his way to the tunnel's mouth and had seen the stream dropping several hundred feet in a narrow waterfall. He was in a heavy daze now; he could not remember much about climbing down the rocks beside the waterfall. It seemed to him that just before he'd reached the bottom he must have slipped on the wet rocks and fallen. After that there were new pains somewhere inside him.

His gut burned hollow with hunger. He'd drunk from the cold streams; he'd finished his Life Savers and he'd tried to eat what scrubby weeds he'd found in this high, barren land. He was dirty and he stank. His chest hurt terribly with every breath now, and he had to take shallower and shallower breaths to avoid pain that would be unbearable.

Hey, God.

Look.

I know you're busy. You've got problems, like, the world and humanity, and all that shit. But you've got to do something for me now. Let me find somebody or let somebody find me. Is that too much to ask? Look, God, I came this far, so you just can't let all that effort go completely to waste. And this I ask in Jesus' name, who is your only begotten son, or however the hell they usually say it—

He stopped and swayed and lifted his head to look upward.

"You hear me, God?"

The energy he spent in order to shout left him so weak that he almost toppled. He stood there and kept swaying and wondered if enough energy would flow back into him to allow him to stumble forward again.

The sky he had shouted at was gray and silent.

Chapter Two

Deputy Joe McBay gave the dispatcher a ten-six, swung from the car with its Cedar County sheriff's insignia on the door, and went into Pookey's Roadside Rest, where the jukebox was playing hard rock, as always. Yolanda, behind the counter, saw him coming and by the time he reached the stool a cup of coffee was in front of him, black, the way he liked it.

"How you doin', Joe?" said Yolanda, smiling. She was a leggy girl with sawdust blond hair in tight ringlets. Her green sweater was tight on her breasts.

"Oh, pretty good," said Joe. "How's yourself?"

"Makin' it," said Yolanda, with a shrug.

Funny, thought Joe, they always greeted each other in this casual way, even though they'd now been to bed together maybe five or six times. She liked it and he liked it. Some of the other birds he'd made out with here in Pickettsville pushed him for a more permanent relationship, and Yolanda probably wanted one, too, but she didn't make a project out of it. She was a little older than he was; mid-thirties, maybe. Ben Franklin had been right in his praise of and preference for older women. And she wasn't all *that* old.

"Makin' it," said Yolanda. "Gettin' along."

"Glad to hear that," said Joe.

"How's it going tonight?"

"Quiet," Joe said.

Joe McBay had the build of a light-heavyweight boxer. His deltoids sloped down from his neck to make his shoulders look narrower than they were. His nose, broken in football practice at Colorado State, was vaguely flattened and a little off center. His hair was dark and he wore it neatly to just below the tips of his earlobes. A biweekly hairstyling at the best salon in town was one of the few extravagances he allowed himself.

He took out one of his little cigarette-shaped cigars, which he puffed but did not inhale since he'd quit regular cigarettes a couple of years ago.

"Hear anything about Fred Garvey?" asked Yolanda.

Joe shook his head.

"Jeez, that's too bad," she said. "I know he's a real good buddy of yours."

"Yeah. Fred's a good troop."

"You couldn't get me up in one of those things," said Yolanda. "I mean, like Fred flies, you know?"

Joe shrugged. "Safer than cars, statistically. And Fred's one hell of a good pilot."

"But he's lost, right?"

"I guess so." Joe sipped coffee. "He'll turn up."

"You two were together in Vietnam, right?"

"For a while. Fred was the flyboy. I was just a grunt. He brought me here, you know."

"To Pickettsville?"

"Yup. I was looking for someplace to go, and we were in touch, and he said this was just the place."

"That was lucky. You're doing pretty good here, I'd say."

"Oh, I don't know. Maybe."

"The way they're talking, you'll be our next sheriff."

"Don't count on it."

"You want to be, don't you?"

"I guess so," said Joe. "But there's no reason Zack Winfield won't get the votes. He's done a pretty good job for fifteen years."

"They ought to elect you instead. And you really

21

ought to run. Everybody in the county knows about you now. After that big drug bust, I mean."

Joe laughed a little. "It wasn't all that big. Truckload of grass, stashed in a farmhouse, and I got a tip on it. Very peaceful bust. No gun, nothing like that. I'm glad to say. The newspaper made it sound bigger than it was."

"Well, it was big enough. And *I'm* going to vote for you."

He laughed fully. "I'll spank your nice little bottom if you don't."

"That'll be nice," said Yolanda, grinning. She moved off to bring another customer a coconut cream pie. Everybody said the coconut cream pies at Pookey's Roadside Rest were really good. They came out of a Seattle bakery. Yolanda came back again. "Seriously, Joe," she said, "I wish you would run for sheriff. I mean, more pay and prestige and everything. It'll be nice to say I know the sheriff. I mean *know* him. You know what I mean."

"I know what you mean, but don't spread it around too much. The church crowd around here carries a lot of votes. And if there's one thing they can't stand it's for somebody to enjoy himself."

"Well, you've got to watch yourself, I guess," agreed Yolanda. She was leaning over the counter now, staying awhile. "Anyway, you wouldn't have to stop at just being sheriff. I mean, what with your college and everything you could move up. Go to Olympia. Maybe, even, like governor or something one of these days."

"If that's what I want," said Joe, smiling.

"Isn't it?"

"I'm not sure it's my bag."

"Well, what *is* your bag."

"I'm not sure of that, either. Wish I were."

"More coffee?"

"Nope. Gotta hit the road."

"See you Saturday?" asked Yolanda.

"Maybe. But I might pull some duty Saturday night. I'll let you know, okay?"

"Duty with some other chick, I'll bet."

"It's a possibility."

"You're a louse," said Yolanda, laughing. "But then all men are."

As Joe approached his car again, he heard the dispatcher calling him. Deputy Carol Jorgensen was the dispatcher. Nice voice. Figure a little hefty, but not too bad. He'd have to look into that sometime. He hoped she wouldn't turn out lez, the way that dispatcher in L.A. had. Long ago, that, not so much in time as in spirit. Another world. One he'd left with a bitter taste in his mouth. But it was fading. Coming to Pickettsville had probably been the right thing.

"Yeah, this is unit four," he said into the mike.

"Joe, listen," said Carol's voice. "You wanted to know right away. They picked up Fred Garvey."

"God, that's good! Where?"

"Out on a logging road. He must have walked in."

"That's a relief. How is he?"

"I don't know, for sure. They took him to St. James' Hospital."

"I'll go see him."

"You're on duty, remember?"

"Don't remind me."

"Okay. How about if I log you in for an official call at the hospital, just to see if everything's okay?"

"Thanks. You're a very good bird, and I'll see that you're properly rewarded one of these days." Joe grinned.

"That's one reward I might turn down," said Carol. Not mad, though.

"Ten-four," said Joe.

That was one thing he liked about this job. The informality. There was a bureaucratic stiffness in big-city police departments you didn't run into here. There were just as many good guys back in the city as there were out here in the boondocks; their hands

23

were tied a little tighter, that was all.

Or was he kidding himself again? Trying to justify his coming here again? Frankly, he missed a lot he'd had back in Los Angeles. The excitement, the professionalism, the promise—the heady air of the big time. And here, in this town of fifty thousand or so way to hell and gone in the extreme northwest corner of the continental contiguous United States there was a sense of having been exiled. The continental, contiguous United States of America. In his mind's ear, he started to hear the melody of *The Stars and Stripes Forever.* He thought of the only words he knew to that tune.

Be kind to your web-footed friends,
For a duck may be somebody's mother—

They'd sung it in Nam sometimes. After all the dirty songs. Not that they sang much. Nam didn't produce any songs of its own. The Civil War generated a lot of songs, and World War I a few less, and World War II not so many, and Korea hardly any. As disillusionment grew, the songs died out. McBay's index of some fucking thing or other. He could go back to school, develop it, and get a Ph. D. Guys had done it with lesser notions.

But he didn't suppose that was his bag, either.

The administrative person at the desk at St. James' was artificially sweet and seemed to be groping for reasons why Joe couldn't go upstairs to see Patient Garvey. She gave up finally. Joe walked into Fred's semiprivate room, which, for the time being, he had to himself. "Five minutes," the old bag of a nurse on that floor said. Fred was lying there with tubes stuck into his arms. One up his nose even.

"Hey, Fred. It's me. Joe."

"Joe?"

Fred's eyes were hollow and his voice was hoarse. He was so thin and wasted away he looked not like a cricket but a praying mantis, turning brown at the end of its season.

"Jesus, I'm glad you made it," said Joe. "You're going to be okay. You're going to be just fine."

"Bullshit," said Fred.

"No, listen. Seriously. You're going to make it, Fred. I'll whip your ass if you don't."

"Come down closer, Joe. Talking's hard. Gotta whisper."

"Sure, Fred. But you don't have to talk. You can tell me all about it later."

"I might not make it, Joe. I really might not make it. I don't know how I know, but I know."

"Don't talk like that, Fred. Hang in there."

"But just in case. You have to know. You ought to go find those things. Somebody ought to. Might as well be you."

"What things, Fred?"

"Bigfeet," said Fred Garvey.

"What?"

"Bigfeet. You know, sasquatch. Those apes."

"Oh, for Christ's sake, now," said Joe.

"I'm serious. I saw the goddam things."

"We can talk about it later."

"No. Now, Joe. Look, I didn't want to say anything to those guys who picked me up. You know how people are. You say anything about bigfoot and they think you're crazy."

"You rest now," said Joe.

"They're in the mountains," said Fred. "In the Kayatuk. Somewhere below the border, west of Stanton Lake, east of the Mt. Baker line."

"That's a lot of territory."

"I know. But I'm not sure exactly where I went down. It would be on a course from Trapper Springs in B.C. to Pickettsville. There was big, high kind of a canyon, all boxed in. You get to it through a waterfall that comes out of a tunnel. Maybe some other entrance, but that's how I got out."

"The nurse gave me five minutes," said Joe, looking at his watch. "It's up."

"Don't go. Jesus! Please don't go—let me finish!"

"All right, Fred. Make it fast, okay?"

"Ten or twelve of the goddam things. Like big apes, just like they say. In caves. I saw them, Joe!"

"I wouldn't doubt you saw a lot of things."

"Don't patronize me, you bastard!"

"Take it easy, Fred. Joe, here, your old buddy, remember? Listen. You get better. I'll come back and we'll work it out."

"I've got proof, Joe. A goddam tooth."

"What do you mean, a tooth?"

"In my jacket. In the closet there, I think."

"Okay, Fred. You've got a tooth. You want me to look at it?"

"You take it, Joe. You get it analyzed or something. It'll show I wasn't seeing things."

"I didn't say you were, Fred. Okay, I'll take care of the tooth."

He knew his voice lacked conviction. So did Fred, bad off as he was.

"Goddammit, Joe!" Fred grimaced as he tried to lift himself, then gave up and fell back again. "Don't you see what I'm getting at?"

"No, not exactly."

"It's Eleanor and Dennis."

"What about them?"

"They're down in Seattle, with Eleanor's folks. I talked to her on the phone, though the goddam hospital didn't want me to. She went there to wait till I showed up. Don't blame her. Anyway, they're on their way here. Look, Joe, the thing is, I've got hardly any insurance. If I don't make it, Eleanor's in bad shape."

"Don't worry about that, Fred. You're going to make it."

"But, you see, in case I don't. She's got to be taken care of. She and Denny."

"Fred," said Joe, "if anything ever happened, I'd always be around."

"I know that, Joe. And I appreciate it. You'd help and all that; I know you would. But she's going to need more than just a hand with things. As much money as she can get, that's what she's going to need.

More than you've got, Joe; more than I'd want from you. So you see how it is with that crazy ape out there."

"What's the ape got to so with this?"

"Money. For whoever finds bigfoot. There has to be. From the scientists or the university or the government or somebody. Or the zoo or the circus or whatever. If I thought I'd pull through I'd go after it. But if I don't pull through, I want Eleanor to have whatever there is. You keep some for yourself, of course, but just see that Eleanor's taken care of, okay?"

"Fred, you know I'll do whatever I can. But it's not going to be necessary. Now for God's sake, get some rest."

"The tooth, Joe. In my jacket. You take it now. I don't want somebody else to get it if I cash in."

"Fred, I'll take the tooth if it makes you feel better."

"Sure, Joe. Sure." He clamped his eyes shut, hard upon his pain. He breathed brokenly and laboriously.

"I'll be back tomorrow," said Joe.

Fred gave a barely perceptible nod and seemed to sink back even more deeply into his pillow.

"You get better. Okay, flyboy?" said Joe.

He had the feeling Fred hadn't heard him.

He checked the closet on the way out and found the tooth in the right-hand slash pocket of Fred Garvey's leather flying jacket. He hefted it in his hand and stared at it. Big, as teeth went. Otherwise, it didn't seem so damned remarkable to him. Just a back tooth from some animal, that was all. A bear tooth or maybe an elk tooth would be about this size. He stuck it into his own pocket.

The floor nurse met him as he came out of the room. She was country-mama fat, had chemically blond hair and a mole on the right side of her chin. Her blue nameplate said Abigail Collins, RN. "You were more than five minutes," she said sternly.

"Yeah. He needed more than five minutes."

27

"He's a very sick man—internal injuries—and he needs complete rest and quiet. They'll operate in the morning."

"If it's so damned urgent why don't they operate now?"

"The doctors know what they're doing," she said.

"Well, I'll be back tomorrow."

"Don't count on seeing him. He may be in intensive care."

"I'll be back anyway. Look, tell me something. He thinks he's dying. Is he?"

"There's a very good chance that he is." She said it almost triumphantly. It proved her point: that she was right, always right, and if somebody had to die to demonstrate that, well, that was too bad, but she was still right.

He needed a drink. It would make him stop thinking crazy things like that. It would dull his senses and make him a little more sane. That was what sanity was: dullness, conformity. Aw, to hell with it. "Good night, Abigail," said Joe, and went on down the hall.

At the end of his shift—the graveyard, midnight to eight—Joe put the sheriff's car in the garage under one wing of the county courthouse and went to the locker room to change out of his uniform. The uniform, dove-gray with lavender piping, always seemed to him gaudy for a law-enforcement officer, and whenever he wore its broad-brimmed hat he thought he ought to be in front of a microphone playing a guitar and singing songs of infidelity on the range. He'd liked the plain blue-black of the L.A.P.D. much better. It made you feel more like a cop. But he wouldn't complain about that or any of the other minor irritations of his job as deputy sheriff for Cedar County, State of Washington, county seat Pickettsville, Pop. 48,379 last time they took count and probably more now. He was still glad to be here; he was still lucky to have this job. Considering all

28

that had happened back in Los Angeles, he was lucky.

He got into his Levi's slacks and checked wool Pendleton shirt. In these parts that was almost another uniform. Even on close-to-formal occasions. Put on a suit and you were either a fag or an outlander. He looked at his off-center nose and gray eyes in the mirror on the back of his locker door. Bulldog chin, Neanderthal brows. Texture of skin: old barn door. One a shotgun had blasted at before. That was the acne he'd had as a kid—the Clearasil never would touch it. And it was lucky he was a man, he thought, because if he'd been a woman he'd have been really ugly. The women's-lib gals had a point there: it was unfair. Ugly men could be attractive to women, but not the other way around. Because women were sex objects. Well, unfair or not, he'd be damned if he'd stop seeing them as sex objects. Where was he supposed to point his libido—at snakes?

The squawk box high on the wall said, "Deputy McBay, please report to Sheriff Winfield's office."

Joe frowned—he'd hoped to get out fast and fix himself a big breakfast in his mobile home at the court—and went upstairs.

"Come in, Joe, huh?" said Sheriff Zack Winfield from behind his desk. "Come in and sit down. Make yourself comfortable, huh?"

Zack Winfield was tall and hefty and had a shock of thick white hair which he wore just short enough to make it bristle. Instead of the gaudy uniform of his department, he sported wool shirts and broad suspenders with the names of chainsaw or tractor companies on them to hold up khaki-drab oiled-canvas logger's pants. Heavy, cleated logger's boots completed his trademark. A lot of people in Cedar County would vote for a man simply because he'd once been a logger.

Joe glanced at his watch, hoping Winfield would get the message. He doubted it. Zack wasn't oversen-

29

sitive to such signals.

"Pretty quiet last night?" asked Winfield.

"Routine," said Joe.

"Uh-huh," said Winfield, nodding. He began to stuff a corncob pipe with Grainger. "The quiet nights always drag out, huh? I know. Used to do it myself. When I started out we had only eleven men. To cover the whole damn county twenty-four hours a day. It was a lot rougher in those days."

"It must have been," said Joe noncommittally.

"Still like the job?" asked the sheriff.

"Sure. Why wouldn't I?"

"Oh, I don't know. Just a feeling I get, maybe. After the big city, Pickettsville's kind of small potatoes, huh? Of course, we're growing. All the building going on and new industries coming in. Lots of Canadian money coming over the border. That part's good. Trouble is, we're starting to get big-city problems. You can't hardly park downtown anymore, and there's a new element moving in. Hippies. All kinds of—you know—ethnics and people like that. More darkies all the time. We always had Indians on that reservation right next to town, practically, but, hell, they keep to themselves pretty much."

"I'd say all this was good for the town," said Joe. "It's been too bland. Like white bread. All the goodness refined right out of it."

"Don't get me wrong, huh?" said Winfield. "I'm as much for minorities as anybody else. I never wanted to take away anybody's rights. But I got to admit the county was a lot more peaceful before it started to bust out at the seams. But in the old days everybody knew everybody else. I mean, you could depend on everybody, huh?"

"What's on your mind, Zack?" asked Joe, looking at his watch again. Back in L.A., Zack's counterpart would have been "sir," but here everybody expected first names. They'd be uncomfortable if you didn't use them.

"Well, nothing, really," said Winfield. "I just

wanted to check on how you felt about everything. And about this talk you might like to run for sheriff. I guess I could just let it go and not say anything, but that's not my way, huh? If I want to know something, I go right to the horse's mouth to get it."

"Okay, Zack," said Joe, nodding. "Let me tell it like it is, too. Chet Anders *has* talked to me about running for sheriff. That's no secret. He says you might be thinking of retiring. Maybe I would like to run. I don't know for sure yet. I haven't made up my mind."

"That's fair enough," said Winfield. His pipe had gone out, and he reached for a kitchen match from the box on the desk to relight it. "Chet Anders is an old fart," he said. "And a lawyer. I never trusted lawyers. You call them in and you make things worse, huh? Now he thinks he's a political boss. Big party chairman. Okay, let me give you my side of it. I have no intention of retiring. I built this goddam department up and, by God, I'm gonna stay with it!"

"Well, Zack," said Joe, "look at it this way. There's an election coming up and *somebody's* going to run against you. If it's me, I don't see how that changes the basic situation."

"Maybe not," said Winfield. "Except that, well, it's different. You came here with a cloud hanging over you, you might say, and we took you in. No complaint—you've done a good job. Some college guys are pretty smart-ass, and you haven't thrown that around too much. But to tell you the truth, Joe, I'm not about to give up my job to some newcomer just because Chet Anders wants to put in a figurehead and run the county himself."

"He'd never do that with me," said Joe, shaking his head.

Winfield smiled a little, softening the lines of his hard, square face. "You say that now. Probably you mean it. But when you sit where I'm sitting things look different, huh? You don't get away from obligations."

"I know how it works. Chet still wouldn't run me.

Nobody would."

"Okay, Joe, whatever you say. Just wanted to sound you out. You want the truth? That's what I believe in—the truth. You'd have a pretty fair chance in the election. The way Chet Anders built up that drug bust of yours—Christ, he made it sound like the French Connection all over again—and the way he goes around spreading nasty rumors about me, you just might have a chance. From my standpoint, it would be better if you weren't on the force."

"Is that what you called me in for? To give me a pink ticket?"

"Now, don't jump to conclusions, huh, Joe? With all the regulations we've got now I can hardly fire anybody. In the old days I could run things the way they were supposed to be run and no questions asked. Besides, Chet Anders would make real hay out of it if you got dismissed for anything short of raping the mayor's daughter. And I don't think you'd do anything like that, huh? I mean I'm sure you're smart enough to keep your nose real clean. Exceptionally clean, maybe. Do everything by the book, huh?"

Joe nodded. "I get it."

"Good. Glad we understand each other."

"Am I supposed to say thanks for the warning?"

"Aw, come on now, Joe. No warning or anything like that, huh? I just wanted to clear the air a little. And maybe show you it might be better not to listen to everything Chet Anders says. Because if I'm reelected—and the odds are still in favor of that—you'd be in a pretty good position here if you were on my side all along. There's one thing I don't do, and that's forget my obligations. So let me know, Joe. Let me know what you decide, huh?"

"I will as soon as I decide it." Joe shuffled his chair back and stood up. Zack Winfield nodded, and Joe knew the interview was over.

In his mobile home—the twelve-foot-wide model with two bedrooms—Joe watched his sausages fry.

He knew that he wouldn't sleep for several hours, and that was the trouble with the graveyard shift: you could never set up a proper sleeping pattern the week you were on it. This morning, as usual, he'd try to kill the time reading before he dropped off. He glanced at the bookshelf in the living room, which was really part of the kitchen, or was it vice versa? Maybe he'd read up on forensic medicine today. Maybe this month's *Outdoor Life*.

The phone rang.

"Yeah?" Joe said into it.

"Morning, Joe. Chet. Hope you weren't sleeping."

"Not yet. What's on your mind, Chet?"

"Got a little something for you here. Hope you can find time for it."

Chet Anders' voice was round and full, like the man himself. It had the beam of his continuous smile in it. It was also, like that smile, faintly contrived— there for effect and not just because it came out that way naturally. For all that, Joe thought, it must have been pretty effective in a courtroom. Chet had apparently done quite well as an attorney. And he seemed to have all the spare time in the world to devote to his local political party chairmanship. "Okay, Chet," said Joe, trying for the sake of politeness not to sound annoyed, "what is it?"

"The university wants a speaker on police procedure. One of their criminology classes, or something like that. I said I'd try to get you. You'll get a play in the paper out of this, and every little bit helps when you're running for office."

"Chet, I haven't said I'll run yet."

"But you haven't said no, either. Also, there's a small fee. You can use a couple of bucks. Anybody can."

"I've already got a couple of bucks."

"Like the nigger, eh?" said Chet, laughing.

Joe frowned. "What are you talking about?"

"You know. The old joke. The nigger's laying there and the boss says if you get up I'll give you a quarter,

33

and he says, 'Boss, ah already got a quota!'"

Joe grimaced. Chet couldn't see that, but he could hear the silence.

"I thought it was funny," Chet said. "Hey, Joe, you're not one to get uptight over ethnic jokes, are you? Goddam, a man used to be able to enjoy a joke once in a while."

"Chet, let's not beat it into the ground."

"Well, don't go and get on this hooray-for-the-minorities kick, just because of the trouble you had when you shot that black guy. That is actually an asset for you, here in God-fearing middle America."

"Chet, I just got off shift, and I'm not in the mood for lessons in politics. If the university wants a speaker, I'll do it, okay? But not to get votes. I haven't really decided whether or not I'll run yet. You know that."

Chet Anders chuckled. "Hey, partner, you can play coy with the electorate if you want to, but you don't have to with me. Anyway, how about next Thursday morning?"

"Okay. I'll be off duty then."

"Good. I'll set it up. See you later, Joe."

Joe went back to the sausages, which had burned a little while he'd been on the phone. He set them aside on paper towels and broke two eggs in the pan.

He'd be ninety years old one of these days, he was thinking, and somehow that incident in L.A. would come back to bug him. Outside of maybe some Charleys in the tall grass in Vietnam, where he'd sprayed automatic fire, he'd never killed anyone. Chances were fair he hadn't killed any of those unseen Charleys, either. So the only one he'd ever had to kill in all his life had turned out to be a black man. A thoroughly innocent black man, at that. And to Chet Anders this was an asset.

He fished with the pointer on the FM band and found some classical music from a Vancouver station. All the Pickettsville stations were either hard rock or country-and-western. This station was playing Mahler's Second. All those little folk tunes in it fooled you. You didn't hear the real guts of the thing till after you'd been listening awhile. He loved Mahler. And if he ever did run for sheriff he'd probably better keep *that* from the voters.

He took the tooth Fred Garvey had given him, dropped it on the table beside his plate, and contemplated it as he ate.

Fred didn't make up wild stories, especially to Joe. They'd hit it off from the beginning in Nam. Same casual and maybe faintly sardonic approach to life. Good communication. They didn't have to explain things to each other in a lot of detail in order to be understood. And trust. Trust in each other they both sensed somehow. When Joe had resigned from the L.A.P.D., and had told Fred about it on the phone, Fred had said, "Why don't you come up here? Great country and very relaxed. No problems like you've got down there. I hear they're looking for sheriff's deputies. I'll look into it for you."

That day in Nam, Sergeant Joe McBay had been pinned down in a clearing, and Charley's bullets, fired from jungle cover on higher ground, were ripping the elephant grass all around him. Along came this little liaison plane and made the goddamnedest, hairiest landing Joe had ever seen. He climbed aboard and Fred flew him out. Later, they got drunk in Saigon together and traded whores. That was symbolic. It made them blood brothers. Anyway, they got along.

Fred wouldn't lie to him about seeing big apes in the mountains, but he might have been hallucinating. Delirious. And the tooth he found could have come from almost anywhere.

He turned it over several times in his hand, examining it.

Joe found the small office—Room 207—down the second-floor corridor of Underwood Hall, the Life Sciences Building. When he'd mentioned bigfoot they'd referred him to a Miss Zia Marlowe. The young woman sitting at the desk in Room 207 looked up as he entered. She was trim and compact. She had short-cut raven-black hair. She wore an off-shoulder blouse and a heavy Navaho concha belt.

"Hi," he said.

She had a bright, friendly smile. He noticed a faintly oriental cast to her eyes. Eurasian? Part Indian? Anyway, exotic. "Hi," she answered.

"I'm Joe McBay, with the sheriff's department."

"Sheriff's department? What have I done now?"

He smiled to show her she hadn't done anything he knew about. "I understand you're an expert on this bigfoot creature."

"Well, yes, I suppose I am."

"I figured there'd be somebody here at the university who would know about bigfoot. Only—" he broadened his smile—"I figured it would be somebody different. You know: a gray beard, leather patches on the elbows—"

"Maybe if I grow a gray beard and get some leather patches they'll take me seriously."

"Sorry," said Joe. "I didn't mean it as a jab."

"I know you didn't. And I didn't mean to shift defensively. I *do* get taken unseriously, though. Especially about bigfoot. Maybe that'll change when I get my union card."

"Union card?"

"Doctorate. Without which, in this business, you just ain't."

"But you're an anthropologist, right?"

"I teach it, as a graduate assistant. While I work on the Ph. D. Now. What can I do for you, Mr. McBay?"

"Joe."

"All right. Joe."

"Maybe you can check something out for me." He took the tooth from his pocket and put it on the desk in front of her. "What would you say this is?"

She turned it around several times, examining it.

"A tooth, obviously. A premolar, I think. From some animal."

"From a bigfoot?"

"It could be. But since I've never seen a bigfoot tooth before—I don't think anybody else has, either—I can't be sure. Where did you get it?"

"That's kind of a long story."

"I've got time to listen."

"Okay, fair enough." He looked around at the small office with its crammed bookshelves and table covered with skull replicas near the window. On a separate shelf were plaster casts of huge footprints. Over her desk was a map of the Northwest with colored pins in it. He looked at her again. "Can we sit down for coffee someplace?"

"The faculty lounge," she said. "Lousy brew, but it's the only game in town."

He liked her walk as he accompanied her out of the building and across a flagstone-paved quadrangle to the faculty lounge. It was brisk and pert, like the rest of her. They traded small talk and a few vital statistics. As a small child, she'd been raised in New Mexico. Her name, Zia, was after an Indian pueblo there. Her mother had been old New Mexico Spanish. Right down from the conquistadores, she had always said. How did she happen to be here at Cascade University? That was another long story.

She was right about the coffee. The Styrofoam cups made it even lousier. He sat across from her at a small Formica-topped table.

"I thought maybe I'd go after some advanced degrees once," he said, "but I got busy and didn't."

"Oh? What was your field?"

"Sociology. Minor in police science."

"I'm encouraged. I didn't know we had anything like that in the sheriff's department here."

"You'd be surprised about cops. Lawyers, psychologists, and one I knew who used to win prizes with flower arrangements."

"It can't be true!" she said, laughing with delight. "It is well known that all cops are fascist brutes!"

"And all anthropologists have beards and leather elbow patches."

"Well," said Zia, "now that we know each other, what's the story on this tooth? I don't dare hope it's real, you know. That would be more luck than even an honest, hardworking, humble scientist such as myself deserves."

"A friend of mine found it," said Joe. "He swears he took it from a bigfoot skull. He's not some kind of nut, and I've always believed whatever he said before. But this time it sounded so far out I just had to check." Some instinct was keeping him from telling her more than that for the moment. Some kind of reticence linked, in some way, to the lurking suspicions about everyone and everything that infected any cop after a while. Call it an occupational disease.

Zia Marlowe examined the tooth again. "Joe, I can't tell you too much offhand. I'm not an expert on primate dentition—if this is primate. It could be. You'll notice the five cusps, arranged in a Y pattern. That's anthropoid or hominid, usually. Oddly enough, it's even more primitive than the four-cusp pattern we find in monkeys. Man has it, apes have it, and their common ancestor undoubtedly had it."

"Then you don't think it's from a bear or some other animal?"

"I don't know with absolute certainty. But this has exciting possibilities. Maybe it could shake a few foundations and knock the ivy loose on a few academic halls."

"I take it nobody ever came up with a bigfoot tooth before, is that right?"

"Exactly," said Zia. "The creature's left almost no hard physical evidence. Some alleged hair, some alleged droppings, all still in doubt. That's why all the controversy, all the disbelief."

"But you think there *is* such a creature."

"There's not the slightest doubt of that," she said. "Not to anybody who's looked into the matter, anyway."

"How did you happen to get interested?"

She finished her coffee, smiled, and glanced at her watch. "All we seem to do is set up long stories, Joe. I've got a class in a few minutes. Rain check?"

"Sure. How about dinner tonight?"

"I'd love it. What are the logistical details?"

"I'll pick you up. Seven. You say where."

"My apartment, all right?" She scribbled an address on a scrap of paper he supplied, then hefted the tooth again. "Can I have this, meanwhile? For a few days?"

"If you take extra-good care of it. It might be valuable—more than just scientifically valuable, I guess. And it's not mine, it's my friend's."

"I won't lose it. Not a gem like this. I'd rather have my paws on this than on the Kohinoor. I want to get some other opinions on it. Ken Schoenfeld over in zoology for one. Joe, if this tooth is what I think it may be, I'd no more lose it than I'd drop and break the Rosetta Stone!"

He walked outside with her and watched her cross the quadrangle, again admiring her brisk, pert walk, and standing there until she rounded the corner of a building and disappeared.

The Time of Snow would soon be upon the Ones again, Self knew. The air was grayer, cooler. The sun was moving south. The time of darkness each day was lengthening. The lone foragers were returning one by one, many with game for the ice caves high upon the slope. The Ones of the troop were becoming just a little more torpid in all their movements.

Another of the Ones had died. Many-Colored Male, with his brindle coat, the mate of Narrow Mouth. He'd slipped on the rocks climbing up to one of the caches, and here was his body, where they'd carried it, laid out in front of the caves. Narrow Mouth was still moaning and dancing about slowly near the body. The others were gathered in a rough arc, murmuring and swaying sympathetically. After a while they'd gather up his body again and put it in a cave or crevice off to one side, where, in time, the flesh would shrivel away from the bones.

Self joined in the whistling song all were singing.

Young One cuddled up against her, and she dropped her arm around his shoulders. He often came to her, for some reason, instead of to his own Giver-of-Milk, whose belly was now fat with another young one. Old One said it was coupling, as she'd done with Big Male, that made female bellies fatten with offspring, but she found that as hard to believe as most of his tales.

You were supposed to feel grief when one of the troop died, and she was showing ritual grief, as required, but in her heart she was pleased that this ceremony was taking place, and that *something* was happening. She'd been decidedly bored lately. She'd tried to seduce Big Male again several times, but his mate, Skinny One, had become even more alert and they'd been unable to get away together.

Young One gestured and made sounds indicating that Many-Colored Male was asleep.

"He will not wake," said Self.

"Some sleep and wake. Some do not sleep and wake." He shook his head and twittered. That meant: "Why?"

"It is the way," said Self.

"I'm hungry," said Young One.

"Not now," she said, and cuffed him lightly.

The moaning and the swaying dance continued. The sky was clear, and a moon nearly full, silvered the gorge. Self looked at the moon. It was the eye of some creature in the sky who had power over the Ones. There were two major creatures in the sky—one with a burning eye by day, one with a pale eye by night. Old One said you could propitiate these creatures by dancing dances of submissiveness

40

before them. Most of the others took Old One's assertions at face value, but Self always questioned them. It seemed to her that things that were—things that happened—ought to have connections with each other. Sometimes she searched for these connections until her brain actually ached with the effort.

Why, for example, was it unwise to show oneself to the Pink Skins? That was one of Old One's favorite admonitions. The Pink Skins were dangerous when they had their firesticks—she could accept that much—but Old One himself had said that they were puny without their firesticks. She was immensely curious about the Pink Skins. Old One would probably cuff her if he knew how curious. She wanted to see a Pink Skin someday. More than that, she wanted to smell and touch one. She had already done so in the sleep pictures in her head. In groping for connections in her mind, she had found several curious links between the Ones and the Pink Skins. The Pink Skins walked erect as the Ones did. They communicated by gestures and by vocal sounds. They picked up things with their hands, like rocks and sticks, and they used them to strike or poke at other things—the way the Ones used branches to probe for marmots in the rocks, or stones to mash saplings into a chewable pulp. Old One said that the Pink Skins sometimes sang and danced, as the Ones did. And he said that they coupled face to face. The penises of the Pink Skin males, he said, were larger than those of the Ones, even though their bodies were smaller. Now that *was* hard to believe!

Thinking about penises brought the tingle of desire back into her loins. She turned her head and shoulders—her neck was not supple—to glance at Young One beside her. How many Times of Snow did Young One have?

She took her arm from Young One's shoulders, grabbed his hand, and gently pulled him away from the group. The others were busy moaning and swaying; no one had noticed. She led Young One to the concealment of her favorite nest of rocks. He murmured at her happily, wondering what this new game was. She reached down and touched his penis. He thought that was a game, too, and tried to avoid her, cuffing at her lightly and scampering just out of reach. She tried to get at him several times, but he continued to avoid her. This was great sport!

She gave up. Young One simply didn't have enough Times of Snow for this sort of thing. When she ceased her efforts, he drifted away and went back to the group.

Self stayed where she was. She looked up at the moon again. She wished the creature with the pale eye would come down out of the sky so she could see all of it. She wished something would happen. Anything. Self knew, somehow, that her mind was quicker than any of the minds of the others in the troop. Now she was suffering from the curse of a quicker mind. Boredom.

Chapter Three

Joe McBay looked at Zia Marlowe across the flickering of two red candles on the table. The Belle Epoque was a new restaurant in Pickettsville, specializing in classic French cuisine. It seemed to be doing well enough, but, Pickettsville being Pickettsville, it was probably not doing nearly as well as all the steak and pizza and hamburger houses.

They had been talking about food. Zia had been able to make out most of the French on the menu. "What this town really needs," said Joe, "is a good kosher delicatessen."

Zia nodded. "True gourmet fare. Lox and cream cheese. Lots of it. On a warm bagel. Escoffier would have gone into paroxysms of ecstasy over it."

They had compared notes on a number of things by now, finding their tastes remarkably similar. Yes, she liked classical music and kind of cottonned toward Mahler. She liked big-band jazz, too. Was that right? Joe had a pretty good collection of it. Her favorite old-time movie actor was Humphrey Bogart, and she considered Laurel and Hardy high art. They were not together on several oddments: Joe didn't know who Braque was, and she didn't know that Stephen Crane had also been a damned good poet. But on the whole their tastes were parallel. The implication, as Zia pointed out, compulsively analyzing the situation, was that they probably shared the same general *Weltanschauung*.

"What the hell's that?" asked Joe.

"Outlook."

"Then why not just say that?"

"And lose my academic standing?"

They laughed.

They laughed a lot.

After a while she was telling about herself again. "I think it was some idea of prospecting for gold that brought Dad to this country," she said. "He came here and set up a small tool-sharpening business. Whenever he could, he went into the mountains to prospect. Not much success. But it led to what changed his life. He saw a sasquatch one day—came face to face with it. Everybody laughed at him, but he was stubborn. He started looking for it again. He got in touch with all the other bigfoot buffs and traveled everywhere to see them and to listen to stories of sightings and look at footprint finds. He spent a fortune and also neglected his business. A lot of people stopped dealing with Dad because they were convinced he was a kook. He died broke and, I think, broken-hearted. Mother died soon afterward. I don't know that she ever forgave him. All those years, though, he kept up this endowment policy for my education, so I was able to go to college. It paid tuition, and by working on the side I could bootstrap it. I found a pretty-good-paying night job to start."

"What was that?"

"Topless dancer."

Joe looked at her bosom. "You had a pretty good endowment for that, too." She'd donned a somewhat urbane pottery-blue shirtfront dress for their date. Joe had risked a jacket and tie and felt a little conspicuous in them.

"Well, I did that and few other things," continued Zia. "Carhop, waitress, assistant at the dog pound. I always liked animals. They talk to me. I'd wanted to be a veterinarian, but all those years of study seemed too formidable at the time, especially financially. Forgive me for telling you more than you wanted to know."

"Go on," said Joe. "On and on."

"Well, after fapping around with this and that I finally got into anthropology. I think because the prof was kind of cute. And I already knew a lot about bigfoot, on account of Dad, which seemed to fall into that category. I got a few scholarship breaks and graduate assignments and took a master's in ethology, or animal behavior as some schools call it. One thing led to another, and there was an offer here at Cascade to teach and work for my doctorate. And this is bigfoot country—he's been moving north, you know—and by now I was as hipped on the creature as Dad had been. It was all just too good to turn down. Anyway, here I am."

"And from here, where?"

She was thoughtful. "I'm not sure. Hallowed halls of ivy someplace, I suppose. My thesis, by the way, is going to be on bigfoot. Some of the old guard don't approve. To hell with them. I might even find the critter one of these days. I'd write my own ticket, then. I'd be up there with Jane Goodall and Dianne Fossey. Maybe even Leakey. Well, we all have our dreams. That's mine. How about yours?"

"Even vaguer than your own. I want to do *something*, but I'm not sure what. Back in L.A. I thought I'd go for rank, maybe even chief someday. It didn't work out. Right now, never mind why. Anyway, I came here to get out of the ratrace. Ever hear of Sam Hoffenstein?"

"No."

"He wrote almost-nonsense verses. He wrote a very short and very wonderful one I've always remembered. 'Everywhere I go...I go, too...and spoil everything.'"

"A man of wisdom."

"Yup, always thought so. So here I am, still not sure which way to go. I'm an artist without an art. A philosopher without a philosophy. A voyager on you-know-what creek without any oars."

"You're quite a guy for a cop," said Zia.

"You're quite a bird for an anthropologist."

"Let's have some more wine," she said.

There was more wine. The main course was oyster-stuffed pork with many accents, grave, acute, and circumflex. Almost as an afterthought they got around to the subject that had originally brought them there.

The tooth, as far as Zia had been able to learn from several of her colleagues so far, was that of no immediately identifiable species. It was definitely primate. "A premolar from the mandible," she said, "if you want it technically. With prominent cusps and a well-defined cingulum. And of course that Y-shaped crease characteristic of the suborder Anthropoidea and the family Hominidae. The relative proportions and the placement of the conids resemble those of a human tooth. But the size of everything is comparable to, say, the premolar of a gorilla. Maybe even larger."

"What's all that mean in plain English?"

"To me it means it's a bigfoot tooth. Not so to my more conservative colleagues. To them it can't be a bigfoot tooth because there just ain't no such thing."

"Maybe there ain't," said Joe. "To be frank, it still sounds far out to me. An ape in the mountains and nobody's ever caught it. Flying saucers. Little green men from outer space."

"Ye of little faith," said Zia.

"Okay. Go ahead. Convert me," said Joe.

The Indians of the Northwest had him in their legends. (He was totem to the local tribe—the Tillamish.) The journal of a surveyor who followed Lewis and Clark reported a footprint he'd seen near the Columbia River in 1811. As explorers and settlers moved west, the reports of such finds became more frequent. Diaries, letters, and yellowed newspaper clippings. Theodore Roosevelt cited one in his book *The Wilderness Hunter*. Settlers near Mt. St. Helens told many tales of "skookums" in their vicinity—tall, hairy men thought to be a special breed of Indians, or, barring that, some kind of evil spirits. One better-documented report told how, in 1884, railroaders captured a young ape, four feet and seven inches tall, in the wilds of British Columbia, named it "Jocko," and put it on exhibit.

The number of sightings increased after the turn of the century. Bigfoot was seen from British Columbia to Northern California, from the coast to several hundred miles inland. A party of miners said two creatures attacked and besieged them awhile in 1924. A Canadian prospector, Albert Ostman, swore in an affidavit that he'd been picked up in his sleeping bag by a sasquatch and taken to a remote valley where he'd been held captive by a family group of the creatures for several days. Psychologists interviewed him and said they thought he was neither tetched nor lying.

A roadbuilder, Jerry Crews, found the first widely publicized footprints near Bluff Creek, California, in 1958. In the next decade hundreds of other prints were found, photographed, or made into plaster casts. Zia said she had well over a thousand sightings noted in her files, most of them from witnesses who could be considered credible.

"Throw out the sightings," she said, her eyes now glowing with missionary zeal. "Call them all lies or hallucinations. The footprints still have to be explained. Prints of many different individuals, ranging from twelve to eighteen inches long. Whatever made them weighs a quarter ton or more and does four-foot strides with perfect ease. They resemble human prints at first glance, but not after you study them. *Something* made those prints. Not a man, not a machine."

Earnest, level-headed, well-qualified people believed bigfoot was out there. Investigators like John Green, a Canadian journalist. René Dahinden, a British Columbia outdoorsman, Peter Byrne, an

47

ex-big-game hunter who now devoted all his time to the search. John Napier, a London primate biologist, formerly with the Smithsonian Institute, had done extensive research and was cautiously convinced. He'd had a film of the creature, taken by a rancher named Roger Patterson in 1967, thoroughly analyzed. The experts couldn't prove it was a fake, though, Lord knew, some of them tried.

"I think it's Krantz at Washington State who really put the clincher on it," said Zia.

"Who he?"

"Dr. Grover Krantz, physical anthropologist. He's made a brilliant analysis of the anatomy of bigfoot's foot from the prints. First, they all lack an arch, and the toes don't taper off as human toes do. They're much broader, proportionately, than human feet. Finally, there's that short, transverse crease in the ball just before the big toe—a character never found in human feet."

She reached into a portfolio she'd brought and took out several photographs and diagrams of plaster casts of footprints. Joe obediently looked at them.

"If we were to design a foot to support such weight in erect locomotion," said Zia, "we'd not only have to give it these proportions, but we'd have to rearrange the bones. There's a sketch here that shows how, with a human foot beside it for comparison. Notice that the first metatarsal is lengthened to meet the phalange of the big toe some distance forward of where it does on the human foot. This would be imperative; the human foot arrangement simply wouldn't work. It's this lengthened first metatarsal that gives us exactly what we see in all the footprints—the crease and the double bulge beneath the big toe!"

Joe sipped his wine and thought about it for a while. He lit one of his little cigars. I probably look like some kind of hit man, he thought, sitting here with this beat-up puss and these cigars.

"Okay, impressive," he said. "But how about the

Piltdown Man? Some people will go to a lot of trouble to work up a good hoax."

"Very well," said Zia. "Let's see what hoaxers would need to put this one over on us. First, they'd have to leave hundreds of footprints throughout a quarter of a million square miles over a period of more than twenty years. With no traces of the hoaxers or any machines or vehicles they might have used. To make the prints with something attached to his own foot, a man would have to carry a three-hundred-pound weight while taking four-foot strides. If he did it by machine, he'd need something costing tens of thousands of dollars. Hollywood technicians have made that estimate. And all the while, mind you, the whole conspiracy—which must involve hundreds of people—is kept a deeper secret than the defense plans of the Kremlin."

"I guess you've got a point or two," said Joe. "Still..." He fished for some rationale to his objection. "Still—dammit, I don't know."

"It's just too crazy to believe, is that it?"

"Something like that," he said.

"Joe, listen to me. There are only two possible conclusions. Either, A, a hoaxer made the prints, or, B, a giant hominid made them. Both conclusions seem absurd. But that bigfoot made them seems *less* absurd. Sherlock Holmes said it. 'When you have eliminated the impossible, whatever remains, however improbable, must be the truth.'"

"It still sounds crazy."

"Give it time to sink in," said Zia.

She turned to him at the door of her apartment, which had its own entrance on the outside of a new, jerrybuilt structure near the campus.

"Goodnight, Joe," she said.

"Just like that?"

She kissed him warmly and firmly. "Like that," she said.

"That's good," he said, "but not good enough."

49

She smiled. "All right, Joe. Let's not be coy. You want to come in."

"Of course."

"But I'm not going to ask you in."

"The calendar, I suppose."

She shook her head. "No, not that."

"Puritan principles?"

"Not exactly."

"What, then?"

"I can't tell you, Joe. Not now. Not yet."

"You don't make sense."

"I know I don't seem to. Can you take it just on faith for the time being?"

"*I* can. But then there's a set of glands somewhere that maybe can't."

"They'll have to. Look, Joe, sometime I'll be able to explain. When we know each other better."

"And when will that be?"

"When it happens. We'll know when it does. We *will* be seeing each other, I hope. For one thing, Joe, we talked about so much tonight, we never got around to the most important thing. Where the tooth came from—how your friend got it. And what's to be done with it. Lots of unfinished business."

"Yeah," said Joe, surveying her openly. "Lots of unfinished business."

Chapter Four

J. Richard Charterhouse III doodled on his scratch pad. It was a nice, fresh, legal-size yellow pad on the polished surface of the conference table, here in the board room of the Cadbury Corporation, which kept its headquarters in Pickettsville, where its empire had originally been founded in a sawmill. On the scratch pad, Dick Charterhouse was drawing a nude woman with absurdly immense boobs. The trouble was that Dick, no artist, couldn't make the right sort of lines, and she was coming out fuzzy, as though she were covered with down. Well, he thought, maybe a downy woman would be another new experience. He'd had one with alopecia once—completely hairless—and it did something to the nerves of her skin so that she really went up the wall when he caressed her. Then there were those Oriental chicks who seldom had much in the way of hair in certain places. And those sultry Italian women who burned in a moody way when you did it. And the English girls. They were the surprising ones. Supposed to be all cold and British and proper, but in bed, Jesus!

Dick Charterhouse had had them all in his day.

In his day? Did that mean his day was over and gone now? Was that what it meant, now that he found himself here, in this frontier whistlestop they called Pickettsville?

A chilling thought. He'd have to do something about it.

The president of the Cadbury Corporation, Wallace P. Kegelmeyer, was droning away at the head of the conference table. He was a tiny man with a head too big for his body and a fantastically well-tailored, soft-shouldered suit. He was on to the subject of those government bastards in Washington again. The others at the table were hanging on his words, because hanging upon Wallace P. Kegelmeyer's words was the same as hanging onto their jobs. And they were good jobs. The Cadbury Corporation might operate from the boondocks, but it was not at all stingy when it came to paying its key personnel. A form of extra-hardship pay, Dick told himself.

"It is imperative, therefore," Kegelmeyer was saying, "that we do all we can to prevent the legislators from declaring the Kayatuk Wilderness a specially dedicated area. It's dedicated enough already, with all the restrictions they've got, and all the red tape you have to go through to pick up a stick of firewood there. They're under pressure from the environmentalists, of course, and that includes everybody from sentimental slobs to downright communists. They have clout, but we have clout, too. There will be a good budget, funneled through the National Forest Products Association, not only from Cadbury, but from other vitally concerned companies. Charterhouse, are you with me?"

"Yes, sir," said Dick.

"You looked kind of absentminded."

"Just thinking ahead, that's all."

"Fine," said Kegelmeyer. "Now stay with me."

The stuffy old bastard, thought Dick. He'd supposed private industry, with its compelling profit motives, might be different, but he found it saturated with the same old opinionated idiots.

He dared let his eyes wander for a moment to the broad windows. The paper-products plant, giving off white smoke that smelled like a blend of pickle juice and rancid popcorn, was in the foreground, and the horseshoe curve of the bay was beyond it. Not much to do in Pickettsville. There were all those mountains you could climb nearby, of course, and there was the inland sea for the boat nuts, but there really wasn't much in the way of good, unhealthy fun. He wondered if he'd done the right thing in coming here, in spite of the fat salary and the stock options.

Dick Charterhouse was patently out of place here with his smoother Eastern ways, his prep-school accent, his preferences for scotch instead of bourbon, bridge instead of pinochle, golf instead of bowling, all the rest. But he'd played roles and taken on protective coloring before, so he'd manage to survive somehow.

Dick was thirty-six, still trim, still athletic, and still rakishly handsome. A gal who was into old movies had once told him he looked like an actor named Robert Montgomery. Another gal had once said, "You know what, Dick? You're *couth.*"

He'd been a Department of Defense Civilian, GS-14, assigned to military intelligence, until about a year ago when the entire intelligence community had suffered another of its periodic losses in both prestige and funds. Dick had told the congressional investigators that no, his section never transferred any funds to that opposition group in that African country—the group that was known to be determined to assassinate any left-wing leaders they could, leaders who were themselves a bunch of assassins, of course—and the congressman had known that this was a lie, but couldn't prove it. Then his own bosses, the sons of bitches, who had ordered him to pay out those funds, had turned around and eased him out of the organization just to placate those damned congressmen. They let him know that they would accept his resignation, saying publicly that it was with great regret, and privately that if he didn't resign things could get very disagreeable for him in the organization. Thank God he had already been tendered his offer from the Cadbury Corporation. Wallace P. Kegelmeyer had great admiration for spooks, whom he considered real patriots. Dick Charterhouse, he thought, was just the man to handle various confidential chores for Cadbury. He brought him in as director of special operations.

"Now, gentlemen," Kegelmeyer was saying, "you all know the situation, but I'll review it anyway. Lumber is getting harder and harder to obtain and, as a consequence, it is damn near worth its weight in gold. When we mention a source of lumber like the Kayatuk Wilderness, we're talking about millions of dollars—maybe billions not too many years from now. Most of our other sources are being harvested out, and what we've replanted won't be ready for another generation or two. Under the present ground rules, we can log the Kayatuk by permit. But now the proposal has come up to curtail, among other things, all logging in the area. Why? I don't know why. So the coyotes can have trees to lift their legs and piss on, I suppose."

There was dutiful laughter.

Kegelmeyer accepted the laughter with a smile, then went on. "I want every man here to brainstorm this thing and think of ways to shortstop that ruling. We've *got* to have the Kayatuk or—and I'm neither dramatizing or exaggerating—we'll be out of business in a few years. We're doing what we can. We're contributing to the campaigns of the right congressmen and we're organizing pro-logging groups all over the country. Maybe we're spreading a little money around under the table—that's something we don't talk about. But I want other ideas. I don't care how far off base they sound; just come up with them. We'll shotgun this. One of our ideas, or a combination of them, is bound to work. I want written proposals by the end of the week. If anybody has any ideas now, I want to hear them."

Jim Tumbler, v.p. for advertising and public affairs, stirred and cleared his throat. He was a sallow ex-drinker with a nose like a purple potato and a pious enthusiasm for Alcoholics Anonymous, which had undoubtedly saved his life. "I was just thinking, Wally," he said, "that maybe some of these congressmen would be more inclined to go our way if they had a better image of us. You know how they are about corporations. They think there's something immoral about trying to make a profit. They see corporations as ogres."

"Yes, you're right. Go on, Jim."

"Well, that's it. We do something—some good work, or something—to help our image."

"What good work? Be specific."

"I don't know. We create a foundation to support the arts or something. Look at all the exposure Ford and Rockefeller get out of that."

"Okay, you work on that. Come up with something definite. Anybody else?"

"Well," said Dick Charterhouse in his well-modulated voice and polished drawl, which, he knew, captured attention more quickly than any bombastic interjection, "I have what you might call a passing thought."

"Let's hear it."

"There are certain prominent environmentalists," said Dick, "who are always bleating about preserving the pristine character of the wilderness. Let's not mention any names, but that of a certain movie actor we'd all recognize comes to mind. I've no doubt that his fatuous pronouncements do a great deal for the cause of the nature lovers, and, indeed, exert a disproportionate influence on a number of legislators."

"All right. What's your idea?"

"It wouldn't hurt us at all to have a dangerous person like this thoroughly discredited."

"How?"

Dick shrugged. "I know a number of ways. Dig into his background for dirt. Get him caught in drug parties or sex orgies. Statutory rape is always good.

55

There are fifteen-year-old girls who will cooperate for next to nothing."

Kegelmeyer frowned a little. "I don't know if I like the taste of this sort of thing, Charterhouse."

"I'd be surprised if you did. *I* certainly don't care for it. But dirty jobs are dirty jobs and sometimes have to be done."

Kegelmeyer shifted uncomfortably in his finely upholstered executive chair, one a shade more elegant than the others around the conference table. "I'll tell you what, Charterhouse," he said finally. "You might have something there, but maybe it would be best if you discussed that sort of thing with me only. *In camera*, so to speak."

"Of course. That's what I meant to do."

The others at the table smiled and nodded and directed glances toward Dick that held exactly the same mixture of approval and disapproval Kegelmeyer's eyes had shown. That was part of the game. Go along with the praise when a colleague earned good graces; gang up on him when he made a booboo.

J. Richard Charterhouse III doodled away the rest of the meeting, sketching mountains after a while, and thinking of ledges, crevasses, chimneys, and cornices. He'd *have* to get out and climb again pretty soon. It was the only thing that really settled his nerves. Too bad his forced resignation from the government had come along just when he'd been invited to join that bunch who were going to take K-2 in the Himalayas. He'd had enough leave accumulated to make time for that, but now, he was sure, it would be impolitic to ask for an extended absence from his relatively new job.

It was a fresh start, here at Cadbury. All the loose ends of his former life had been gathered together and finished off in neat little knots. That went for Gladys, too. What the hell, she'd wanted the divorce all along as much as he had. They'd parted friends.

Well, he thought, at least the weekend was coming up. Thank God it's Friday. Tomorrow he could drive down to Seattle and meet that cute gal TV reporter he'd found there. She was not as elegant as such gals were apt to be in the larger cities, but she was better than anything he'd seen so far around Pickettsville.

"That's all, gentlemen," said Kegelmeyer, rising. "Have a nice weekend."

Dick Charterhouse would try to do just that.

Nurse Collins had the duty tonight in intensive care. From her station at the hub she could see all the patients through the glass and monitor their appearance in addition to checking them at brief intervals. It was difficult work, and the time went slowly. She couldn't even get away to the ladies' room to look in the mirror and imagine she'd lost some weight or to primp. Fortunately, there were only two patients this evening. There was that cardiac case—an old man who, in her estimation, should be allowed to expire quickly instead of taking up valuable hospital space, and the pilot named Garvey, who had crashed his airplane in the wilderness.

She was not supposed to divert her attention even momentarily from the patients, but she'd had enough experience to handle this shift by instinct, almost with her eyes closed. She kept an open gossip magazine in her lap and read a few paragraphs from it—mostly picture captions—between periodic checks.

About a third of the way through her shift, she glanced at Fred Garvey again. He lay there quite still with the BP sock on his arm, ready for instant use, and with an IV tube taped in the crook of his other arm. Patient Garvey had had his ripped and punctured insides put together again, and Nurse Collins rather expected him to pull through. But in this particular moment, when she glanced at him, something about his skin color did not seem quite right to her. She had an impression that the blue was beginning to show.

She went quickly to Garvey's bed, stethoscope

57

dangling from her neck. He was breathing shallowly and irregularly—it sounded like Cheyne-Stokes coming on. She checked his blood pressure immediately. Down, way down. Alarmed now, she went to the emergency override microphone on her desk and said, "Dr. Portman, code twenty-five. Code twenty-five, Dr. Portman, please." She hoped young Sheldon Portman wouldn't be tied up down in emergency. He was a pretty good young doctor, but he was much too conscientious and looked harried all the time.

She went back to the patient. His skin was definitely getting bluish now, and his breathing had become almost imperceptible.

Well, you never know, she thought, looking down at the young man with his cricketlike features drawn and gaunt. She'd have sworn this one would pull through and the old and wasted one in the other bed would have terminated long ago. She heard the elevator doors down the corridor open and shut, and turned her head in time to see young Dr. Portman rush into the room. He'd made it quickly, for a change, but Nurse Collins was fairly sure that he was already too late.

The ceremony in the crematorium was brief and almost pleasant, Joe McBay thought. This is the way I'll have it done when my time comes, he decided. There was a box with Fred's remains in it up front, ready to be rolled through the portcullis-like door to the vault. The room itself was rather like a small chapel, with a dais and lectern front and center.

Eleanor Garvey sat beside him. He held her hand. She was dry of tears now and had even, he'd noticed, shown several flickering though pleasureless smiles. She was small and slight, as Fred had been. She was a plainly pretty woman with calm eyes and a brave mouth. She had not brought Denny, the boy, to the ceremony. "I don't want him to have another dark dream to come back to him," she had said.

At the lectern, the Reverend Bob Hagen finished his vestpocket eulogy. Fred had often said that he wanted absolutely no religious folderol if he ever bought the farm, but Eleanor had brought in Bob Hagen anyway. He was young and neither obtrusive nor sanctimonious. Joe decided that Fred wouldn't have minded his being there, after all.

"And so," said Hagen, "Fred Garvey was a man who sought what we all seek, high in the sunlit silence of the sky..."

Afterward, Joe drove Eleanor home, to the small rancher in a birch thicket not far from the Pickettsville airport, where Fred had kept his plane.

"Don't forget, El," he said, "if you need any help just call. For things like moving or whatever, okay?"

"I will. And thanks, Joe." She pressed his hand fondly.

"What are your plans?"

"I don't know yet. I still can't think. Funny, I've known this might happen sometime, and I've gone over it a hundred times in my mind, but now that it's really happened I'm not sure just what to do. I suppose I'll go back to my parents' place in Seattle. For now, anyway."

"Look, El," Joe said somewhat uncomfortably, "Fred told me he wasn't leaving much, and that maybe finances wouldn't be so good for you."

"I'll get along somehow, Joe."

"But I think you'd better know about this ... well, this discovery of his. That tooth he brought back."

"Those creatures he thought he saw?"

"Maybe he really saw them. I don't know. If he did, and if this tooth should lead to those apes, or whatever they are, there may be some money in it. You're entitled to a good part of that. The tooth's really yours, as a matter of fact."

"You keep it, Joe. Fred gave it to you. You keep it."

"Okay. But, remember, if anything comes out of this, you're going to share it."

"That's nice of you, Joe. And thank you. But I think I just want to make a fresh start. I don't know if I can take the sadness of remembering Fred and everything about him."

"Let's say it's for Denny, then. If there is anything."

"All right. We'll do it that way."

"And keep in touch, El. Let me know where you are and how you're getting along."

"I'll be in Pickettsville for a while yet. Maybe I can even hang onto the house." She studied Joe for a moment. "You've been a really good friend, Joe."

"Well, Fred and I *did* get along, I guess."

"To Fred, and to me, too."

He met her eyes and saw what was in them. He realized that possibly she herself didn't quite know what was in them. "Sure, El," he said awkwardly. "A good friend. I hope I'll always be."

"Fred and I used to wonder why you didn't get married."

After a moment's pause, Joe said, "I'll tell you why. I just never felt that magic click they talk about. I'm not sure there is such a thing."

"There is, Joe, Take my word for it."

He shrugged. She withdrew her hand from his. They rode on in silence.

Joe McBay rode out the rest of his graveyard shift, and then he had two days off. He saw Zia Marlowe each evening. They dined at less-expensive restaurants than the Belle Epoque, and Zia said she couldn't have him feeding her all the time and offered to pay her share. He laughed that away. They had drinks after dinner, usually in the Logger's Lounge of the Pioneer Hotel.

Joe's favorite cocktail was a Rob Roy, and he'd introduced her to it. She sipped one now and looked up at him and said, "I don't think you realize what a bombshell we're holding. Do you know how many people have been looking for the sasquatch, and for how long?"

"Oh, I've got an idea. I read all that stuff you gave me. I'm even becoming a true believer. Well …maybe."

"That's the thing about the squatch." Her eyes always brightened when she got back to her favorite subject. "Most people never look into it, so most people just shrug it off and assume there's some rational explanation other than the one that there really *is* a sasquatch. But you see the importance of finding it, don't you?"

"I guess so. Big splash if it's brought in. Some bread involved, no doubt."

"Joe, listen to me. Anthropologists don't like the term 'missing link,' which is a layman's concept. It implies an over-simplified line of evolution, from ape to man. It's much more complicated than that. Think of lines like tree branches, going up, spreading out, intertwining. Present-day apes aren't man's ancestors—they're his cousins. And sometimes pretty remote cousins, at that."

"I had all this in school once." He grinned. "I'm not sure I paid much attention to it."

She matched his grin. "Well, pay attention now, will you? Leakey, in the Olduvai gorge, gave us a big breakthrough. He found evidence of an ancient primate species that could be in very close cousinship to man, and not far from the common ancestor. All the answers aren't in yet, in spite of his marvelous work. There are still a lot of blank spots, and bigfoot, if found, would fill in one of those blank spots. He'd be, for the first time, what we might call a living fossil. We could study not only his physical characters, but his pathology, his behavior, and all the rest. The more we'd learn, the more we'd know about *Homo sapiens* himself, and what really makes him tick. Where he came from—and possibly where he's going. Textbooks would be rewritten, not only on anthropology, but on psychology and philosophy and ethics and maybe even economics. The average person wouldn't feel it right away, but the knowledge that would come out of this find would eventually touch, in one way or another, every human being on our planet! For the better, I hope. The more man knows about himself, the better he'll be able to survive as a species."

Joe's grin became faintly sardonic. "What are we doing? Saving the world?"

"I think so. Yes, I think there's a good chance of that."

He laughed. "Now I *do* need a drink." He took a long sip of his Rob Roy.

"Joe," continued Zia, "I *know* bigfoot's out there somewhere. I've gone to every possible source for backing so that I could go look for him. Foundations, universities, the government, everybody. I've spent hours putting together presentations that are big, fat theses in themselves. No luck. The answer always is: 'This is all very fine, but there just ain't no such critter.' You see, until now, there never has been any real physical evidence. The sightings, the footprints, a few bad photos, a controversial film. Now we've got something concrete. That molar of yours. We've got more than that. We know where to look. At least, I presume we do. Your friend Garvey, I suppose, told you where he saw those creatures. That might make you the only man in the world who knows where to look. You haven't told anyone else, have you?"

"Not a soul. Fred's widow may know—but she's not interested. And, by the way, she's supposed to share in anything that comes out of this. I promised that. That's partly why I took the tooth back from you in such a hurry. I haven't decided what to do yet, but meanwhile I don't want the information to get out. Somebody might decide to steal a march on us."

Her eyes became earnest. "Joe, we can find bigfoot. At least we'd have the best chance anybody's had so far. I know what to do—I've made enough detailed plans for an expedition, Lord knows—and you know where to go. This is the brass ring, Joe, and we'd better grab it now. It might not be there next time around."

"What do you suggest?"

"We'll need backing. For people, for equipment. A small group—five would be good—and they'll have to be pretty sharp people with certain specific skills. It's not just a bunch of good ol' boys on a weekend hunting trip. Bigfoot's shy and elusive; he'll be deliberately trying to avoid contact. Probably with cleverness and intelligence, like those Japanese holdouts who spent years in the Philippines after the war. We'll need a helicopter, a base camp, supplies, field equipment, tranquilizer darts—I've got it all listed. It will cost as much as fifty thousand dollars."

Joe grinned and fumbled in his pocket. "I haven't got that much on me, right now."

"Neither have I. But I might be able to dig it up. That tooth of yours makes a difference. That and the fact that you can take us to where it came from."

He frowned slightly. "You're assuming I'd like to go along on this expedition of yours."

"Well, wouldn't you?"

"In a way. It would be a nice hike."

"You know it's a lot more than that."

Joe rubbed the blue nap on his jaw. He hated to shave twice a day, but maybe he ought to. "Zia, I've got to give it to you the way it really is, okay?"

"Always, I hope," she said.

"All right. I'm still not one hundred percent convinced that ape's really out there. Ninety-eight or ninety-nine, maybe, but not a hundred. I'm even less sure we'll find it if it is. That's a lot of wild country to cover. As for revolutionizing science and the course of human destiny...well, maybe you're just a little carried away with that. Finally, I'm not sure I could find the time to do it. How long would it take, anyway?"

"That depends on how much you know about

where the creatures are. If you just know a general area, we might need as much as thirty days."

"Zack Winfield wouldn't give me that much time off. Not to go look for a sasquatch."

"Why don't you ask him?"

Joe laughed. "Go look for an ape in the mountains? He'd have me on a couch, getting evaluated, the same day."

"Joe, if I put an expedition together, will you tell us where to go?"

"I don't think I rightly should. I told you—some of this belongs to Eleanor Garvey."

"I'd see that she got her share."

"You would. But somebody else might not."

"Joe, you're being stubborn."

"I guess I am. I guess I have to be."

"You just *can't* let this thing drop! Not the way things are now!"

"All right," said Joe. "I'll make a deal. Wait a few days. Maybe I can find a way to get some time off. If I can, we'll go out and look for bigfoot. Okay?"

"If that's the best I can get, I'll take it," Zia said.

He took her home again, early, about eleven, received her dutiful goodnight kiss, and went home, frustrated and unsatisfied. He did not press her for an explanation of her refusal to invite him in. He had decided that Zia was choice, as birds went, and worth a bit of stalking. He made his pass; she parried it; he bided his time. In some respects it was even better this way. Fact was, he enjoyed her immensely even without taking her to bed. He'd enjoy her a hell of lot more, of course, if he could make out with her, but meanwhile it wasn't bad; it wasn't bad at all. He'd be patient.

Catching Sheriff Zack Winfield in the corridor, Joe sounded him out. "Got a moment?" he asked.

"Hello, Joe," said Zack. "How's it going, huh?"

"No complaints. I was thinking about a little relaxation, though."

"How do you mean?"

"It might be nice to get out in the woods. I've always been kind of a camping nut."

"Fine," said Winfield. "I like the woods myself. I can hardly wait for hunting season every year. Hell, I grew up in the woods. Did you know I was a logger when I was thirteen? I could handle a mankiller before I was full-grown. Know what a mankiller is, huh?"

"I don't think so."

"It's a chain-and-bar winch. A real sonofabitch if you don't know what to do with it. Okay, you go ahead out in the woods. Good for a man. Take plenty of whiskey. You need a day or two off?"

"I was thinking of a little more than that."

"How much more?"

"Oh, a month, maybe."

"*A month?*" Winfield stared, astonished. He slipped his thumbs in under his broad suspenders.

"Well, this is kind of an extended trip I have in mind. Sort of a scientific thing. Nature study."

"For Christ's sake!" said Winfield. "Nature study!"

"I just thought I'd ask," said Joe, as though about to shrug.

Winfield ran his palm over his stiff white hair. "Joe, you haven't been here long enough for that much leave time." He gimleted Joe with one narrowed eye. "When you earn it, you can have it. You were gonna go by the book, remember?"

Joe let the shrug develop. "By the book," he said.

He thought he'd be able to see Zia again, now that he was off the graveyard shift, and maneuver himself into her apartment or her into his mobile home. Either venue would be fine for what he had in mind. When he tried to set up a date, he learned she had to attend a seminar in Seattle. He rustled up Yolanda, the waitress, instead. Yolanda was exceptionally passionate, and Joe tried not to show her that in spite of this he was mildly bored. He tried, as a matter of fact, not to admit that to himself.

One evening Chet Anders dropped around to Joe's pad, just before Joe was about to go out and cruise around town to see if he couldn't develop someone other than Yolanda. He stepped out of the shower he'd been taking, wrapped a towel around his middle, and built scotch on the rocks for both of them. Chet was in his usual dark courtroom suit; he wore a wildly flowered tie and a heavy gold chain with a Masonic emblem across his bellied-out vest.

There were some preliminary remarks and a few sips. Then Chet said, "Look, Joe, what's this about asking Zack for a whole month off?"

"You must have the place bugged!" said Joe, staring.

"Zack told me himself. He thought it sounded strange. A month off for nature study. Is that what you really said? Nature study?"

"That's what I said. What in hell's wrong with it?"

"Oh, nothing, nothing. Though it sounds a bit strange to me, too. I listen to a lot of testimony, and I've developed a pretty good ear for sour notes. But the main thing is, Joe, as far as Zack's concerned, you want to play it cool. Don't irritate him too much. He's afraid of you, you know, Joe. He knows damn well you might take him in a race for sheriff. And he's got some power as sheriff, never forget that. He could find ways to shoot you down if he got scared enough and mad enough to do it."

"Chet," said Joe, after thinking that over, "I didn't ask for all this fuss. I came here to get *away* from the ratrace, remember? I'm still not sure I want to run for sheriff."

"That's good," said Chet, nodding, making accordion folds that appeared and disappeared in the fat under his chin. "Keep suggesting that. It's always good to play a little hard to get. The voters like it."

"Fuck the voters," said Joe wearily.

"Of course," said Chet. "But never let them know it. And stay a little mysterious, a little aloof. Always make 'em think you've got your mind on big, serious things. You haven't got time for nonsense, for the picayune. Look, did you really mean to take time off for nature study?"

"That's what I said, isn't it?"

"Uh—yes. But it still doesn't sound right. It means something else, doesn't it?"

"All right, Chet," said Joe, lighting one of his little cigars. "I'll level with you. I thought I'd go out looking for bigfoot."

Chet went into sudden rolls of laughter. He slapped his knee. "That's good, Joe! Bigfoot! The sense of humor is good! Never make it too sarcastic, though. Not for the voters."

"I'm not joking. I'm perfectly serious."

It took Chet a moment to absorb that. A puzzled stare washed away his laughter. "You're not!"

"A friend of mine saw the things," said Joe. "Somebody I believe. I think I know where they might be."

"Joe, please!" said Chet, looking pained. "In the first place, there's no such thing as bigfoot. In the second place, even if there were, you'd ruin everything by going after it. Nobody's going to vote for a nut for sheriff!"

Joe finished his drink, rose, and said, "Is this how it'll be if I run for sheriff? You telling me what I can or cannot believe in?"

"Joe, that's unfair. All I'll ever do is give you political advice. And damned good advice, I might add. I put the prosecutor in and the state representative from this district. If you don't believe my advice is always good, ask them."

"Chet," said Joe, "I think I'll go finish my shower. Wash off a little film of sticky stuff I somehow ran into."

Chet put down his drink and went to the door, walking heavily, pompously, as though crossing the floor of the courtroom to address the jury. He turned at the door. "I'll level with you, too, Joe," he said. "If I had another candidate who's had the favorable exposure you've already had, I wouldn't be playing footsie with you this way. For your own sake, Joe, be nice. Try to get along, okay?"

"That's what I thought I was doing."

"You weren't, Joe," said Chet, shaking his head solemnly. "You weren't. Bigfoot! My God!"

He muttered his way out of the door.

Dick Charterhouse crossed to his office door to greet his visitor—a Miss Marlowe from the university—at about the same time the visitor entered. He did not believe in the pose of being at one's desk, if it wasn't necessary, and pretending to be busy, so that the visitor felt apologetic and a little off balance right away. He preferred a more subtle approach. Seem harmless at first; be charming and agreeable. Start tightening the screws later, if need be. The other fellow would be way off guard by then.

Miss Marlowe looked unexpectedly attractive. Compact, fresh-smiling, elusively exotic features. Dressed and groomed in good taste, too. "Hello. I'm Dick Charterhouse." He extended his hand.

"Zia Marlowe. How do you do."

"Come in. Sit down." He indicated the armchair beside his desk, then went around the desk to his own swivel chair. "Coffee? A drink, if you'd like—"

"No, thanks." She put a hardcover portfolio she'd brought beside the chair. "I won't be taking up much of your time. Not on this first visit."

"Oh? That's a disappointment." He smiled as he sat.

"As a matter of fact," said Zia, "I hope I've got the right person. I asked our grants writer whom to see and he suggested you, but he wasn't sure you'd be the one."

"I probably am," said Dick. "I've got the garbage-can job around here. Anything nobody else knows what to do with, I get. So fire away." He continued to study her, with pleasure. He liked the tweedish suit she wore and the old-fashioned cameo pin on the lace of her blouse. It suggested walks in the countryside in Connecticut. From her accent, however, he didn't think she was Eastern. Maybe the getup was a ploy; maybe she'd done some homework on him and donned it just to please him. That's how he would have played it if he were she, and after something. After something she undoubtedly was. Everybody was after something.

"I think first you ought to know who I am," said Zia. "I teach anthropology as a graduate assistant, and I'm not here officially from the university. I'm on my own. I have to make that clear so there's no misunderstanding later."

"All right," he said, still smiling. "You're on your own."

"I've got to start with a word that might make you laugh and decide immediately that I ought to have my head examined. I hope you'll wait to hear what else I have to say."

"When in doubt, say what you have to say. Even the truth—as a last resort, of course."

She smiled. Then she said, "Bigfoot."

He stared back for a moment. "The...uh... legendary monster out in the woods?"

"Yes," said Zia. "Though not legendary, and possibly not so monstrous."

As briefly as she could, she told him of her researches, and of the accumulated evidence that pointed, without doubt in her mind and in the minds of some other experts, to the existence of the creature. She told him of the tooth that had recently been found and explained that a deputy sheriff named Joe McBay knew where there might be a band of the creatures. "With this new data," she said, "I could start hitting some of the foundations again—the ones that have turned me down before. But that could take months. So, frankly, I thought of the Cadbury Corporation. At least it's right here in town. A shot in the dark, I suppose, but anyway worth a quick try."

Dick was thoughtful. She could glimpse what she was sure was a good intelligence in his clear, healthy-looking, cobalt-blue eyes. Handsome devil, she thought. She wouldn't let that prejudice her. He didn't seem too conscious of it, so that was a plus. "I take it," said Dick, "that you're after something that will cost money. What kind of money are we talking about?"

"I estimate fifty thousand. Everything's itemized in my presentation." She picked up the portfolio.

"Later," said Dick, waving his hand. "Miss Marlowe, what makes you think Cadbury might be interested in something like this?"

"The publicity. The very favorable publicity. Cadbury would be a scientific benefactor."

He smiled again. "If the search succeeded. If not, Cadbury would have egg on its corporate face."

"Yes," said Zia, nodding. "I'm not going to be foolish enough to absolutely guarantee success. But for the first time, now, the chances of finding bigfoot are *extremely* good. You see, a pilot went down in the wilderness recently and walked out. He saw a colony of the creatures and brought back a tooth—a premolar from a skull he'd found. I've seen the tooth, and it's absolutely authentic."

"In your opinion?"

"In mine, and several others."

"But it could be open to controversy?"

"Possibly. Not all scientists agree on everything. Some have axes to grind—if only to support what they've always said, even if that's wrong."

"Could I arrange to have this tooth checked out myself? I happen to know some very good lab people for that sort of thing. I used to be with military intelligence, and we had access to some pretty sophisticated analysis techniques. I still know people who would help me out."

"That might be a problem." She frowned slightly. "The man who has the tooth doesn't want to let it go. He has various reasons—some of them cogent, I suppose. But I have photographs and measurements of it. Complete data."

"That might do. Of course"— his smile flickered on again—"I'm jumping ahead, here. I haven't said I'd do anything about this yet. You'd better tell me a little more of what you have in mind."

"Well, since I've studied the creature so thoroughly, and for such a long time, I may be one of the few people who knows exactly how to go about finding it, without scaring it off, for one thing. All this is in the presentation, carefully referenced. All I'm asking now is that you give it a fair study. Quickly, though, I hope. The expedition should get under way before the middle of October. The weather will be impossible if it doesn't."

Dick Charterhouse took the portfolio and flipped through it. He paused now and then to read a passage more thoroughly. He did this until Zia found herself fidgeting. He looked up at last. He smiled to palliate whatever sting his words might have had otherwise. "Miss Marlowe—Zia—did you actually think you could walk in here and tap Cadbury for fifty thousand dollars, just like that, and, if I understand you correctly, in a few days' time?"

She smiled back. "It didn't cost anything to try."

"They could use you in sales," he said. He put the portfolio down again. "All right. Now let me be fair with you. A lot of people here would have to approve before anything like this could go through. Second, as the person submitting this, I myself would have to be convinced of its merits. To be crude about it—what's in it for us? On the other hand—and I'm telling you this against my better judgment—there *has* been some talk about here about taking on a good

71

work of some kind for the sake of our public image. You seem to have hit the timing right in that respect, anyway. I'll tell you what, Zia. I *will* study your prospectus; I can promise you that much. I might do some poking around on my own for further information. But no promises beyond that. And you must understand that all this can't possibly happen in the next day or two."

"Since at the moment I have nothing," said Zia, "anything at all is gravy."

"Good. And now let's make it even better. What are you doing tonight?"

"I have a date."

"Can you break it and have a date with me instead?"

"Is that a condition?"

"Of course not. You'll get a full hearing, date or no date."

Zia considered that for a moment, then said, "In that case, all right. I can't resist the chance to sell you on this a little more. Joe will understand, I'm sure. He's the man I have the date with. He also has the tooth. That's neither here nor there, I suppose. All right, Dick, it's a date."

J. Richard Charterhouse III showed an easy smile. He had the air of a man who feels always in control of himself and of everyone and everything around him. He seemed secure in a feeling of natural superiority— a superiority that was obviously actually there—but, with good taste, he didn't flaunt it. Zia liked him. She was also, for some reason, a little afraid of him. Maybe that added to her liking. These things could get elusively ambivalent.

"I'm very glad you dropped in," said Dick, after they had arranged time and place for the date and he had accompanied her to the door. "Where have you been hiding yourself in Pickettsville all this time, anyway?"

"Second ivory tower on the right," said Zia, laughing.

72

Chapter Five

Self slowly and cautiously approached the large object that lay askew, like a downed cow, in the long snowbank down the gorge, many steps from the caves. Big Male, going out to forage, had discovered it. Wonder of wonders! It must have dropped from the sky. It must have happened when the wind was howling; no one had heard it drop. Old One had warned against approaching it too closely. He himself had ambled down to it for a look, and he had detected a sharp odor he associated with Pink Skins.

They must now all be alert for the presence of the Pink Skins, he said. Every Time of Snow the Pink Skins came closer; there seemed to be more of them each season, spreading themselves inexorably out into the wilderness.

She stood now at about a rock's throw from the object, feet spread as she studied it, her hands stroking her breasts, which lately had been growing more prominent. Self did not know why she seemed to be more curious about anything strange than most of the others; she sensed that her head, inside, worked with greater ease than their heads, and she also sensed that whenever this was exhibited the others resented it, for some reason. Take the business of counting. There were grunts for one, two, and three, and once Self had lined up some stones and invented a new grunt for four. Those to whom she tried to teach this new concept had merely growled and threatened to cuff her.

And now, having surveyed the wrecked airplane a little further, and seeing that the snow had covered much of it by now, Self dared to take a few more steps toward it.

Where did the Pink Skins obtain the many strange objects they used? Self wondered. No such objects were to be found lying about, as sticks and stones suitable as implements were. There was a correlation here somewhere. Sometimes the Ones themselves combined the things they found to create new objects. The fir-bough beds in the caves, for example. You could make things stay together by twisting them around each other in a certain way. Perhaps, therefore, the Pink Skins made their objects by putting together the objects they had found in a very skillful and complicated fashion. More than that, perhaps they made little objects, then combined these to make bigger objects, then combined the bigger objects to make still larger forms, and so on and so on, till one could no longer keep track of the process. Letting this concept take form in her mind was just a little painful, yet, in a strange way, she enjoyed it. In that sense it was a little like the pain she'd experienced when Big Male had penetrated her. One's own head was really full of marvelous entertainments; she wished some of the others would realize this.

A few steps more, and Self would be able to touch the curious object in the snow. She stopped and waited for courage to take those extra steps. There was a kinship between her kind and theirs, something beyond the fact that both walked truly erect and vaguely resembled each other in physical form.

Blurred pictures, none fully formed, swirled through her mind. Some came from things Old One had said; others came out of nowhere—perhaps, in some incredible way, from her very bloodstream.

74

There had been a day, unimaginable Times of Snow past, when the Ones had roamed broad savannahs, locomoting easily on their broad, sturdy feet, rising erect to peer over the tall grasses with stereoscopic vision other animals lacked and to see game in the distance. There were bands of bigfeet, circling deer or bison, cooperating, running them down. And then there were the Pink Skins, who used objects in their hands in order to kill—sharp sticks they could throw—and who hunted down all animals, including the bigfeet on rare occasions. Swarms of Pink Skins, their numbers increasing all the time. Generation after generation, they killed many bigfeet. The bigfeet who remained began their many long migrations, withdrawing always farther into the lonelier mountains, higher and higher in their flight, learning to survive among the harsh rocks and the ice and the snow, adapting slowly, and developing the customs, such as the lone foraging and storing of food in frozen places, that made survival possible. Their huge jaws had originally been designed for grinding vegetable matter, but now they increasingly added meat to their diet, and, over countless generations, their canine teeth and their incisors became sharper to enable them to tear at food before they chewed the pieces into a digestible pulp. There were other adaptations. As they foraged in the lower country of the Pink Skins, they moved by night, and their eyes learned to see well in the darkness. Their coats of fur grew thicker to protect them from the bitter cold. Their hands became more dextrous to enable them to climb rockfaces, and their fingers and thumbs moved slightly toward opposition with other for easier grasping and manipulation of objects, though not as extremely as in the hands of the Pink Skins. Because many of the characters of their savannah days remained—the big, broad, archless feet, for example—they were not yet fully adapted to their new environment, even though they had now dwelt in it for eons. Their numbers were slowly and constantly dwindling. Whatever might help increase their numbers was good; whatever might tend to diminish them was bad. She knew that this so, though she had no idea how she knew. What would it be like, she wondered, if the Ones could somehow live in harmony with the Pink Skins, as they did with each other, and thus avoid their slow, constant, and almost imperceptible aggression? But that was one of her more nonsensical mind-questions; one of her wilder dreams....

She took the several final steps forward and slowly reached out and touched the flank of the big object in the snow. She withdrew her hand again almost immediately and waited. Nothing happened. The object did not move, nor did it seem to threaten her in any way. Old One *could* be wrong. It was possible there was no danger in it.

She touched the thing again. It was completely inert. Running her hand along its smooth surface, she moved forward until she came to an opening in its side that was rather like the mouth of a small cave. There were other remarkable shapes and forms in its interior; she could make sense out of none of them.

Araggh! Here was a curious object! Here on the floor of this little cave. It was the size of a small rock, but its edges were completely square. It was light in weight. Its surface was a little slippery—some kind of bark, wrapping whatever was inside. She scratched at its surface, and the covering came off easily under her fingernails.

Marvelous! There were other wrapped objects inside, and she could open these, too. A small, flat bar she uncovered smelled edible. It was dark brown in color and slightly brittle. She tasted it. It had the sweetness of wild honey and another captivating flavor. Self ate the rest of the chocolate bar quickly and in great delight.

She spent the next few hours that morning at the strange object in the snow, eventually touching or smelling every part of it she could reach. She had encountered nothing dangerous in it, and perhaps the Pink Skins themselves were not so fearsome as Old One made them out to be. They were, after all, quite puny compared to the Ones, and she'd certainly be able to vanquish one if it were imprudent enough to attack her. Maybe some would attack and some would not. At any rate, she was now more curious than ever about the Pink Skins themselves.

At last she left the object in the snow and headed back toward the caves. Her first impulse was to tell the others of the marvels she'd found, but suddenly it came to her that they would disbelieve, and growl, and try to cuff her for going so near the object and endangering all of them. She decided she would keep her experience to herself. That wouldn't be easy. There was a stirring urge within her—as always—to give an account of what she'd seen and done.

The moon was high and the stars were diamond chips spilled prodigally on the sky. Driving home from the courthouse shortly after midnight—he was on the swing shift, four to twelve, now—Joe looked up at this display and took in the pleasant sight of it while he had a chance. There weren't many starkly clear nights in this moist air of the coastal Northwest; a starry evening was rather an event.

He drove a three-year-old Datsun 280Z, liking its shift-stick control and race-car handling. He knew stretches out in the country where he could take it up to 120 without getting caught—the other sheriff's deputies were no problem and would extend him all the courtesies of the trade, but the state patrolmen could be hard-nosed about it.

Joe wasn't ready for sleep yet. He never was at the ends of any of his shifts; it always took him several days to get into the rhythm of each weekly change. Right now, the swing shift had turned out to be unhandy. It didn't allow him time to see Zia in the evening. There was a conspiracy taking place somewhere to keep him from making time with Zia. (These were the same conspirators who clogged the roads he wanted to enter from a sidestreet, or who filled the line at the bank in front of him with men with canvas sacks and complicated transactions; he envisioned minor gods in togas dancing around a glade in nutty fashion and chanting: "Let's frag Joe McBay!") First, that seminar in Seattle. Second, her date with this character from the Cadbury Corporation who just might come up with funds for the expedition. Then the hours by which they lived out of phase. One thing or another.

She'd called him to say that this Dick Somebody-or-other at Cadbury was very interested and that she now felt optimistic about getting a grant. He wanted to have the tooth for a while. Joe said he was sorry, but he wasn't going to let the tooth out of his hands just yet. He heard the frown in Zia's voice when she said that this was very disappointing to her.

He drove along the crest of a hill now. From here he could look down upon much of the town, laid out as though in miniature upon a sand table. It followed the scimitar curve of the bay and filled the gently rising slope toward the foothills of the Cascades to the east. It was on I-5, the highway from Mexico to Canada, and most people who drove past were on their way to somewhere else. It did not attract a great many tourists. Joe swung into the mobile-home court, which was built in a stand of tall cedars, and nosed the Datsun into the driveway of his own unit. He left the car, found his house key, and put it into the lock of the front door. The door swung open as he pushed, and before he had turned the key. Thinking he must have left it unlocked, he stepped inside.

Joe was never sure whether he actually saw movement in the dimness of the room or merely sensed someone's presence there. He was aware of someone else for one pulsebeat. Then there was a very loud noise in his skull, followed by flashing lights, and what he could only think of as a grayout. He was not unconscious, but then he wasn't really conscious, either.

He was—

—on the floor—

On his hands and knees—

—on the floor.

He couldn't quite remember falling there. There was a pain in his head and the rockets were bursting high above Ft. McHenry. There was blurry movement above him. Somebody was stepping past him and leaving by the still-opened door. He fought with his own mind-and-nerve complex to regain control of himself.

When at last he made it, swaying, to his feet again, his head ached terribly and the side of his neck was numb. He switched on the light. A quick glance told him that the room was in order; if anything had been disturbed it was too small for him to detect at the moment. He breathed hard until some of the dizziness went away. He slowly lurched back to the bathroom, supporting himself with his fingertips on both walls. He dry-heaved in the bathroom. He stared at himself in the mirror. It took a moment for his eyes to focus properly. They looked a little wild. He thought his skin had a greenish tinge.

Some minutes and one good stiff drink later, Joe felt that he had the energy to examine all of his rooms more closely. By now he had found the bump near the top of his head, and his fingers had come away sticky when he'd touched the tender spot. He was sure, however, that there'd been no fracture—his vision was quite clear now, for one thing—and if he were treated there would be a report and more hassle than it all was worth. The newspaper might even think it was funny. "Deputy Zonked in Own Pad." Something like that. To hell with it. He'd surprised a prowler, and the prowler had fled.

Everything of value was still in place. His Nikon camera and its accessories were still on the shelf where they belonged. His electric portable typewriter was on its stand. His two bottles of scotch were still in the cupboard. His pile of *Playboys* and *Penthouses* was undisturbed. In his bedroom, his Patek-Philippe dress-up wristwatch, which he hardly ever wore, was still in its little lacquered oriental box in the drawer.

He looked for the tooth. He'd put it in an ordinary envelope and dropped it among his socks and belts and gloves.

It wasn't there.

He rummaged among the socks. It definitely was missing. Had he put it somewhere else? He searched a few other places. He searched again, this time more carefully.

He went back to the kitchen-living room, poured another drink, sat in his armchair, belted the drink down, and said to himself, "I'll be a sonofabitch."

"Let's take a ride, huh?" said Sheriff Zack Winfield, climbing into the passenger seat of Joe's unit just as Joe was ready to leave on patrol.

"Where to, Zack?"

"Most anywhere. I want to talk. Cars are good to talk in, huh?"

He did not say anything else until Joe had reached the edge of town and headed out the Ski Area Highway, toward the mountains. He spent the time lighting his corncob pipe and filling the car with its licorice-smelling smoke.

He said finally, "I kind of thought, at the time, that all this business about nature study sounded like a bunch of bullshit."

"I see. Sounds like you've heard things."

"Yup. Sure have. Bigfoot. You want to go out and catch yourself a bigfoot, huh?"

"I've been thinking about it," admitted Joe. "Who told you?"

"A little bird."

"Let's not play games, Zack."

"It's no game. A little bird. That's what you call them, isn't it? Birds. In my day they were dames or broads or tomatoes. Yup. It was a little bird who told me everything."

Joe glanced at Winfield and saw his self-satisfied smile. "All right. Who?" He was trying to remember whether he'd told any little birds about bigfoot. Not Yolanda; he was sure he hadn't said anything to her.

"This little bird," said Winfield, at a leisurely pace, "is a smart little bird. So smart, in fact, she's a college professor. Or something close to that, anyway."

"Zia Marlowe?" Joe was astonished.

"The same. That's some name, huh? Zia. Looks like she might be part Indian. But cute as a button. I'd like to be in your shoes, Joe, though you probably have them off when you're with her."

"I can't believe it," said Joe, taking his eyes off the road momentarily several times to stare at Winfield.

"Now, Joe, I wouldn't be telling you anything Zia herself wouldn't confirm, would I, huh? She came to me, Joe, and she told me about your getting hold of some tooth, and about these great plans the two of you have to go after the critter."

"It doesn't make sense for her to do that," said Joe, bewildered.

"Why, I think it makes pretty good sense. From her standpoint, anyway. You told her you couldn't get time off to go out traipsing in the woods with her. She came to me to explain everything and ask me to give you that time off."

"Oh, Christ," said Joe. "I knew she had lots of initiative, but this is carrying it too far!"

"You would like to go look for that imaginary ape, though, wouldn't you?"

"I don't know, Zack. Some ways yes, and some ways no. If I were absolutely convinced it exists, I think yes. There's an obligation to Fred Garvey's

81

widow—but never mind all that. The point is, I don't think the chances of bringing anything back are good enough. At the moment, that's how I see it. I'm still thinking it over."

"Well, you're right about one thing. You won't bring anything back, because there ain't nothing to bring back, huh? Look, I been going out in this wilderness all my life, and I'm damned if I ever saw a bigfoot or came across real proof anybody else ever saw one."

"Okay, Zack. I don't get time off to go on a wild-ape chase. I figured that in the first place. So what's the problem?"

Winfield started laughing. His pipe went out again. He sucked on it noisily, then began to tap it on the dashboard ashtray to get the dottle out.

"What's so funny?" asked Joe.

"What's funny," said Zack, "is that there *is* no problem. Because you *are* going to go out and look for that ape."

"What?" said Joe.

"This is more fun than a fucking barrel of monkeys," said Winfield.

"Let me in on the joke so I can laugh too," said Joe.

"I'm assigning you to go out after that ape," said Winfield.

"*Assigning* me?"

"Well, you see, the way it goes," said Winfield, leaning back and slipping his thumbs under his galluses, "is like this. This smart little bird, Zia Marlowe, is a very nice young lady, and if she wants to whip up a scientific expedition here in my county, I think she should have our support. Now you and I, and any sensible person, knows there's no bigfoot. But there have been reports of something or somebody taking domestic animals and scaring the hell out of people. Could be rustlers. We still have 'em, you know. It's worth an investigation. At the same time we can provide protection for the folks on the scientific expedition. I've decided to call it a special project and put a deputy on it. One of my real whiz-kid deputies. Guess who, Joe."

"I'll guess more than who. I'll guess why. It gets me out of the way. And when everybody learns I'm looking for bigfoot they'll twirl their fingers at their temples and say, 'Poor Joe McBay! To think we ever even considered the idea of voting him in as sheriff!'"

"Always knew you were sharp, Joe. Real sharp, huh?"

"There are two little bobbles to your plan, though, Zack. One, Zia might not get the funds and there might not be an expedition. Two, I just might decide not to go on it."

"You mean disobey a direct order, Joe? That wouldn't be playing it by the book, would it? Now in spite of all these new regulations I can still get rid of somebody for disobeying a direct order."

Joe stared at Winfield for a long moment, then said, "You think you've got me by the balls, don't you?"

"I sure have," said Winfield. "And whether I start squeezing or not depends on you, huh?"

"I'm *sorry*, Joe!" said Zia, aghast. "Really! Please forgive me! I had no idea there was all this between you and Zack Winfield!"

They sat at one of the small tables in the faculty lounge, drinking the tepid coffee that tasted of Styrofoam.

"Zia, I don't want to drive this into the ground, but you can see where I'm sore as hell, can't you?"

"Of course. And you have every right to be." She reached across the table and squeezed his hand. "I was very precipitate; very foolish. I can never apologize enough, but I can explain. I really thought I could persuade Sheriff Winfield to give you the time off; I realized it would be difficult for you to ask for it on your own behalf. I wasn't trying to pressure you into it—you could have still refused if that's what you finally decided."

"Well, it's done now. What can I say?"

"You could belt me one across the chops, I suppose."

"It's not my year for whips and chains," said Joe.

"Joe, please try to understand that I thought I was doing right. Especially since Dick Charterhouse has now as much as said that Cadbury *will* put up the money for the expedition. Frankly, I'm surprised at that. But I'm awfully glad, too."

"I've got to be honest," said Joe. "I've got mixed feelings about it."

"Joe, listen to me. You may be in a better position than you think. If we find bigfoot—correction, *when* we find bigfoot—you'll be public hero number one and an absolute cinch for sheriff or maybe even better."

"That's what it all hinges on, isn't it? That little 'if,' and that little 'when.'"

"Joe, bigfoot exists. The tooth is authentic. That means Fred Garvey's story is true or close to true. And, knowing bigfoot's out there, I know how to bring in the irrefutable evidence that he exists. Ever hear the verse about the purple cow?"

"Yes."

"'I never saw a purple cow, and never hope to see one. But I'll say this much, anyhow—I'd rather see than be one.'" Joe laughed as he quoted.

"A newspaperman named Gelett Burgess wrote that. So, a practical joker got a cow, painted it purple, gilded its teats, brought it up into the poet's office, and said, 'There!' Well, that's what I'm going to do. Shove bigfoot in the faces of all the wise guys and say, 'There!'"

"Zia," said Joe, sighing, "Zack Winfield's got me by the balls, and you've got me over a barrel. This position is not conducive to comfort."

"I'll make it up to you, Joe. I'll make everything right."

84

"Do you mean that?"

"Not in the way your eyes are suggesting."

"Oh," said Joe. "For a moment I thought all this was going to be worth it."

It occurred to Joe, as he thought things over in the next several days, that the situation did have its advantages. The prospect of being in close contact with Zia Marlowe out on the wilderness for thirty days held promise. He still seemed unable to make it with her in normal surroundings; maybe the wilderness would be a more favorable setting.

He met with her at least once a day, getting progress reports on her efforts to obtain a grant. Apparently the people at Cadbury had been impressed with her presentation, and especially with the photographs and description of the tooth she'd submitted. They still wanted to see the tooth. Joe frowned and said he didn't think he could let them have it. He wasn't sure why he didn't tell her honestly that he believed it had been stolen.

Zia arranged a meeting with Dick Charterhouse at a luncheon in the Turkle Burkle Sandwich House, whatever the hell that meant. Joe had a hamburger Swiss cheese melt on toasted rye. There wasn't time for much to be said, but Dick questioned him closely about Fred Garvey's account and about the tooth. Dick apparently had been very busy checking everything: the hospital records, and both Fred's and Joe's backgrounds. Joe guessed that he was keeping his promise to Zia to work fast, which meant that he wanted to please her, which in turn probably meant that he wanted to make out with her, as Joe did. Joe wondered if by any chance he already had. That would really zing the old ego.

Joe refused to give Dick the exact location of Fred's find, and Dick seemed to understand his caution. Fact was, he didn't really have it pinpointed. He calculated that there would be an area of at least two hundred square miles to be searched, though this could be narrowed down a bit by eliminating some of the obviously impossible places.

It still bothered Joe, somehow, that Cadbury was coming through so quickly. Dick explained this partly at least by saying, "You're lucky, you know, both of you. Zia walked in just when we were looking for a vehicle like this. The idea jolted Wally Kegelmeyer at first, but he saw its merits once I explained them."

On the last day of his swing shift, Joe had two beers in a tavern, shot one game of rotation at the pool table with one of the city cops, and then went home for a good sleep. He rummaged in the fridge, found some Danish Havarti cheese, took a box of crackers from the cupboard, poured a small glass of milk, opened a camping magazine. To make room, he pushed aside a pile of unpaid bills on the kitchen table.

The tooth lay there. No envelope.

Just like that. He stared at it in surprise, picked it up, and rolled it in his fingers. He had absolutely no recollection of removing it from its envelope and putting it there. But that must have been what had happened.

I must be starting to rot on the vine already, Joe told himself.

They drove to the Indian reservation. "I just want you to see the totem pole there," said Zia. The reservation was a few miles outside of town, and it was difficult to tell when you crossed the line and were on the reservation. There were sharecropper-like shacks and at least two wrecks of old cars in every yard. The tribal center was a group of well-kept buildings the federal government had paid for. There was a tourist shop nearby—trinkets probably made in Taiwan—and the big totem pole stood in front of it.

"Reading from bottom to top," said Zia, "we see Bear Mother, the wolf, the raven, and the dogfish. At the very top is sasquatch. The lower ones represent the principal phratries of the Tillamish tribe; the sasquatch—which I grant you looks more like a goat by Picasso—represents the soul of all the Tillamish. They've always known about the sasquatch. When I came around to ask questions, one of them said to me, 'Oh. The white man finally got around to hearing about it, I see.'"

An old, fat Indian who had apparently been drinking came near and stood there swaying and staring at them.

"Hi," said Joe. "Is Tom Quick around?"

"Tom? No, he went to Utah. Big intertribal conference. He's always off on something like that. You folks want to buy some genuine Tillamish beads?"

"No, thanks," said Zia. To Joe, she whispered, "The Tillamish don't do beadwork—never have."

On the way back, she said to Joe, "Who's Tom Quick?"

"He's their lawyer. Young fellow. Pretty good troop. I've seen him in court. He doesn't seem like an Indian. Hell, none of 'em do."

Zia nodded. "They've lost something. Of course, I don't expect them to stand around with their arms folded in blankets and say, 'Ugh!' Still, they *are* wearing the white man's ways now. I think that's what I mean. They don't actually have the white man's ways—they're just wearing them."

"Do you think any of them has ever seen a sasquatch?"

"If so," said Zia, "I don't think he'd let the white man know it."

Dick Charterhouse had arranged a dinner for three in the Cedar Room of the Pioneer Hotel. Joe studied Dick as they sat at the table. He saw how Zia kept looking at him with her eyes a few lumens brighter than they had to be, and he decided that the

87

reason he couldn't like Dick altogether was plain and simple jealousy.

Otherwise, he realized, he might have liked Dick fine, just fine. Maybe the man had a touch of snobbery that wasn't quite to Joe's taste, but on him it looked almost good, like his Brooks Brothers suit and his regimental-stripe tie. He'd gathered a few facts concerning Dick by now, but from Zia and the man himself. Dick had many skills Joe admired. He had boxed and fenced and learned to shoot. He knew the martial arts of the orient—judo, karate, aikido, takewondo, and also, apparently, had picked up plain old back-alley dirty fighting. He'd parachuted and skin-dived and held a light-plane pilot's certificate. Perhaps his greatest passion was mountain climbing. He'd soloed Rainier by the difficult Willis Wall route.

Dick cut himself a bit of Beef Wellington, the specialty of the house, and ate it European-style, his fork pronated in his left hand, his busy knife in his right.

"Very well, good friends and dear companions," he said at last, showing a lopsided smile that was full of rakish charm. "There's no point in letting the suspense drag out any longer. Zia, brace yourself."

"I'm braced and breathless," she said.

"The Cadbury Corporation," said Dick, measuring the words as he payed them out, "has decided to accept your proposal."

One beat. Chimes ringing. Zia flushed excitedly. "Oh, Dick!" That seemed to be all she could say in the clutch of emotion. She knuckled a spot of moisture away from the corner of her eye.

"There are a few conditions, of course. We might as well have a clear understanding of them right now, at the beginning. First, it will be known as the Cadbury Expedition. That will be cranked into all the publicity. The corporation will receive a twenty-five percent royalty on any direct returns—films, promotions, and so on. It's all in the contract, and you'll have a chance to go over it thoroughly. There's nothing I would call unreasonable, and I'm sure you'll be in agreement, but if there are any questions, please bring them to my attention, and we'll negotiate if necessary. Does that sound all right so far?"

"I suppose so," said Zia. "I don't know what you mean by promotions. I hope it's not bigfoot T-shirts or anything like that."

"It might be. Dolls, T-shirts—who knows?"

She shuddered. "Well, beggars can't be choosers. What else, Dick?"

"Funds will be in a special account, and I'll countersign all checks for equipment and other expenses. You can have office space at Cadbury, if you wish, for the preliminary work. I'll be working with you, full-time, because I've been assigned to the project. In fact—and we might as well get this clearly established right now—I'll be director of the expedition, and I'll be calling the shots."

"Does that mean you're going along with us?"

"My dear Zia, I wouldn't miss it for the world. I thought you understood that. I hope you don't object."

"Certainly not in any personal way," she said. "But I had planned on a team with members qualified in certain fields, and the more versatile they are, the better. I know a veterinarian, for example, who's also a fine outdoorsman and, best of all, a bigfoot buff. We want to keep the group down to about five. That's important. Fewer people will be able to move faster and there will be less chance of alarming the creatures."

"I understand all that," said Dick, nodding. "I went over your presentation quite thoroughly. As for myself, I must confess I can't contribute much in the way of scientific knowledge, but I have other assets. I'm quite at home in the mountains, and"—he grinned—"I can even cook pretty well. I'll insist on garlic and marjoram as part of our commissary."

"We'll hold you to that," said Zia. "What else?"

"The next person we'll need is a first-rate cinematographer. I have someone in mind, name of Pete Hollinger. He's in Hollywood, and his field is documentaries. I've worked with him before and know his abilities, so I think we'll have to use Pete. I've already contacted him, and he's willing."

Zia looked disappointed. "I'd planned on an archaeologist I know whose hobby is films."

Dick shook his head. "No amateurs. It's too important."

"All right," said Zia, with a little frown. "But we're using up our quota fast. You, Joe, this cameraman, myself. And I'm the only scientist. I'd hoped we'd be able to make a thorough study of the creatures when we find them. Observe behavior, take biological samples, compile some statistical data. That's in the presentation, too."

Dick, still smiling, shrugged. "I'm sorry about the quota, but that's the way it is. You get to pick the last member, though. Maybe that vet you spoke about."

Joe, who had been listening, quietly shifted in his chair as a signal that he was about to speak. "I think we'd better have a guide," he said. "I'm enough of an outdoorsman to know that a professional guide on something like this is a necessity. All we find won't do as much good if we can't get in and out in one piece. And, believe me, the country we're going into is unforgiving. We need someone who knows it like the back of his hand."

"I believe I agree with that," said Dick.

Zia sighed. "I suppose I'm forced to agree with it."

"The best man I know," said Joe, "is Emory Greer. He's licensed and well experienced, particularly in the northern Cascades. I've worked with him through our volunteer mountain-rescue unit. He's right here in town—runs an outdoor equipment shop.

He'd rather be out in the mountains, I think, but that doesn't support him and his wife. Anyway, I recommend him."

"Sound him out, then," said Dick. He glanced at Zia. "Is that all right with you?"

"It'll have to be," she said, with an air of resignation.

"Good!" said Dick. "We're off to the races! The rest is just putting all the nuts and bolts together. Do I mix metaphors? I probably do. It's all too exciting for one to sit here and compose proper rolling prose."

Everyone laughed. It was time for liqueur and coffee. Dick ordered Grand Marnier. Zia followed suit, and Joe ordered Calvados.

"A toast!" Dick said.

They raised their glasses.

"To the Cadbury Expedition and its complete success!" said Dick.

They drank.

Chapter Six

Joe McBay was constantly surprised at the effort required to put together a wilderness outing for five people for thirty days, even with the specialized equipment that had to be procured. He was not ready to complain about this, however, especially since Sheriff Winfield, assigning him to the expedition, reduced his patrol work (causing the sergeant who had to revise the schedules to grumble a bit) and allowed him time to assist Zia in her preparations. He considered that good duty.

Declining Dick's offer of office space Zia worked out of her cubbyhole on the second floor of Underwood Hall. The head of the life sciences department somewhat reluctantly went along with all of it, including her leave of absence. She began to compile lists, file invoices for the purchase of equipment, and use the long-distance phone for procurement and the gathering of information. Once she called all the way to Nairobi to ask a game curator his opinion concerning the tranquilizer to be used.

The problem with the tranquilizers (as Joe learned in what was more or less a spectator's role) was that their effectiveness was based on both species and weight, known factors in other animals, but conjecture when it came to the sasquatch. Estimating a typical full-grown sasquatch to be three hundred kilos, Zia thought at first of using succinyl choline chloride in the amount recommended for grizzly bear: 1.2 milligrams per kilo. It took several minutes for this drug to take effect, however, and kept the animal down for only six or seven minutes. The dosage was also critical and could easily amount to too much or too little. The man in Nairobi recommended M99, a newer morphine derivative which, he said, could knock out an elephant in two minutes and keep it tranquilized for fifteen. Its added advantage was that the beast could be revived with an antidote at any time, which lessened the possibility of killing it with an overdose.

Having decided upon M99, Zia spent another hour on the phone finding a source for it, and then ordering a CO_2 gun plus a supply of three-and-a-half-inch hypodermic-needle darts with expansion tablets to activate their pistons. Next came the drawn-out business of obtaining the permit for the purchase of the drug.

And so on, and so on.

Dick Charterhouse would be consulted about the purchases from time to time, usually by phone.

"Do we really need this tranquilizer equipment?"

"Of course," said Zia. "We *must* have these biological samples. Hair, skin, blood, body fluids. Especially blood. With the Sarich-Wilson tests we can find out exactly where the creature stands in relation to man. The samples will also be absolute proof of the creature's existence."

"Why can't we simply shoot one and have the carcass hauled back by helicopter?"

"Shoot one?"

"Well, I don't find any pleasure in killing animals—which is more than I can say for some humans, by the way—but in this case it seems justified."

"What if it turns out to be human, or very close to human?"

"All right, Zia," said Dick. "We'll do it your way."

Further permits had to be obtained from various agencies so that they and their equipment could enter the Kayatuk Wilderness. Ordinarily no vehicles, including aircraft, were permitted. Zia was able to procure an okay for helicopter supply to the base camp and for overflight reconnaissance, but not for subsequent landings except in case of emergency. Meanwhile, in close conference, they all selected a site for the base camp from a detailed map and chartered a helicopter to fly to the spot and survey it. It was on a knoll in a broad meadow by a stream and seemed eminently suitable.

"What we'll do," Zia explained, "is make helicopter searches and then hike from the base camp to any promising areas, one at a time. We ought to minimize the use of the helicopter. It could easily frighten the creatures off. They might be lost forever, then."

As the equipment arrived it was stored in warehouse space provided at the Cadbury paper-products plant. There was clothing in assorted sizes: thermal, underwear, wool shirts and trousers, sweaters, knee-length parkas, eight-inch Alpspitz boots, and tenpoint crampons in case ice slopes or glaciers had to be climbed. Dick himself ordered the eleven-millimeter perlon climbing rope, the carbiners for hooking and fastening (he called them "beaners"), and the ice axes and pitons and jam nuts. He went into a long dissertation on why jam nuts were generally superior to conventional pitons, and they took his word for it. There were the big tents and the electric generator for the base camp; there were the individual Alpine tents for their sorties out from the base camp; there were Kelty frames for packing in and softer Chouinard knapsacks for climbing.

By now Joe had revealed to the others the area in which Fred Garvey had crashed. It was to be kept a tight secret; Dick cautioned all hands never to mention it to anyone, and especially not to reporters during any of the interviews they now found themselves giving with increasing frequency. Zia agreed with this policy, averring that there must be a hundred sasquatch hunters in the Northwest who would like to steal a march on them.

In the midst of all these weighty matters, Dick, at a luncheon conference, came up with a trivial point, though he was properly apologetic about it.

"The discoverer gets to name a new species, isn't that so?" he asked Zia.

"That's the custom," she said.

"Well, our good president asked me to be sure to mention this. Genus and species, I believe. If bigfoot's genus turns out to be *Homo*, let us say, Wally would like him called *Homo kegelmeyeriensis.*"

"Poor beast!" said Zia, laughing. "What are we doing to him?"

Emory Greer was in the back room of his shop, sharpening an Italian-made ice ax for a customer. The steel was made to withstand subzero temperatures, and it had to be ground without being heated excessively. Expert climbers knew this and brought their axes to Greer for sharpening. He used a felt wheel on which an abrasive powder had been cemented; it tended to grind and polish at the same time.

Greer was a huge, muscular man; his skin was like supple leather stretched tight over his thews. He had deep creases in his face, a thin, determined mouth, and overhanging, bushy brows which shaded pale, eyes.

He would rather be out in the mountains than here in the shop, he was thinking—a thought that came to him at regular intervals—but if he *had* to be confined like this, the work of sharpening ice axes was not too bad. It beat waiting on customers and listening to their boring tales, usually about how much whiskey they'd drunk or what other sins they'd committed on their ridiculous little camping trips. He preferred to leave waiting on customers to Dahlia, who was much better at it. She was out there now, selling packs of dried mountain rations to a couple of young men. He wished she'd push a few goose-down jackets or something equally expensive upon them. The shop hadn't taken in much in the past month, even with the hunting season approaching.

On the high table, beside the grinding wheel, Greer kept an open Bible from which he read as he worked. He was up to Ecclesiastes now, and still had a long way to go before he could say he'd read the Bible whole, which was what the Pillar of God Church demanded all its members do. They even sold them these special Bibles which could be carried anywhere and opened for reading in one's spare moments. Once a month Greer dutifully canvassed residential neighborhoods to sell Bibles, pass out tracts, and bring more followers into the fold. That also was expected of all true-believing PGs.

Switching off the grinding wheel for a moment, in order to inspect the edges of the serrated side of the ax, Greer heard laughter from the other room. He frowned, as he usually did when he heard laughter. He looked through the partly opened door. Dahlia was leaning across the counter, very close, he thought, to the two young men, sticking one foot out behind her and wiggling it, putting her little finger into the corner of her mouth in a shameless provocative gesture.

Greer watched flatly, expressionlessly, the only sign of his anger a slight compression and further thinning of his lips.

"Y'all come again, you hear?" Dahlia was saying to the two young men.

"We sure will, honey!" said one.

"Love that way you talk!" said the other.

There was one more flurry of laughter as they left the shop. Still smiling, Dahlia straightened herself away from the counter. She was beginning to be plump now in her early thirties, but the effect was sexy. Dahlia looked like a bouncy, cuddly little playdoll, and she knew it. She wore her bluejeans low and tight, and the top two buttons of her plaid flannel shirt open. She slid out the cash drawer now and dropped the bills and change she'd just collected into it.

Greer came into the room with toed-in moccasin steps. "I saw that there," he said. "I heard you."

She looked up. "What are you sayin', Em?"

"Tempting them two. I saw you."

"Oh, for Christ's sake, Em" said Dahlia, "let's not start that again."

"How many times I told you not to use the name of our Savior in vain, woman? I *saw* the way you was acting. You think I don't notice, but I do!"

"Em, what in hell"—she pronounced it "hay-yull"—"am I supposed to do? Be grouchy like you and drive all the customers off?"

"You know what I'm talkin' about, Dahlia."

"No, I don't! When you get like this I'm sorry I ever left Texas. Back home, folks are friendly, like they're supposed to be!"

Greer drew a deep breath and then intoned: "'For the lips of a strange woman drop as honeycomb, but her end is bitter as wormwood, sharp as a two-edged sword!'"

"Em, you're enough to *drive* someone to sin! What would you do if I ever *really* done anything with anybody?"

Greer's deep-set eyes burned with white fire as he stared back at his wife. He was fishing for an answer. Something appropriate from the Holy Word. He didn't suppose that in their three years of marriage Dahlia had ever gone all the way in cheating on him, but he knew well that in her mind she had succumbed to the desire to do so, and that was practically the same thing. She had not seemed such a Jezebel when he'd first met her. That was how she'd exercised her guile. She'd taken on that air of meekness deliberately to entrap him.

He'd been vulnerable when she'd appeared. After a

lifetime of sin he'd been born again by joining the Pillar of God Church, and it was the pastor himself, the Reverend Ernest Osterman, who'd said he ought to take unto himself a wife, cleave to her in holy matrimony, settle down, and do God's work here in town, as all PGs did.

He'd picked Dahlia up where she'd been hitchhiking into town. A man had brought her to these parts, then abandoned her. She'd been coming to Pickettsville, where, she'd heard, there was work in the salmon cannery. He'd bedded with her the first night, drenched in guilt afterward, but also evilly delighted with the pleasure he'd known. She'd done things he'd never known, were done. It had been God's way of trying him. After their marriage, the outdoor-equipment shop was Dahlia's idea. She had the Devil's cleverness when it came to business, and she handled most of the details. Occasionally, these days, he guided hunters or backpackers into the mountains, but it wasn't anything like it had been before. The Reverend Ernest Osterman assured him he'd chosen the right path and that he would know glory on the day of judgment. He dutifully gave ten percent of his income to the Pillar of God Church.

Before Greer could find a suitable quotation with which to answer Dahlia this time, Joe McBay walked into the shop.

"Hi, Em; hi, Dahlia," said Joe. He wasn't in uniform this evening, so it probably wasn't an official call. When one of the sheriff's men called in uniform it usually had something to do with the volunteer mountain rescue unit. Rescue missions gave great joy to Greer; they got him out into the wilderness again, where there was all that space for a man to swing his elbows.

Greer nodded a greeting to Joe.

"How you doin', Joe?" Dahlia asked brightly.

"Fine, just fine, Dahlia," said Joe. Greer sensed that Joe's return grin was merely friendly. He'd never figured Joe McBay for a threat, and this placated him somewhat. "Em," said Joe, "can we talk somewhere?"

"What about?"

"It'll take time to explain. Maybe we can go out and get a beer or something."

Greer frowned and nodded toward the workshop. "We can talk here good as anyplace. Come on back."

He shuffled chairs in the workshop, and Joe sat upon one. Joe began by explaining that he had a job for Em, and then he went on to outline the events that had led to the formation of the Cadbury Expedition. "We want the best guide there is," he said. "That's you, Em."

Greer took his usual long pause before speaking. He dredged up words with difficulty and mistrusted them when he found them. "Bigfoot, huh?" he said finally.

"That's right, Em. What do you think about him? Think he's out there somewhere?"

"Myself, I ain't never seen the critter. But I've heard tell lots about him. Him and the tracks he's made. I got an idea as to what maybe bigfoot is."

"What's that, Em?"

"One of Satan's demons, that's who. It says so in Revelations. 'The Devil, as a roaring lion, walketh about, seeking whom he may devour.'"

"I'm not sure bigfoot's all that fierce," said Joe. "Anyway, we intend to find out exactly what he is. It could mean a lot to you, Em. Maybe even make you famous. You'd have more customers than you could handle."

Em thought that part of it over for a few seconds. "Folks I could maybe show the light to and save," he said, nodding.

"I suppose so," said Joe.

"I'll go with you, then," said Greer.

"Good. I'll get back to you with the details. When we start and all that. It'll be pretty soon."

"Bad time, right now, for the mountains."

"We know that," said Joe. "But we can't put it off. Anyway, that's one of the reasons we need a man like you."

"This here woman professor," said Greer. "Is she a Christian?"

"I don't know. Probably. I never asked her."

"There's some of these scientific people who are godless and do the Devil's work. They preach that man's descended from monkeys. That ain't what the Bible says."

"Well, whatever the truth, Em, Zia's not the kind to push anything on you. You'll like her, Em. And you just may get more out of this than you ever dreamed of. There could even be a fortune in it."

"'He that trusteth in his riches,'" said Emory Greer sternly, "'shall fail.'"

"Okay, Joe, okay, Zia," said Pete Hollinger, holding his Angenieux with its 12-to-120 zoom lens at the ready, "what you do now is pile some of those boxes in place, okay? Joe does the piling; Zia makes, like, notes and things on the clipboard. Got it?"

They were in the warehouse where the equipment was piled. Zia looked at the clipboard Pete had given her and said, "But we really don't do it like this, Pete."

"Do it, schmoo it," said Pete Hollinger. "It has to be this way to tie the scene together. Okay, let's run through it once more, then we'll try a take."

Zia glanced at Joe, and she and Joe traded shrugging smiles. Pete Hollinger had them doing that fairly often by now. He'd checked into the Pioneer Hotel, Dick Charterhouse had called a meeting to introduce him, and at several meetings after that Pete had explained how he'd be shooting the preparations for the progress of the expedition so that the end result would be, as he put it, "one of the greatest documentaries of all time! Dynamite! Pure dynamite!"

100

Pete was short and fat. He was built out of two globes, a large one for his body and a smaller one for his head. His skin was smooth and fair and his eyes were innocent blue. He wore loud plaid sports jackets that made him look fatter.

"Is he famous or something?" Joe had asked Dick Charterhouse. "I don't follow movies much."

Dick had smiled. "Not exactly famous. But he's established in the movie industry. He's done big documentaries. He grew up in the business and he knows every facet of it, including photography. He produced some institutional films for Cadbury, and that's how I got to know him."

"Do you think he's the best we can get for the expedition?"

"Maybe not the best. But he's quite competent, and I know I can handle him. I don't have to spend a lot of time figuring out someone new. Don't worry about Pete. He'll do a good job. He has to—he needs a success for a change."

Having finished shooting the brief sequence in the warehouse, Pete Hollinger nodded and said, "Dynamite! Okay, that's all at this location."

"Can we get back to work now, Pete?"

"Dick said I could have you all morning. Didn't he tell you? Look, I was thinking we ought to get something on these Indians near town. We could shoot you getting info on bigfoot from the chief or something. Somebody with a good costume is what we need."

"We haven't checked with the Indians," said Zia, "and we don't really have to."

"So what's the diff?" asked Pete. "Make a hell of a scene. Movement, color, production values—"

"Let's just go get some coffee," said Joe.

He was seeing more of Zia Marlowe than ever before these days, but the curious conspiracy to keep him from making it with her was still working. The irony of it was that she liked him, he knew, as much as he did her, and that went for the physical side of it,

101

too. He could tell that by the way she looked at him, and sometimes brushed against him, and, indeed, by the warmth with which she kissed him now and then. But whenever he managed to maneuver her to his place or hers, there was always some last-minute development to block a touchdown. The calendar, one week. Another time, a headache. Or she really needed her sleep. Once, when he'd brought her home, she'd looked at him ingenuously and said, "Joe, something like this has to be exactly right, and tonight, to put it bluntly, I'm simply not in the mood."

After Pete had shot the warehouse scene, he drove her home to change her clothes. Pete had wanted them both in rugged outdoor garb—for production values or something. She let Joe into her apartment, said she'd only be a few moments, and went to take a shower.

Joe lit a small cigar and looked around her one main room, with its kitchenette partitioned off to one side, and its hide-a-bed sofa against the wall. There were excellent watercolors of animals—deer, bear, cougar—on the walls, and when he squinted more closely he saw her signature in the corner of each. There was a classical guitar standing in one corner, and brightly lacquered Mexican gourds festooned some of the molding. There was a poster about saving the whales. There was a clay model of a sasquatch eighteen inches high atop one bookcase.

He inspected the statue more closely. The face was brutish, part simian, part human. The forehead was low, the eyes deep-set. It stood fully erect, bent forward very little. "The only mammal, except for man, who walks truly erect," Zia had said. From listening to her he himself was becoming something of an expert on bigfoot. He still found it hard to accept that the beast really existed. He wondered why. Maybe, in some subconscious way, he didn't want the beast to exist. Maybe it was too close to some kind of truth about man he didn't want to hear. Hard to say.

When Zia finally came out of the shower she was, to Joe's eye, absolutely breathtaking. A big red towel was tight across her swelling, upcurved breasts. It reached down to just below her pubic region, creating maddening shadows there. Her golden thighs glistened and there were tiny drops of unblotted bathwater still upon them.

"Just another minute," said Zia, crossing toward her closet, "and I'll get something on and make lunch for us right here."

He followed her as she crossed the room, and, reaching her, took her by the shoulders and turned her so that she faced him. She stiffened and looked up at him with her eyes switching back and forth almost imperceptibly.

"Zia?" He pulled her body forward, against his.

"Not now, Joe." She shook her head quickly.

He kissed her, but she did not respond eagerly. She drew her head away and said, "Really. Not now."

"Not ever, I'm beginning to think," said Joe.

She closed her eyes for a moment, as though in difficult thought, then opened them again. "I think I'll have to tell you now. I knew I'd have to, sometime."

"Tell me what?"

"The reason. The big reason. You've got to understand."

"I'm listening."

"Joe, I like you. Very much. Maybe close to love—I'm not sure. It's wonderful when we're together, and I think about it all the time."

"Then why don't we do something about it?"

"It's because of me, Joe. Because of the way I am."

"Dammit, whatever it is, say it!"

"Joe, listen to me. There's a bad gene in our family. Our blood clots too readily. Father died of thrombosis—so did his father. I've inherited this tendency. And I was warned about something quite early, Joe. The pill. The magic pill that brought about the great

103

sexual revolution of our time. I can't take it, Joe. It exacerbates this condition. There is literally the possibility that taking the pill would kill me."

"Well, I'm sorry about that, but there are other ways to keep from getting pregnant."

She shook her head. "None a hundred percent effective. I can't afford to take even a long chance. Not right now, anyway, when I'm determined to get that doctorate. All else is subordinate. That's how it's been with me, Joe. Always."

"Always?"

"This is what I'm trying to tell you, Joe. I've indulged in love play, as I suppose anyone has. But I've never gone all the way. I'm twenty-five years old and still a virgin."

He stared at her. "I'll be damned," he said finally. "I'll be goddamned."

"We can make love, Joe—after a fashion. Up to a point, I suppose you'd say. If you'd like. If you insist on it."

"Of course I'd like!" he said. "Though insisting on it doesn't sound like much fun. I want to make love to you somehow, but—but—"

"Yes. There'd be a 'but,' wouldn't there?"

"I don't know!" he said angrily. "Dammit, all this puts me off balance!"

"Joe, you had to know about it. We've been getting closer, so you had to know before it became even more difficult. Someday, when I feel I can risk having a child, sometime when the situation permits, yes, I'll go all the way with you. Or somebody else if you're no longer around. Whatever happens naturally. But you must understand the way it is now."

"I'm trying, dammit, I'm trying."

"And *I'll* understand, Joe, if you want to back off. Go somewhere else for what you want. We can continue being friends, I hope, the way we are now."

He took the top edge of the towel and slipped it down below her breasts. Her nipples stood erect in large pink nests.

"If this is what you want, Joe. But it won't be the best. It's my fault. I've made the moment awkward."

"Goddammit, then!" said Joe, bringing the towel up again. "Let's have some lunch and get back to work!"

"I'm sorry, Joe. Don't be angry. The right time will come. I promise you that."

"Yeah. Sure. The right time will come." He spoke flatly, and without conviction.

Pete Hollinger sipped at his fourth scotch and soda and looked at the stupid people in the stupid bar—the Loggers' Lounge of the Pioneer Hotel in where-in-the-hell-is-Pickettsville, Washington, Nine-eight-bla-bla-bla; he couldn't even remember the zip code. This was really the boonies. *Everybody* here was a logger in one way or another. Everybody wore wool shirts and clodhopper boots. The bartender had a big black beard and was dressed like Paul Bunyan. Pete had already asked him where the action was; he'd suggested the town's one massage parlor.

Once more, Pete swiveled partly about on the barstool, which his ample buttocks covered thoroughly, and surveyed the booths and tables. There were one or two passable foxes, but they seemed totally wrapped up in their dates.

The mural on the far wall caught his attention. There were loggers hacking away at tall evergreens, with the snow-capped Cascades in the background. The mountains reminded him of that mean-eyed guide, Emory Greer, he'd been introduced to—he'd cast him as John Brown at Harper's Ferry. And that reminded him, in turn, of that plump little Cornish game hen he had for a wife.

His next sudden recollection was that Emory Greer had been sent to Seattle to procure some kind of camping equipment. He was to stay there overnight, Pete seemed to remember.

Pete dropped a couple of bills on the bar and left the Loggers' Lounge.

It was only a short walk to the Trail Hut, which was the name of Greer's establishment. Pete went past the closed storefronts of the J.C. Penney and the Woolworth and the Pay 'n' Save and all the clothing and shoe stores on the main drag, close to deserted, even at this early hour, and then he went down a couple of other streets until he came to Greer's place, which, he saw, was still open.

The plump little pigeon (what the hell was her name—some flower) was in the shop as he entered, at a desk near the rear, going over books. She looked up. Her smile was sudden and bright. "Oh, it's you, Mr. Hollinger! I declare!"

"Pete, for God's sake," he said, laughing.

"Well, sure. Pete. And you call me Dahlia. They used to call me Doll for short back home sometimes, but I'm a big girl now, you know what I mean? I guess you're lookin' for Emory. He's not here. He went to Seattle and won't be back till tomorrow." By now she had risen and was standing before him, wriggling a little, tossing her head this way and that, putting her hand on her hip and dropping it again. Keep it up, baby, thought Pete, you'll find the right pose yet.

"I wasn't specially looking for Emory," he said to her, smiling and showing his dimples. Her air of being slightly flustered amused him. Back on his home turf he wouldn't have given her a second look, but now, after a second look, she *was* kind of cute and sexy, and, more importantly, she was *here*. Taking her would be like shooting fish in a barrel. "What time do you close?"

"I was just about to."

"Well, it got kind of lonely for me at the hotel, so I thought I'd look up some company. Want to go out somewhere and have a couple of drinks?"

"That would be right fine," said Dahlia. She pronounced it "rat fan." "But I don't expect it would look so good. Not that we'd be doin' anything wrong, you understand—"

"No, of course not," said Pete.

106

"But this is a pretty small town and some folks might see us and get the wrong idea. You could just stay here and we could talk. I've got some beer in the icebox. You like beer?"

"Sure," said Pete. He despised the stuff.

The small apartment was upstairs, just over the store. The furniture was schlocky, as he'd expected, and there were reproductions of genuine oil paintings of sylvan scenes and flowers in vases on the walls. There was a framed embroidered motto near the door that said, "Believe on the Lord Jesus Christ and ye shall be saved." Pete had often wondered what the difference was between believing *on* and believing *in*. Maybe Dahlia would turn out to be a religious nut?

"I'll get into something a little more comfy," said Dahlia. He'd been waiting for it.

He sat on the worn floral-printed sofa, an open beer can on the flimsy coffee table in front of him. She disappeared.

He'd better get what he could now, there wouldn't be much nooky once they started out into the mountains. The gal professor was attractive, but he didn't get the right vibes from her. He had an idea she was making it with Dick Charterhouse, anyway. Well, he'd been on location before when there was nothing around in the way of amusement; it was one of the hazards of his trade.

Dahlia appeared at last in a diaphanous negligee thing with, so help him, fake ostrich feathers on it. He could smell her cheap musky perfume all the way across the room.

Within almost too short a time she was cuddled against him and he was stroking her soft pubic hair and feeling it moisten. He found her clit, which was excitingly prominent, and fingertipped it lightly till she moaned. He hoped she had no lower-class objections to sixty-nine. Pete liked sixty-nine even better than regular screwing. His cock was just a little short for regular screwing.

He nibbled on Dahlia's tits.

"Do you think I have a good figure?" she asked.

"Dynamite, love, dynamite," said Pete.

"I always wondered if I could get in the movies sometime. I do some pickin' and singin', you know. Some folks say I sound just like Dolly Parton."

"I'll get you an audition sometime. I know everybody at the networks."

"You're cute as a bug's ear, Pete," said Dahlia. "Just as cottonpickin' cute as a little old bug's ear."

They were coupled like a pair of Spanish question marks when a key rattled in the door. Emory Greer brought his towering frame into the room. There they were, naked on the ratty couch, staring at Emory in surprise.

Greer stared for a long, painful string of moments, and then he roared: "The Lord Jehovah guide me in this here my moment of shame!"

"Now, look, Em," said Pete, hastily worrying himself into his shorts and then his trousers. "I know this looks bad, and, okay, sure, it is bad, but—"

"Disciple of the Devil!" roared Emory Greer. He rushed forward, grabbed Pete by the shoulders, and pulled him erect as easily as though he'd lifted a pillow. Pete stared back at him in hollow-eyed terror. He was, in this moment, more frightened than he'd ever been in his life.

Greer shoved Pete back, then backhanded him hard across the cheek. Pete felt the jolting pain all the way into the pulp of his molars, cried out, "No! Please!" and dropped to the floor. Greer picked him up and backhanded him the other way. Pete dropped a second time. He put up his pudgy hands and said, "Please, Em, please!" Tears came down his fat cheeks. "Look, Em, I'll do anything to make it up! I can get you a good job! In the movies—you could be in the movies, Em! Just don't do this, Em! Let's talk it over! We can work something out!"

Greer picked him up once more and drew his hand back a third time. But this time he did not strike. A curious relaxation came over his deeply lined face

108

like a sudden, queer shadow. The look frightened Pete very badly.

"Em—look—I was wrong—I admit that—"

"Shut up!" roared Greer. "You too, Dahlia. We are going to do what the Word teaches us. First thing, I want to hear both of you ask for forgiveness!"

"Sure, Em! That's only right!" said Pete eagerly. "Forgive me, Em. Okay? Forgive me—"

"Say it in God's name!"

"In God's name, forgive me."

"You, too, Dahlia."

"In God's name, forgive me," said Dahlia quickly.

"And now both of you," said Emory Greer, trembling to keep his fury down where he'd put it, "are gonna clothe yourselves."

"Sure, Em. Sure. Anything you say," said Pete.

When they were dressed, he had them kneel at the coffee table, across from each other. He folded his hands and looked up at the ceiling.

"Merciful Father," he said, "we're all sinners till we get ourselves born again, like you know, and we ask your forgiveness for our sins. And specially now we ask you to forgive me for wanting to murder, which is about the same as doing it, and these here two servants of yours for the awful thing they was doing. We ask that you let them see the light of your countenance and the wickedness of their ways they've took on to themselves. We ask..."

Later that night, in bed with Dahlia, Emory Greer was strong and fierce in his lovemaking. For maybe the first time ever with Em, Dahlia really enjoyed it.

Chapter Seven

Self pushed through the dimness of the long tunnel at the lower end of the canyon. Here, the glacial stream, fed from the ice cliffs above the caves of the Ones, widened as it tumbled through the gorge. It would emerge soon and drop as a long, slender waterfall to a valley below, a place of greenery and of other living things. She had been to the far end of the tunnel before, but she had not yet descended into the valley. The few brief sorties she'd made so far into the outer world had been by way of the cliffs hemming in the gorge, and then along a circuitous route downward to the timberline. She had, on these occasions, been in the company of an older creature, teaching her to find her way.

Now, at last, Self had decided to make her first foraging trip on her own. She was not sure just how this compulsion had come upon her; it had begun with faint, restless stirrings deep inside her, and then, suddenly, this morning, she had known that it was time for her to make the journey. As nearly as she could observe it was always that way when any of the Ones left the gorge. A restlessness, a puzzled and dissatisfied air, and then a sudden departure. It was well that the urge came along, to different individuals at random. That kept a steady supply of meat coming in to the ice caves.

And when Self had started forward—the others glancing at her indifferently, but knowing quite well that she was about to forage—she had begun to tingle with excitement. It was a sensation unlike that she felt when she was about to enter into sexual activity with a male. She'd done it with two males now, Big Male and Broken Foot, with both several times, and that she had done it finally made her feel both sad and wise. She was more confident in her movements now, and a little less playful than she had been before. Her breasts seemed to be growing larger, and she loved to stroke them now and then with the palms of her hands.

There was something about her last copulation with Big Male that made her want to open her mouth wide, stretch it horizontally, and make the odd sounds of relief and pleasure that Old One said the Pink Skins also made upon occasion. Big Male had approached *her* this time, and had led her to the same nest of rocks. And then, as he was breathing hard and pumping himself into her, his mate, Skinny One, had suddenly appeared and had begun to leap up and down in a fury, howling in anger and baring her fangs. The sight of it should have frightened Self, but somehow it only made her want to produce the whinnying pleasure sound. Big Male had withdrawn, stood erect, and had then turned to face Skinny One, himself grumbling and growling. Skinny One had screamed at him, charged, and then broken off the charge a few feet away from him. The mock charge was a favorite device of the Ones, and Self had seen it many times. Big Male had then begun to make sweet, chirping, placating sounds, and that had struck Self as irresistibly amusing; she had made the laughter noise openly, and quite loud. Skinny One at that point screamed curses at her, too. Self had boldly stood in place and faced Skinny One defiantly. Skinny One had not charged—not even one of the charges that obviously would be broken off at the last instant—and had finally lowered her eyes, pretending she had suddenly noticed something of vital interest on the ground beside her. There was nothing on the ground but rock and moraine, all of it quite motionless.

Moments later, Big Male put his arm around Skinny One's shoulders and led her away. As they disappeared, she was cooing and snuggling against him, as though nothing had ever happened.

Much time passed before Self could stop making the laughing sounds, even though she was alone now and making them purely to herself.

"It is the way of the Ones," Old One had said, "for mate to remain with mate. The offspring of the Ones grow slowly, over many Times of Snow, and mate must be with mate in order to protect them in this long period of helplessness until they can fend for themselves."

He hadn't said it exactly like that, nor all at once, like that, but those thoughts were the essence of his message.

Self picked her way along the irregular rock footholds paralleling the stream, and emerged at last at the far end of the tunnel. There was a ledge here, with a groove worn in its center, where the water spurted out and then dropped several hundred feet in a long silver stream.

With great care Self began the long descent down the cliff along a route beside the waterfall. Because of her immense weight she was, like all the Ones, a slow and not very agile climber, but to offset this there was within her—indeed, within all of her species—a well-developed instinct for finding obscure footholds. It was also quite natural with her to employ such techniques as bracing, quickleaping, and chimneying without conscious thought.

There were several times during this descent when Self thought she might slip and fall, as Many-Colored Male had recently done. But each time she managed to cling to the rock, pressing herself flat against it to bring her center of gravity in, until her heart stopped racing and she could go on again.

After reaching the floor of the lower canyon, she

began to stride downslope, leaving the pool into which the waterfall tumbled. She moved along swiftly, roughly beside the stream, feeling the softer vegetated earth of this lower level beneath her broad flat feet. Instinctively she sought harder places on which to tread so that she would leave as few traces as possible. Another admonition of Old One—try not to leave footprints. But since the Ones were the greatest and strongest creatures in the wilderness and could easily vanquish any other creature that tried to track them down, Self could not see the sense of this. She walked carefully nevertheless. It was the way of the Ones.

A flicker of sly movement in an aspen thicket far down the canyon caught her eye. Her heart began pounding again, this time with excitement. There was a kill down there somewhere!

She turned her head this way and that, her immobile neck forcing her to turn her shoulders with it, and tested the direction of the wind. This was a necessary precaution she also understood by instinct. The Ones, who lacked the keen sense of smell of other hunting creatures (just as the Pink Skins lacked it, Old One had said), gave off a strong body odor by which they often identified one another in the darkness. (And the Pink Skins stank, too, said Old One; a sour, fetid odor, like rotting vegetation in a swamp.) To keep from warning game of their presence, they found it best always to approach a prospective kill from the downwind side.

Luck was with Self today. The wind blew toward her from the thicket.

Crouching slightly to make herself less visible, and also to improve her balance, Self trotted forward now in silent six-foot strides. The creature that had moved was one of the gray, sharp-faced animals that slunk about everywhere in the wilderness, themselves looking for kills. Having seen her quarry clearly now, she was able to keep it in sight almost constantly as she loped toward the trees. But now, apparently, it had spotted Self; it tried to scuttle deeper into the thicket. It began to make high-pitched, yipping sounds of fear.

Self propelled herself toward the coyote pup in a final rush, then leaped and came down upon it, her chest and belly striking the ground, her arms shooting forward, her hands grabbing the squirming, terrified creature and holding it fast and firm.

She drew it closer to her face and, mildly entertained, examined it at close range. It was soft and tiny and still making its terrified screeching sounds. It was trying to bite at her with its little needle teeth. Self felt herself admiring its courage; what was almost a feeling of affection for the little creature was starting to glow and grow within her breast. (On the savannahs, long ago, coyotes, or creatures like them, had followed the Ones, not fearing them, grateful for scraps of meat thrown to them, and sometimes coming near to let the Ones fondle them. How had she known that?)

Affection or no affection, the creature was game. Her first, fairly caught. She held it in one hand, then took its head between the thumb and forefinger of the other hand and twisted neatly. The creature jerked spasmodically in her grip several times before it became still. She brought it to her mouth, bit off one hindquarter, and began to chew, finding the morsel warm and delicious. Old One had been right when he'd said that one's own kill was the tastiest of all....

From VIEW, Sunday supplement distributed to 203 newspapers coast to coast each week:

THE GREAT WILD APE CHASE
By Kevin Burkley, Outdoors Editor

Well, they're after bigfoot again.

It seems to be seasonal, like steel strikes or the World Series.

We've just attended a press conference on the

114

eve of the Cadbury Expedition to root out poor bigfoot once more somewhere in north-central Washington State.

Cadbury's the company who sells you those two-by-fours that seem to keep going up in price, year after year. They must be doing well; they have enough to throw away, apparently, on a quest to find this imaginary hairy ape of the mountains.

The latest expedition is headed by playboy sportsman J. Richard Charterhouse III, and is given scientific respectability by Ms. Zia Marlowe, anthropologist and graduate student at Cascade University. Filmmaker Peter B. Hollinger, whose last vehicle was *Teenage Sex Around the World*, is going along to take pictures, and guarding the flanks, apparently, are mountain guide Emory Greer and deputy sheriff Joseph McBay of Cedar County, Washington.

The expedition will employ helicopters and other modern equipment. They swear bigfoot is out there and they swear they're going to bring him back.

They all do.

I have roamed the wilderness for many years, and still do so, whenever I can get away from the deskbound chores that provide bread and butter and keep my two teenagers in such necessities as hour-long phone calls and that godawful music. I have never seen a bigfoot. But I will tell you what I have seen.

The heady wine of the great outdoors does something to a man. He begins to see shapes in the clouds, demons in the shadows, saurians in every shimmer of the high, still lakes. It is no wonder that the early trappers and explorers came into civilization with tall tales of mountains that danced, or geysers that sang, or men that walked like bears or bears that walked like men.

What else is there to imagine at a lone campfire on a crisp autumn evening?

I have caught myself doing it. I dreamed of a cougar letting me scratch its belly like a tabby cat one night—and almost reported it as fact. You sleep well in the cold, thin air and your dreams seem very real.

The bigfoot buffs—they're usually hipped on flying saucers and the Loch Ness Monster, too—have been telling us for years about this giant ape, supposed to be ten feet tall, often seen but never captured, in the wilds of the Northwest. They've come up with footprints and photos that wouldn't fool my old Uncle Josh, without his bifocals. They say we can't explain away the footprints.

Well, there is much that *they* can't explain away.

I have checked some of these questions with qualified scientists, and I presume they know whereof they speak. Others are based on plain common sense. Here they are:

1. How come no piece of the creature—no hunk of bone or hank of hair—has even been brought in and duly certified for what it was?

2. How come no one's ever stumbled over a carcass? The beasts must die sometimes, like anyone else.

3. How come something as huge, and presumably as hungry, as bigfoot can find sustenance in the protein-poor Northwest? There isn't enough game left these days for the grizzlies, let alone some giant ape.

4. How come he can survive the bitter mountain winters when there's definitely nothing to eat? *Primates do not hibernate.* Put that in your monkey's paw and squeeze it.

5. How come an ape in this part of the continent, anyway? There aren't even any related species till we get down toward South America and find a few monkeys.

The how comes could go on and on, but these few are enough.

I suppose the bigfoot legend endures because people want it to. We're all looking for our roots these days, and I suppose it makes folks happy to think of some evolutionary ancestor practically in their back yards.

116

My great-grandfather, Francis Patrick Burkley, was, I've been told, a tobacco-spitting, sourpussed, whiskey-drinking, opinionated old curmudgeon. No one you'd invite to tea, God rest his soul. But I'll take him any day over a fierce and foul-smelling ape.

I say leave the legend in peace now, for a change. We're getting tired of it. Use it to frighten the kids once in a while and make them eat their rutabagas if you must. But let us grownups get on with the grim business of meeting modern life, which tempts us with enough will-o'-the-wisps of its own.

I heard a distant howling in the wilderness the other weekend. It was a banshee wail—the lonely cry of some grotesque spirit such as you see on totem poles. Or was it just a coyote? No. It couldn't have been. Who would sit up and listen if I prosaically reported hearing a coyote call to the moon?

I am sorry if I spoil the fun of believing in bigfoot for anyone. It's just that I, old crotchet that I'm becoming, prefer the palpable truth to thrilling drive-in-movie nightmares.

Chapter Eight

Kendall's Corners was represented on most road maps by the smallest type of dot shown in the legend. An unpaved road crossed the blacktop secondary highway here, to peter out presently a few miles on either side of it. The principal structure at the crossroads thus formed was Bert Kendall's gas station and general store, along with Kendall's Tavern, and then the seedy cabins of Kendall's Motor Court, where the broken neon sign said, in blinking red each night, ACANCY, whether there was a vacancy or not.

Bert Kendall himself decided to help his daughter, Monica, with her usual job of tending bar in the tavern tonight. He wanted to watch those five crazy bigfoot hunters who were spending the night in the cabins, and who would fly into the wilderness by helicopter, of all things, early the next morning.

Bert hadn't believed it at first when Joe McBay had called on him some weeks ago to make arrangements for this, but now it had actually come to pass. And that was fine as far as Bert Kendall was concerned. He'd put the word out, and folks had flocked in tonight, some from pretty far away, just to get a look at these odd interlopers. Practically all the loggers from the camp in Wolverine Canyon were here. He liked loggers. After a few beers they didn't at all mind spending their money.

He drew foaming schooners from the taps and set them on the bar for Monica to take to the tables. It was nice to have a big night like this when he'd thought the season was well finished. He was a bald, rugged-faced man, short of stature, but still muscular from his own logging days, years ago. The belly under his white apron had begun to bulge lately, so that he had to wear his belt buckle down below it. He could still hold his own, though, with anyone who wanted to start trouble. Sometimes, on Saturday nights, he had to.

Kendall kept glancing at the five bigfoot hunters who sat at two tables bunched together. They had two pitchers of beer on the table, but none of them seemed to be drinking much of it. The roly-poly one, who had breezy, big-city manners, had asked if he had anything stronger, and when Bert had explained the state's licensing laws, the fat man had said, "Christ, this *is* the boondocks!" He'd taken a supply of hard-boiled eggs and pickled Polish sausage back to the table with him.

Bert Kendall knew the young deputy—Joe McBay—who'd originally contacted him, and who'd been out this way on patrol before that. He'd never given Bert a hard time, and he hadn't even taken anyone in that night some time ago when the free-for-all started and Bert put in a call for help.

He knew Emory Greer, too, who had visited Kendall's Corners in the past when taking camping parties up into the bush. Em had always been a real silent type you never knew quite what to make of, and Bert had the feeling he'd grown surlier and maybe even a little tetched since he'd got religion.

The tall, handsome fellow who seemed to be quietly in charge—Charterhouse, that was his name —somehow looked dressed up and tailored even in his wool shirt and hiking boots. The gal with the short, dark hair and animated eyes looked kind of cute in her wilderness getup.

As far as Bert Kendall was concerned, he wished all of them luck in their search for bigfoot, though that wouldn't mean a damn thing. They'd have a better chance of finding an elephant.

A big, pale-blond logger with close-set green eyes

pounded on the bar with the flat of his hand. "Hey! How long does a guy have to wait for a beer around here?"

"Keep your britches on, Vern," said Kendall. "I'll get to you in a second." He'd have to watch Vern Topelius and his big black-bearded friend, Kaarlo, again tonight, he supposed. Those two crazy Finns had started trouble here before. Finns were as bad as Swedes. The Norwegians were the roughest, though. Them and their damned silly expression: "Oofdah!" When you boiled it right down, anybody but Anglo-Saxons, and maybe a few Krauts, *American* Krauts, anyway, had to be watched for possible odd behavior.

Kendall slid two beers to the Finns, wiped the bar, and amused himself looking at the sasquatch hunters again.

"Look, kids, I've been trying to explain this all along," Pete Hollinger was saying to the others at the table. "I just can't shoot most of these things when they actually take place. Half the time I don't know they're ready to take place, and almost all the time they don't work out visually anyway. Like everybody climbing in the chopper tomorrow. You've all got to do it several times so I can get some angles to pick from."

"Sometimes," said Zia, with a smile to cover her annoyance, "I think the main thing we're dong is trying to make a movie instead of trying to find a sasquatch."

"I know how you feel," said Dick, reaching over to pat her hand. "But the film's pretty important, just as the press conference was."

"Those stupid questions they asked!" said Zia.

"And what they printed was even stupider," said Dick. "But, as our PR man, says, the only bad publicity is no publicity at all."

Joe smiled. "We're on the way finally. That's what counts."

There had been times in the past few weeks when Joe had thought the jump-off date would never arrive. Equipment hadn't been delivered on time; bureaucrats hadn't come through with the necessary permits until the last minute. Until a few days ago Pete Hollinger had been in bed with a cold. He wasn't sure how Pete was going to hold up under the rigors of the hike that was before them; with Dick Charterhouse, he'd planned for everyone to become conditioned to the outdoors during their initial sorties in the first few days, but he wondered if Pete would ever get in shape.

At least they seemed to have put together a congenial group, except perhaps for Pete and Greer, who scowled at each other a little too often. And everyone was familiar with the basic plan of operation by now. To save flight time and expense they'd stage out of Kendall's Corners, where the supplies had already been trucked in and lay now under tarps in the big horse pasture across from the gas station. Making several relatively short trips, the chopper would lift both them and their supplies to the base-camp site the next day. It would be a comfortable base camp with most of the amenities, and with a radio to keep them in touch with Pickettsville. Each day when the weather permitted the helicopter would fly in and take two of them—enough of a load—on reconnaissance over the remoter parts of the Kayatuk Wilderness. They'd search either for Fred Garvey's downed plane or territory resembling that he'd described. With *really* good luck they might come across a sasquatch itself or his traces. Meanwhile, if aerial spotting showed an area to be promising, they'd hike there and explore it afoot. Generally, they'd try to use the chopper as little as possible. Zia was convinced it would frighten any sasquatches off if it came too near them.

Emory Greer sat by himself at the far end of the tables, peering out at everyone from under the overhangs of his brows, saying little, glancing sternly at Pete Hollinger once in a while.

"I'm almost sure bigfoot will turn out to be something close to what we now think him to be," said Zia. "A hominid primate, closer to man than any other nonhuman species, next to man in intelligence among the primates. His adaptations will have come from a long period in his present environment or one similar to it. It's probable he reached this continent from Asia when the land bridge existed ten or fifteen thousand years ago. He was pretty much in his present form at that time. I suspect reproductive isolation from a common stock that may have also produced the yeti, or Abominable Snowman of the Himalayas. He may be related, also, to the sinanthropines, found in China."

Emory Greer stirred. "Can I ask you something, Miss Marlowe?"

"Of course, Em."

"Does all this you're sayin' mean that this ape—which maybe is out there and maybe ain't—is an ancestor of human beings?"

"That's oversimplifying it, Em. The best likelihood is that he's not an ancestor at all."

"But you say they both come from the same ancestor, right?"

"Even that isn't fully known yet. In a broad way you could say that there was a forerunner for all the primates, perhaps *ramapithecus*, ten million years ago. We don't really know just when the earliest phylogenetic splitting began."

"I believe that man was made by God our father," said Greer.

Zia nodded. "There are many scientists who share your belief, Em."

"He was made separate from monkeys, in God's image."

"That may yet turn out to be true, in a way," she said.

122

"Then why do you go around teachin' the other way?"

"I don't, Em. At least not exclusively. I try to pass along everything that's been thought out or discovered, quite often whether I agree with it or not."

"Well, you ain't gonna convince me it happened any way except like the Bible says."

Greer deepened his frown, lowered his eyes, and settled back into his silent pose once more.

Dick Charterhouse, in a rather transparent move to change the subject, abruptly and brightly asked who would be chief cook during the expedition. It was a point that for some reason hadn't been decided yet. This received more animated discussion than it was worth—anything to keep Em from precipitating a theological debate again—and in the end it was decided that Dick and Zia, who both readily volunteered, would share the cooking.

As this discussion came to a close, a tall, slender man entered the tavern by the front door and paused there for a moment to look around the room. When he saw the members of the expedition, he headed immediately toward their table. Joe, sensing someone's approach, turned his head. The man reached them and halted.

"Hello, Tom," said Joe.

The newcomer nodded. "Joe." He surveyed the others. He was thirtyish—possibly older. Hard to tell sometimes with Indians. He wore a sheepskin-lined jacket and had an old weather-stained Stetson racked back on his head; a dark forelock showed under it, like a hanging spear.

"This is Tom Quick, everybody," said Joe. "Counselor Quick, right, Tom?"

The Indian half-smiled. "Just Tom'll do."

"Tom's the attorney for TITE," Joe explained. "That means Tillamish Indian Tribal Enterprises. Sit down, Tom. Have a beer."

Tom nodded thanks and sat. Joe found a pitcher

and an empty glass and poured for him. Zia kept examining him with frank interest, and now she said, "Tom, I have a feeling you came here specifically to see us."

"Yes, ma'am," said Tom.

Zia laughed. "Ma'am? Am I getting that old and decrepit?"

"This is Zia Marlowe," said Joe. "She teaches anthropology at Cascade."

"I know," said Tom. "I know who all of you are."

"Looks like maybe you do have something in mind, then."

"Yes, I have, Joe. I wouldn't be coming all the way out here just to get a free beer."

Pete Hollinger, munching on Polish sausage, had also been studying Tom Quick. "I've been trying all along to get a few Indian shots for our film," he said. "Indians, bigfoot, the wilderness—it all fits."

"That's true enough." Tom wiped foam from his lips. "As a matter of fact, Mr. Hollinger, sasquatch happens to be the main totem of the Tillamish."

"Yes." Zia nodded enthusiastically. "You call him Squapappek. Other tribes around here have him as Sayatkah, Seeyahtik, Sasquatl, and so on. The term 'sasquatch,' is undoubtedly a corruption of one of these variations."

Tom looked amused. "You've done your homework, Miss Marlowe."

"Maybe not enough of it. I've been meaning to find out more about the sasquatch in Tillamish lore—there's some literature on it in the dissertation files, but not much published—but there hasn't been time. There never is, for everything I want to know."

"Well," said Tom, "you probably know this much, then. Sasquatch is the principle *skaletut*—or spirit, for the layman, as contradistinct to the shamanistic spirits, which are totem to the various societies."

"You're losing me," said Pete, laughing.

"Put it this way, Mr. Hollinger," said Tom. "Sasquatch is the symbol of good luck and good fortune for the entire tribe. As he avoids harm and flourishes, so do we. The funny thing is that it really seems to work that way."

"'There is more in heaven and earth...'" quoted Zia, shrugging.

"That's right, Miss Marlowe," said Tom Quick. He tasted his beer again. "Maybe I'd better begin at the beginning. You're all familiar, I suppose, with the gains we American Indians have made in recent years. We've still got a long way to go, but there's been progress. Some of us, like the Tillamish, have become almost completely assimilated. We have our tribal enterprises—fishing, oyster farming—and we have our engineers and our teachers and our administrators and our lawyers, like myself. A lot of this is much to the good, and I certainly wouldn't throw it away. But there's one thing we lack before we can achieve anything that's truly great—worthy of what we are. Can any of you guess what that is?"

"Capital?" asked Dick.

Tom shook his head. "Not that. It's racial pride, or, for the Tillamish, in a narrower sense, tribal pride. When I say 'race' I mean any minority group, a true race or not."

"Yes," interrupted Zia. "Race is an outmoded concept anyway. Darwin said race was an incipient species. In *Homo sapiens* all the variations don't even approach speciation yet, and possibly never will. We much prefer the term 'stock.'"

"Well, whatever we call the group," said Tom, "I'm speaking now of its pride. The pride that comes from customs and traditions, from the history and the spirit of the group. From their religion, as often as not. The Jews have always had it—it's part of their genius. The blacks and chicanos are acquiring more of it all the time. To a lesser degree, there's pride of ancestry in Americans of Irish descent, French descent, Italian descent—well, you name it. This brings us back to the Indians."

"Hey, I'm serious about getting some camera

shots," Pete reminded him. "I don't suppose you have any real Indian costumes, do you?"

Tom ignored that and continued. "The Indians," he said, "are broken up into so many different tribal cultures that they've never really been able to get together on their pride. They're as splintered as the Protestants, or perhaps the Arabs. I've only been able to concentrate on my own tribe, the Tillamish. I've been making deliberate efforts to restore their old customs and traditions. Our names, for example. Today, we are John Smith or Bill Jones or, if you will, Tom Quick. We are imitation white men instead of Indians."

"Tom," said Dick Charterhouse, "if you don't mind, I can't quite get to weeping over this. I've got absolutely nothing against Indians, but I haven't got time to campaign for their lost rights, either. I hope this doesn't sound unfriendly; I don't mean it that way."

"You've got your problems, Mr. Charterhouse," said Tom, smiling, "and I've got mine."

"Exactly," said Dick.

"But may I finish what I came here to say?"

"You go right ahead, Tom," said Zia. "We really *are* listening."

"Well, as part of the effort to become Indian again, I've been working to restore what you'd call our religion. Like Shinto or Tao or Buddhism, it's not a religion in the sense of the Western world. But it is spiritual. It does enable us to relate to the mysteries of the universe. There's magic in it—as there is in all religions—and I have found that much of this magic works. I have personally found great satisfaction and a sense of peace in our old ways. So have most of the others who have actively joined me in this movement. We've revived the old tales, brought back the old ceremonies. It's been a unifying force to tie us together and give us the pride and sense of purpose we've been lacking."

"Hey, Tom," Greer interrupted, "can I say somethin'?"

"Sure. Go ahead."

"Instead of all this, you should be believin' on the Lord Jesus Christ."

"There's a lot he said I *do* believe in," Tom answered easily. Greer sank back into his surly cocoon. Tom continued, "One of the most important tenets of the Tillamish belief is that the prosperity of the tribe is directly linked to the wellbeing of its totem, the sasquatch. Strangely enough, this seems to be true. There was a report last year of a sasquatch shot by a hunter and lost when it fell into the rapids of a gorge. That very day one of the leaders, who was about to secure an important construction contract for TITE, suddenly and mysteriously died. I could mention a number of other coincidences, but it would take too long. What I'm trying to tell you is that I *do* subscribe to the shibboleths and symbols of the tribe, and so do all of us who have returned to the old ways. Some of our people, who haven't been exposed as much as I have to the white man's other religion of logic and science, find it even easier to believe than I do. It's really on their behalf that I've come here this evening."

"Come for what, Tom?" Dick was looking at him almost suspiciously now. "Let's get to the bottom line."

"I'm here," said Tom Quick, "to ask all of you to give up your search for this creature."

Dick Charterhouse stared at the young Indian archly for a long moment, and then laughed. "Did you really think we'd drop everything, just like that, at your request?"

"No," said Tom sadly. "But I had to ask. I had to try."

"I don't get this," said Dick. "What does it matter to you if we go looking for bigfoot? Even if we find him?"

"The white man will exterminate his species," said Tom. "As he's done, almost, with the buffalo. Or the passenger pigeon, or all the African species that are vanishing now. Aside from any sentimentality, he's tinkering with the ecology of the planet. 'Thou canst not stir a flower, without troubling of a star.' Francis Thompson. Anyway, exterminating. The white man always does."

"You've got it all wrong," said Dick, shaking his head. "We're not even going to kill a bigfoot if we don't have to."

"But you will kill it. You or other white men. In time. And when it vanishes, so will the Tillamish. You can call this a self-fulfilling prophecy if you wish, because those who believe will despair and die out of that despair, but the bottom line—as you call it—is that we *will* come to an end when the sasquatch does."

"Tom, listen to me," said Dick earnestly. "In all due respect for your religious feelings, if that's what they are, I must say that from our standpoint your demand is quite unreasonable."

"I'm sure it seems that way to you. Frankly, I didn't at all expect you to respond to my request. But the council of shamans said, 'You must speak to them, Tom. In their language, in their way.'"

"Okay, you've spoken. Have another beer."

"I will. Thanks."

Tom Quick was pouring his second beer when the huge young logger with the pale-blond hair came lurching to their table, followed by his black-bearded companion. He stopped to look down at Tom with an ugly twist to his mouth and said, "Hey, big chief, what the hell you doin' here?"

"I'm sitting with my friends, sir," said Tom mildly. "Any objections?" The answer was soft; his eyes were not.

"You're friggin' aye I got objections," said the logger. "This is white man's country, chief. There's

128

lots of places for Indians to get stupid drunk back in P-ville. Not here."

Dick Charterhouse turned his head slowly to face the intruder. "We're having a private party here," he said, also softly, but with bedrock underneath. "Now, you be a real gentleman and go back to the bar and have a drink on me. The whole house, in fact. Okay?"

"Butt out, fancy boy," said the logger. "I'm talkin' to this blanket-ass Indian here."

Dick, smiling amiably, rose from his chair. He was over six feet, but the top of his head came up to above the level of the logger's nose. "What's your name?" he asked.

"Huh? Vern Topelius. What's it to you?"

"Mine's Dick Charterhouse," he said with easy charm. "I just thought it would be nice for us to be introduced before I knock the living shit out of you."

"What?" Vern simply couldn't absorb what he'd just heard.

Dick's knee came up, catching Vern full in the crotch. Vern gasped and doubled over in pain. As his head came down, Dick swung a short, hard right to the side of his jaw. It knocked Vern aside, reeling.

But Vern did not go down. He regained his balance and then charged at Dick, shouting something that sounded like "Yow!" His big arms came forward to engulf Dick. Dick sidestepped and sent a jab into Vern's midriff. Vern said something that sounded like "Oof!"

The big blond logger tried again. He swung mightily at Dick this time with a long arching right. It caught Dick on the head just above the temple and sent him staggering to one side. Seeing Dick off balance, Vern leaped forward and kicked at his thigh with his heavy boots. He caught a vulnerable spot in the muscle there, and Dick involuntarily bent his leg and grimaced with pain.

Joe, still in his chair, stared at what was going on and wondered whether he should jump up and give

Dick some help. Maybe not, he thought; Dick seemed to be holding his own and would probably prefer to continue that way. Joe glanced at Tom Quick. Tom was watching silently. Impassively. As an Indian should, thought Joe.

The two men squared off and began to circle each other, each crouching a little. Vern kept his arms wide and hooked; Dick was making tiny ovals in the air with his hands raised in front of his chest.

"For God's sake, somebody stop this!" said Zia.

"Let 'em be," grunted Emory Greer from the end of the table.

Pete Hollinger was looking at it through a partial frame he'd formed by putting his thumbs together and his other fingers vertical. Dammit, it would have to happen here, where he didn't have his camera, and where the light was no good anyway.

Vern kicked out sideways at Dick's groin; something of a karate kick, but much clumsier. Dick grabbed his leg, twisted it, and pulled him off balance. Vern fell to the floor. Dick stepped forward and kicked him hard in the side. Miraculously, Vern gathered his feet under himself and came charging upward, butting Dick under the chin with his head, then slamming his palms to Dick's cheeks, his fingers reaching for Dick's eyes in order to gouge them.

Joe had vaguely noticed Vern's bearded companion turning away from the fight a moment ago, and now he saw him coming back again with a pool cue in his hand. On a pillar near the table hung a red fire extinguisher, the size of a big whiskey bottle. Joe sprang from his chair, grabbed the extinguisher, pulled the pin, pointed the nozzle at the bearded man's face, and squeezed the handles. A yellow stream of fine powder smoked out of the extinguisher and into the black-bearded man's eyes. He dropped his pool cue and staggered back, cursing and knuckling at his eyes.

At precisely this moment, Dick shoved Vern away from him, and, as Vern shuffled backward, threw a combination of three short, hard, well-aimed punches that caught Vern on both sides of his jaw. Vern's eyes glazed over and his hands dropped. Dick kneed him in the crotch again, swiftly, viciously, once and for all. Vern went down, dazed and writhing in pain.

Some of the other loggers started forward from the back of the room.

Joe took his wallet from his back pocket, flipped it open, and showed his badge. "Okay, that's all!" he said. "Next man who tries anything gets taken in!"

One logger stepped forward hesitantly.

"Go ahead, try me," said Joe. "I haven't had *my* fun yet."

The logger scowled and stepped back again.

There was much milling about before it was really quiet again. Bert Kendall came bustling out from behind the bar and supervised as the bearded Kaarlo and Vern's other friends assisted Vern, bent over and retching, out of the main room and into the clear air of the night. There was presently the whine of starters and the growling of gearboxes as pickup trucks pulled away.

"Goddammit!" said Bert Kendall. "I knew them two would start something! You okay, Mr. Charterhouse?"

"Maybe I broke my hand," said Dick, looking at his bruised knuckles. "Otherwise, no damage."

"Here," said Zia, taking his hand. "Let me do something about that for you."

"First-aid kit behind the bar," said Kendall. He waddled in that direction, and Dick and Zia followed him.

Tom Quick came up to Joe. "Tell your friend thanks for me."

"Sure," said Joe.

"It wasn't his fight," said Tom. "He didn't have to."

131

Joe shrugged. "Maybe he enjoyed it."

"Maybe he did," Tom nodded. "I wish he hadn't stepped in, though. I can't do what I should, which is feel I owe him one."

"You don't owe him anything."

"Well, even if I did, I couldn't."

"What's that supposed to mean, Tom?"

"We're on different sides from here on in. Not just Mr. Charterhouse and myself. All of you, and all of the Tillamish."

Joe regarded him evenly. "Tom, you're not thinking of doing anything foolish, are you?"

"I'll only do whatever I have to, Joe. To me, it won't be foolish."

"Okay, now, Tom," said Joe, shifting his stance, keeping his eyes firmly upon the Indian. "I don't like to warn you—especially since I'm not sure exactly what you have in mind, if anything—but I think a warning's called for, here and now. Don't try to interfere with us, Tom. Dick's pretty good at handling trouble, as you just saw, and you know that I am, too. Something else, Tom. I'm on official duty with this expedition. I'm an officer of the law. I'll use that if I have to, Tom."

Tom's slight flick of his head to one side was the same as a shrug. Indians don't shrug.

Alone in his cabin late that night, Joe looked up into the darkness over his lumpy bed. Through the thin curtain across the front window he could see the intermittent flashing of the red neon light that said ACANCY. It sounded like some obscure disease, he thought.

Zia's eyes had shone with sympathy and maybe a little more than that as she'd fondled Dick's hand to feel for broken bones, and then bound it and applied ice. She'd looked up and said, "My God, Dick, you were fantastic with that man!"

"I've had all the educational advantages," said

132

Dick dryly. "In crummy bars all over the world."

She'd laughed as though he'd just said one of the few really funny things she'd heard all week.

Dammit, thought Joe, what if he got to her first?

All those little pieces on the floor. Hard to pick up one by one; better use the vaccuum. Those little pieces, Joe, are the shattered remains of what used to be your ego.

When at last he slept, he dreamed of sasquatch.

Chapter Nine

Splendor—that was the only word for it.

Zia Marlowe, alone at the stream, splashed icy water on her body, shivered with pleasure that was spiced with a few sprigs of pain, then quickly stepped out of the shallow water and to the shore, where she wrapped herself in the oversized towel she'd had the forethought to bring into the wilderness.

She kept looking all about her, first in one direction, then in another, still marveling at the vastness of the land and the cathedral magnificence of all the great peaks and the long slopes and the sharply cut random valleys that formed the watersheds.

The place in which she had bathed was hidden from the camp, which was on a knoll perhaps a hundred yards away. A grove of alder stood between her and the camp. Here the silver water flowed around a gentle bend, forming a shallow pool. She'd long ago considered the practical matter of her personal care on the trail; the only answer was that from time to time she'd have to break away from the others and find what concealment she could.

Dry and dressed now, she trudged upslope toward the camp. The weather this day was miraculously clear, with a deep-blue sky and a few long rolls of cumulus cloud floating over the windward ridges. They were now well settled in the base camp. They had spent the first day flying back and forth between the camp and Kendall's Corners, bringing themselves and the equipment in. On the second day, thick gray cloud and howling rain had advanced upon them out of nowhere and they had spent the time putting the camp in order. Eddie Lorenzo, the helicopter pilot, said on the radio that maybe he'd be out the next day, maybe not. Weather forecasts didn't mean a thing as far as the mountains were concerned. He'd fly out when and if things felt right to him, in his bones. They'd better not expect him every day, on schedule.

By now they'd made what amounted to a practice sortie out of the base camp, getting themselves used to backpacking together across the rough terrain. Greer had led the way to the top of a long ridge. It had been an easy climb, as climbs go, but it had also been exhausting, especially for Pete Hollinger. Zia had watched him puff along behind the rest, cursing and complaining. When he'd asked them, several times, to reenact their single-file passage up the slope so that he could photograph it, she was sure he did so not so much for the film sequence as to afford himself a rest.

Greer passed out grunting instructions in mountain lore. Spread on the sun cream thick; the burn here could be as bad as the beach or worse. Ration your water; you sweated under your clothes here and became thirsty in short order, but you had to resist the temptation to empty your canteen all at once. Give yourself plenty of salt. And watch your footing. Everything around here from rock slides to lava tubes.

During a pause, Greer trained binoculars on a cliff face high on the ridge across the valley. Pete Hollinger, who usually tried to avoid Greer, Zia noticed, happened to be beside him on this occasion. "See that white patch there?" said Greer. "Know what it is?"

"Haven't the faintest," said Pete. He squinted in that direction but saw nothing that struck him as photographable.

"Hawk poo," said Greer.

"What?" Pete almost laughed.

"Hawks never poo in their nest," said Greer solemnly. "They got jet propulsion. They put their little butts up and shoot it right out of the nest—only birds who can. It makes them splotches on the cliff, and that's how you know where they are."

"I'll remember that next time I need a hawk," said Pete.

Greer frowned at him, trying to decide whether or not that had been sarcasm. When Zia moved out of earshot, he said to Pete, "You read your Bible today?"

"Haven't had a chance."

"Well, don't forget it. You know what you promised."

"Okay, Em. I'll get around to it." Pete turned so Greer wouldn't see his frown . Pain in the ass reading that Bible every day. But his promise had kept Greer from crippling him or maybe killing him, so it was worth it. What bothered him most, though, was the way Greer had sold him the damned Bible for eight dollars and twenty cents. That had been extortion.

So far, during their brief preliminary sorties, Greer had found deer tracks, cougar droppings, and a colony of marmots in the rocks. But, as actually they expected, there hadn't been the slightest sign that a sasquatch might be around somewhere.

They'd returned to the base camp at an early hour from their last sortie; Dick had volunteered to prepare the meal, and Zia had wandered off to bathe. As she reapproached the camp now she saw that the folding table had been set up in front of the main tent and that metal dishes filled with food had been set upon it. From behind the tents came the lawnmower snarl of the portable gasoline generator.

Dick had put a number of dried and canned rations together into a tasty stew. "The spices make all the difference," he said proudly. They gave him the compliments a cook always expects. They ate, they talked, they glowed with well-being in the high, thin

136

air. When darkness came, they built a campfire and sat around it. Thin cloud cover appeared, obscuring most of the stars, hazing the edges of the moon.

Dick fetched a bottle of Chivas Regal from the stores. "All right, Zia, let's have some music," he said.

She brought her guitar from the tent and ran off an introductory arpeggio in A minor. "This is a New Mexican folk song. It's about a pretty little lark, imprisoned in a golden cage and longing to be free."

She sang:

> "En una jaula de oro,
> "Pendiente de un balcon,
> "Una trista calándria,
> "Lloraba su prision."

She plucked the strings deftly and rolled her tongue over the Spanish words. Joe couldn't understand them, but he could see the imprisoned lark when he heard the sad, sweet melody. Zia was extraordinarily beautiful, he thought, as she sat there playing and singing, her skin ivory in the moonlight, her dark almond eyes deep as the night. He saw Dick Charterhouse watching her closely, his own eyes gleaming, and he thought it would be nice if Dick would break a leg and have to go home.

Joe and Zia sat together later when the others were busy with personal chores. The last of the fire logs flickered gently.

"There's a sense of escape, isn't there?" said Zia, gazing toward the dim silhouettes of the mountains. "Like the lark in the song. All this space—all of it yours."

"It hits me that way, too," said Joe. "Always did. 1 grew up with lots of space around. Colorado. There was a time when I thought I'd be a guide, something like Em."

"How did you happen to become a policeman?"

"I don't know. How does anybody become any-

137

thing? I was assigned to the MPs for a while in Vietnam. When I came back I decided to finish college under the GI bill. They had some good courses in criminology and police science. One thing kind of led to another."

"You must have found the Los Angeles force a lot different from Cedar County."

Joe smiled a little. "Different is the word, all right."

Suddenly he wanted to tell her everything—crack the valve and let off some of the steam that had been building up again. Maybe, childishly, he wanted sympathy. Maybe he just wanted her to know him better. Feel closer to him. Maybe that would lower the barrier a little. Anyway, he wanted her to know.

A little before midnight, Joe and his partner had received a report of a liquor-store two-eleven in progress only a few blocks away from where they were cruising. The partner was a burly Litvak named Drozd. He pumped iron and posed before his mirror at home, rippling his huge muscles. He didn't drink or smoke, he ingested jars and jars of vitamin pills, and he ate things like wheat germ and sunflower seeds. He stood by, frowning, whenever Joe stopped off for something like a hamburger or a pizza. That stuff'll kill you, he would say. I agree, Joe would say. But he'd be damned if he'd give it up.

Taking the call, they sped to the location, jolted to a halt in front of the shop, and wondered if the robber was still inside. They couldn't see him. Drozd, senior to Joe, called the shots. He'd rush the front door and Joe was to circle around to the back.

There was a shadow in the alley—a shadow in the shape of a man. Joe shouted his warning; several times, he remembered. The shadow would not halt. It moved into a patch of partial light coming from the back of another shop down the alley. Joe saw the fugitive more clearly then, and he would never forget

138

exactly what he saw. A black youth, eighteen or nineteen, maybe, Rangy build; good for basketball. Bright-green pants with flaring bottoms, a sports shirt with big purple flowers all over it.

The youth spun around, took a gun from somewhere—maybe he'd been holding it at his side all along—and began to lift it. Into firing position. As Joe thought. As anyone would have thought.

Joe's gun was already drawn. He crouched, shoved it forward with two stiff arms, aimed by feel rather than sight, and squeezed the trigger three times in succession. The youth was thrown back as the bullets struck, and then he dropped. By the time Joe reached him sticky blood was already beginning to spread on the pavement.

The shock came when Joe's partner arrived, followed by a short, fussy man in spectacles who was the liquor-store proprietor.

"My God!" said the proprietor. "That's Jerry!"

"Who's Jerry?" asked Drozd.

"The kid who works for me!" said the proprietor.

The days of Purgatory followed. Joe had to turn in his badge while the incident was investigated by Internal Affairs. It got to the front pages of most of the newspapers. TV news shows had shots of Joe walking through the halls on his way to various hearings and interrogations. The chief and the mayor himself offered brief comments.

The kid, Jerry Tattersall by name, had worked in the liquor store at night while studying retail sales in the tech school by day. He'd been an honor student in high school. The robber had fled just before Joe and his partner arrived, and the kid had grabbed the .25-caliber automatic that was in the shop and had rushed out the back door in pursuit. Why he'd turned, under the partial light, and lifted his pistol that way was a mystery. Internal Affairs kept doubting he'd done it. Joe's best guess was that in all the confusion young Jerry Tattersall hadn't quite known what to do. Knowing the reasons wouldn't help much now, anyway. Jerry Tattersall—whom everyone said had been a fine young man indeed—was dead, and Officer Joseph R. McBay had killed him.

Joe was cleared of blame at the hearing. Hundreds of citizens cried, "Whitewash!" And the media, in reporting this, implied that they thought so, too. The chief and the mayor tried to explain, but their statements came out limp.

Joe's captain—a thin, serious older man with horn-rimmed spectacles—gave Joe the truth that someone had to say. "Yeah, Joe, you're cleared, but it won't ever be the same for you. Not with this on your record. You'll be passed over for promotions for ten years to come. The way things are these days—and I wouldn't want them again like they were in the old days—you just can't shoot an innocent black man, no matter what the circumstances were. Want my advice? Resign."

Telling all of this to Zia now, Joe held the little cigar he'd lighted between his teeth, crapshooter style, and took in the fragrance of the smoke he was careful not to inhale. Drozd had never approved of the little cigars, even though Joe didn't inhale.

"The worst of it is," said Joe, "that this whole damned thing between blacks and whites was never my quarrel. I made buddies of black guys in Vietnam. I was raised where there weren't many blacks, so I was never exposed to all the usual prejudices. Not that I was militant for black rights or anything. I could never feel guilty over the remote possibility that some great-grandfather of mine might have kept slaves. But at the same time I never saw blacks as blacks, never cared if my daughter—if I had one—married one; might have married one myself if the right black gal had come along. So why couldn't this have happened to some damned bigot instead of me?"

Zia said, "What can I say, Joe? We all have bitter

spots somewhere in us. I suppose this one has to be yours."

"The kid's mother. The kid himself, dead. My problem was nothing compared to that. But that didn't make it feel any better. I thought it might go away after a while when I came to Pickettsville. It didn't. And—get this—Chet Anders calls it a political asset! Makes me look like a tough law-and-order man to the rednecks, he says. In their hearts they've got no use for niggers anyway, he says. I get sick when I think about it. And I wonder. Do I really want to be sheriff—or move on to whatever that leads to—under those terms?"

"Do you?"

"Goddamned if I know," said Joe. "Goddamned if I know right now."

The helicopter hung like a guppy over the ridge, then dipped toward the clear landing space at the foot of the knoll, a little upstream. The air was cold but windless; the light of morning was somewhere behind the cloud cover, which glowed with a nacreous sheen.

Greer, Pete, and Zia rummaged in the chopper for some extra small supplies the pilot had brought.

Kodak 7247 film, which blew up nicely from sixteen to thirty-five millimeter for Pete.

A folding saw, much handier than an ax (which the camping permit required you to carry) for Greer.

A box of Kleenex for Zia. Imagine, with all those supplies she *did* remember to bring, forgetting the Kleenex!

Joe and Dick walked back toward the camp with the pilot.

Eddie Lorenzo, the chopper jockey, was small and slender and walked with a rolling stride, as though he could never quite adjust himself to the unyielding ground. He wore a World War II RAF mustache, its ends shooting off like upcurved sparks from the sides of his face. He used his hands a lot as he talked and

141

had a streetwise accent from some Eastern city, probably Brooklyn. "Well, like they say, never a dull moment," said Eddie.

"Meaning what?" asked Dick.

"Had to make like a broken-field run through a bunch of mountains to get here. Big hunk of weather, just sitting there, over a range. Ever hear of the laws of nature? They're suspended out here. Yeah. That's what it is."

"But you evidently made it all right," said Dick, and his accent, directly up against Eddie's now, sounded more aloof than ever.

"Sure. No real sweat. Just a pain in the old garbanza, never being sure."

"Have some coffee. You'll feel better."

"Thanks, I will. In fact I could use breakfast to go with it."

"Coming right up," said Dick. "You can't very well go looking for bigfoot on an empty stomach."

"I can't even look for my socks in the morning on an empty stomach. I got all these black socks, see? Saved 'em from the army. But the carpet in my pad is black. You ever try to find black socks on a black carpet first thing in the morning?"

"I've had every experience in life but that one," said Dick.

"Yeah," said Eddie, nodding in solemn agreement to the implied proposition that things could get complicated. "I should get married one of these days. Maybe I'd get some other color socks for Christmas."

"That seems as good a reason as any to get married," said Dick.

"Yeah," said Eddie. "Yeah. Well, where do we go today?"

"There's a sector northwest of here I'd like to cover. I'll show you on the map."

"Maybe you'd like to see those tracks instead," said Eddie.

"What tracks?"

He turned and pushed his hand vaguely toward a

distant line of mountains. "Over there someplace. That's the detour I had to take to get here. I could have hopped over some of the peaks, I guess, but that would have used even more fuel. I don't even want to be heading out of here with most of my fuel used up. That would interfere with my living forever."

"You didn't answer my question."

"What question?"

"About the tracks."

"Oh. Yeah. Well, here I am, coming across this slope, minding my own business." His slightly cupped hand, in midair, became the helicopter in flight. "And here's this big stretch of snow on a north slope—probably there year round. So I see this line of tracks angling across it, maybe for almost a mile or so. I figure they're bear tracks, so I don't really pay much attention to 'em."

"What made you think they were bear tracks?"

"What else?" Eddie shrugged deeply. "I don't think bigfoot tracks because—no offense, Dick—I just can't believe in bigfoot. But I do get this impression that the strides are pretty long. So I dip down a little and take another look. I don't measure or anything, and it's hard to tell, but they still look like somebody said to this bear, 'You may take a couply hundred giant steps.'"

"I never had time for games," said Dick. "And I still haven't. So if these are bear tracks, we'd just be wasting our time."

"Whoa!" said Joe. "We don't *know* that they're bear tracks. We'd better have a look."

"You're paying for the whirlybird," said Eddie, shrugging again.

"I suppose we can check it out if you think it's worth it," said Dick. "All right. Let's get Eddie some breakfast and then we'll go flying."

Steep mountainsides surrounded the helicopter, making it tiny. Joe looked at the towering rockfaces and at the evergreen-dotted valley below them. The helicopter sped forward at a tilt, the whump-whumping of its blades echoing and reechoing from the mountainsides.

Dick sat beside Eddie Lorenzo in the copilot's seat; Joe relaxed in the rear. Eddie had explained that if only two passengers came on each reconnaissance the flights could be longer and cover more territory.

Now the little aircraft emerged from the deep V of the mountains and began to skim across a broader, flatter valley. A huge snowbank glistened a short distance ahead of them. Eddie pointed to it and curved the chopper to head directly toward it. As they neared the snowslope, Joe could begin to see tracks like a dotted line drawn in shaky freehand diagonally across it. Moments later the chopper was hovering over a portion of the tracks, the downward airstream from its blades making a wide circle of stirred-up snow powder directly below them.

Joe peered down through the bubble. "That does look like one hell of a big stride. Hard to tell from here, but those steps must be four feet apart. Set her down, Eddie."

"Wait a minute, Joe," said Dick, turning toward him. "We can't do that. This is Wilderness Area. We can't land without a permit."

Joe looked at Dick with a touch of surprise. This sudden concern with the letter of the law didn't fit him somehow. He must have been warned by Cadbury not to take the slightest chance of besmirching the holy corporate name. "Call this an emergency," said Joe. "Hot pursuit. Sheriff's investigation. I don't know. Just put her down, Eddie, and we'll justify it later if we have to."

Dick shook his head. "We'd better do this the way we've already planned. Let Eddie fly us back and we'll hike in here."

"That'll take days! The tracks could be gone by then. Look, Dick, I'll take the responsibility. Put her down, Eddie."

"Make up your minds, you guys," said Eddie.

"Put her down," said Joe.

The chopper settled on the snow a few yards away from the line of tracks. Joe and Dick scrambled out of the bubble, heads lowered below the whirling blades. The air was shockingly cold, even through their parkas and layers of wool shirts and sweaters. The glare of the snow made them squint.

Joe, with Dick close behind him, halted and peered down at the nearest footprint. "I'll be damned," he said softly. "I'll be goddamned."

Dick was also staring down. "Yes," he said, nodding. "Yes, indeed."

The print in the snow was quite clearly that of an immense bare foot. It was humanlike, perhaps eighteen inches long, perhaps nine wide. The prints that led to it and those that followed were all delineated clearly.

Joe nodded several times. "I guess I'm a believer, now."

"It looks that way," said Dick. He frowned and sounded reluctant.

"Let's try to put this together. The creature came up from the valley, onto this snowbank, then walked upslope toward that saddle. He knew where he was going—the tracks keep a more or less straight line. Let's see if we can find where. Then we'll get Pete out here to take pictures."

"All right, I'll go along with that," said Dick.

Joe glanced at him quickly. There had been an overtone to his last remark. He'd go along with it, and that was fine. It would be ridiculous for him not to go along with it. But he'd had to say it like that: in the way of a superior making a concession to a subordinate. What he'd really been saying was that he was the honcho; he was the one who called the shots. Joe shrugged mentally. If the role of honcho made him happy, let him have it.

After they had examined several of the tracks,

they returned to the helicopter, which took off again and began to crisscross the area. The line of tracks, they saw, reached the crest of the saddle, where the snow thinned out and then disappeared. On the southern slope there was rocky, sterile soil with nothing but Alpine weeds growing upon it until it reached the timber level of a broad, irregular valley. Joe considered another landing to look for continued tracks, but finally decided it might be better not to risk frightening the creature off—if, indeed, it was nearby—with the sound of the chopper. The best move now, he thought, would be to have Greer examine the tracks to determine how old they were, or to make any other deductions that might prove useful, and then to have Pete photograph them.

"Back to camp," he told Eddie.

Dick frowned as though he felt *he* should have given the order....

They dropped the bombshell of their news back at camp and watched the explosion. Zia's eyes glistened until Joe was sure that tears would appear. Pete Hollinger kept saying, "Dynamite! Dynamite!" Greer frowned mightily. In this case, it was his way of smiling.

Eddie made three return trips to the site of the footprints, transporting two passengers each time, so that toward the end of the day all hands had been able to examine the footprints closely. Pete Hollinger used a can of film in his Angenieux and a roll of stills in his Minolta. Greer figured the tracks weren't more than a day old. Zia agreed with Joe that they shouldn't try to follow the trail by helicopter.

That night, after Eddie had taken off again for Pickettsville to beat the deadline of the darkness, they opened maps and conferred at length under the camp lanterns. There was a stretch of relatively level country at the lower end of the huge watershed the tracks had entered from the north. They would check this more closely tomorrow, but for now it seemed an ideal site for a subcamp. From here they'd be able to explore the entire area on foot. Dick wondered if they ought not file for another special landing permit, but finally agreed that this would probably mean excessive delay.

"This luck!" said Zia. "It's almost too good to be true!"

"Take it and shut up." Joe grinned. "The odds had to fall right sometime."

"I know," said Zia. "I've been exposed to the theory of probability and all the other logic and science there is. Just the same, I feel a sense of mystery now. As though there's a tablet somewhere, and written on it, in those Hebrew letters that look like CWL upside down, it says we're going to find our bigfooted friend!"

"You ought to be thankin' God for this here luck," said Greer.

"It wouldn't hurt," said Zia, with a smile.

"Everybody put their head down and I'll lead the prayer," Greer said.

They went along with it.

Greer lowered his head and shut his eyes down to wrinkled slits. "Dear Father in Heaven," he said, "we offer our thanks for this here bounty which Thou has graciously bestowed upon us. If it is Your will that we get to this here critter, yea though it be an imp of Satan, I guess that there is exactly what we're gonna do...."

Later that night, when all were in their tents and the camp was quiet, the thin cloud broke apart like a frayed blanket, and the moon became visible, riding cold and aloof in the sky over the wilderness.

Far across the mountain range, Self looked up at the moon and struggled, in her mind, to find some meaning in its mystery. Restless this night, she had emerged from her cave, and she was wandering aimlessly among the scattered boulders strewn on

147

the floor of the high canyon. She was queerly hungry again. Not for food of any kind—she'd eaten well enough the day before on juniper buds and frozen salmon—but specifically for the warm, still-wriggling taste of coyote pup, like the one she'd caught on her last brief foray.

Old One had once said something about hunger of this kind. Or had it been Giver-of-Milk? It meant she had the seed of a young one within her. And it was true that she hadn't bled recently—so maybe she did. If so, she must take a mate. But who? Big Male would have difficulty getting away from Skinny One. Broken Foot might accept her, but he was bland and stupid and she might find him difficult to endure, day after day. Young One, for whom she held genuine affection, wasn't yet mature enough. Yellow Fur, with his tawny coat that set him apart from the others, was a possibility, but Yellow Fur had never shown much interest in her. She'd seen him on occasion try to caress other males until he was cuffed away. Very young males often caressed one another, or even mounted each other sometimes in mock copulation (as did young females, too), but it was somehow unseemly for adults to behave in this fashion.

Self, who had an unusual grasp of cause and effect, saw the problems she'd be facing if she truly now carried a young one in her belly. It would grow and her belly would protrude and the others would mock her for it. They would always do this when there was no mate. When the time came she would crawl away somewhere, give birth, and bring the wet and scrawny creature back to show it. They would despise it. They would not feed it, nor would they play with it later when it became playful. They would no longer share food with Self from the community stores but would insist that she find her own fodder for herself and her offspring. She'd seen this happen to another female known as Waddling One long ago. Waddling

One had had to take her child and wander off on her own.

Perhaps by now Waddling One had found another troop somewhere. Old One said there were other troops, far to the north. Or perhaps Waddling One had simply perished in the wilderness. Her carcass had fallen and the coyotes or the raccoons or the carrion hawks or the grubworms or the earth itself had soon devoured it. The rain and mist and howling wind had eroded away whatever was left. It was as though whoever died that way had never existed. It was as though all of them, in the scheme of things, were not meant to exist. That was bad. To decrease was bad; to increase was good. No one knew why. It was the way, that was all. . . .

She looked up at the moon, sallow, bloodless. She began to sing softly. It was a reedy, whistling song. She began to sway in a curious dance, her shuffling steps timed to the beating of her pulse.

Remarkable about the moon. You could not see it move, yet move it must, for when the night had passed it had gone from here to there. How could anything cross the entire sky without moving?

Chapter Ten

Sheriff Zack Winfield and Attorney Chet Anders sat in a corner booth in the Loggers' Lounge of the Pioneer Hotel. Anders often used this booth, hidden from passing view, for meetings or interviews he didn't want widely advertised. His diamond pinky ring sparkled on his fat, well-manicured hand as he held his bourbon and water. He smelled of bay rum, which he preferred to modern after-shave.

"Well, Chet," said Winfield, with a knowing smile, "how's the power-behind-the-throne business, huh?"

"Powerful as ever," said Chet, chuckling. "I wouldn't be surprised if I put in five or six candidates next election. I've got somebody in mind for senator—not state senator, but a real senator, all the way to Washington."

"That's fine, Chet. Even if you are the other party." Winfield ran his callused hand over his shock of stiff white hair. "Glad you got yourself a good stable like that. Kind of makes up for havin' nobody to run for sheriff, huh?"

"I wanted to talk to you about exactly that," said Chet. "Maybe you can already guess some of what I want to say."

"I try not to guess, Chet. I try not to decide anything till I know the score. You learn that, bein' sheriff."

Chet nodded and sipped his drink. "I expect you do. And I'd say you've done a pretty good job, on the whole, in the past fifteen years. I hope you understand there was never anything personal in it when I thought I'd back somebody else for your job. Just that you're one party, Zack, and I'm the other. That's politics."

"Which I never liked much, I don't mind tellin' you. You got to watch yourself too much. Drop a cussword and you lose the church vote. Bust somebody for growin' pot and all the young people say you're a pig. Try to enforce the zoning laws or the fire code and the whole damned business community is down on you. You spend half your time worryin' about this kind of thing instead of doin' your job."

"That's the way things are, Zack; that's the way they are." He shifted his butterball frame heavily on the upholstered booth seat. "Anybody who doesn't want to play the game can, under the principles of our fine democracy, take his ass somewhere else. Like young Joe McBay. I must say he's been a great disappointment to me."

"That so?" Winfield feigned surprise.

"I told him not to go chasing off after bigfoot. It wasn't bad enough that he did, but there had to be all that publicity on it. He's a dead duck now. Statewide. Nationwide."

"I'm glad to hear that," said Winfield.

"I've got something to say that might make you even gladder."

"What's that, Chet?"

"I'll make a deal with you. Switch parties and I'll support you for sheriff. With me running the campaign you'll be a shoo-in."

"Switch parties, huh?" Winfield was thoughtful.

"I wouldn't even ask that if I wasn't committee chairman. And if I didn't have so many votes lined up, no matter who runs on our ticket. Plus the fact that the committee will go along with whoever I pick. Anyway, you don't have any real attachments to your party, do you?"

"Well, I've been with it all along. Got a lot of good friends in it."

151

"You've got friends in our party, too. As for platforms and all that bullshit, both parties are the same here in Cedar County. People hardly ever vote on issues anyway. They vote for the man first, the party second, and if these two don't mean much they usually flip a coin."

"I don't know, Chet," said Winfield, running his thumb along his cheek. "I'd have to think this over."

"Do that. But don't take too long. I could still find another candidate to run against you. Somebody might come along even better than Joe McBay."

"Better than McBay, huh?" Winfield found his corncob pipe and began to stuff it with Grainger from his foil pouch. "Well, I'll tell you somethin', Chet. He was *never* right for it."

"He looked pretty good to me before he flipped his stack over this bigfoot thing. Young, smart, nice appearance, and just the right stand on law and order. Firm about it, but didn't shove it down anybody's throat."

"Yeah, that's how he came on at first. But I noticed things after a while. Things he said and did. He told me he favored bussing once, and affirmative action. He thought the Indians should get a better deal. As for that nigger he shot, it still bugs him, did you know that? He sends a check to the kid's mother every payday. That's a fine, Christian thing to do, of course, but it means he secretly feels like the rest of the left-wing crowd—that blacks should get special breaks just because they're blacks. Know what he really is? He's a goddam closet liberal, that's what he is."

Chet belched softly and sighed. "I still could have pulled votes with him, though. Too bad he went off after that ape." He looked at Winfield suspiciously. "Of course, it just might be you had something to do with that."

"It might be," said Winfield, grinning.

"Which makes you smarter than I thought. For

152

somebody who doesn't like politics, you do pretty good at it."

"I try," said Winfield.

"You do all right. All right. Well, now that we've had our talk, why don't we make a night of it?"

Winfield looked at his watch. "I ought to get home to the family."

"There are, uh, a couple of new girls at the massage parlor. Up from Seattle—temporary help. They wouldn't be around to talk later. And I've got my little lodge out at the lake."

"That so?" Winfield rubbed his cheek again. "Well, maybe I could have some sudden business come up and have to stay late, huh? By God, Chet, I haven't had a strange piece of poontang in a long time!"

"Stick with me," said Chet. "You'll get lots of goodies you haven't had in a long time."

The first day's search out of the new base camp turned up nothing of much interest. The only living things they saw besides themselves were several rabbits and a few white-tailed deer in the distance. Greer drew a bead on one of these, not to shoot it, but just to see if he could have. The range was too long and he lowered his gun.

Using the helicopter, they had moved most of the tents and the bulk of their supplies and equipment to a site by a stream in the lower end of the long watershed valley. It rather resembled the original base-camp site. Their plan now was to push up the valley slowly, examining every stand of timber and every offshoot canyon along the way. Carrying supplies for several days, they would bivouac each night and continue searching each morning. Greer figured they could cover two or three miles of valley each day and reach the northern end of the valley in maybe a week or a little more than that.

They halted now and set up their bivouac camp an hour or so before it would be dark. Greer was building the fire when he suddenly rose from his hunkered-down position and peered into the distance. "We got company," he said.

Joe had been washing his socks in a bucket of water from the stream. "Where?"

"Over there, where them birds got flushed. He'll show in a minute, whoever he is."

Seconds later a figure appeared, trudging toward them. "He's got a horse," said Joe.

"Ain't a horse, it's a mule," Greer said. "Horses ain't worth a damn up here."

By the time the newcomer reached them, everyone had gathered together into a group to meet him. He was a small, full-bearded man of fifty or more, with what appeared to be an eagle feather stuck at a rakish angle into his hat band. Blanket rolls, evidently filled with supplies, were cinched to his mule.

"Howdy! I sure didn't expect to find anyone else out here!"

"Nor did we," said Dick Charterhouse, nodding a greeting.

"Harry Yates is the name. What in heck are you folks doing out here this time of year, anyway?"

"We were wondering the same about you."

"Me? I'm lookin' for gold. Thought you could tell. You folks don't look like you're prospecting, so it must be somethin' else."

"It is, Mr. Yates," said Zia. "Come on, have dinner with us. We'll tell you all about it."

"Why, that is nice of you, and thanks," said Harry Yates. "Guess I will visit a spell. Be nice to have somebody to talk to besides this mule for a change."

By the time the prospector had unpacked and tethered his mule, introductions and handshakes had been performed. He went at the rations they shared with him with an air of great appreciation. The dried and prepacked mountain meals, simply heated in water, provided a pleasantly varied menu.

"Beats hell out of bacon and beans," Harry Yates said.

"I didn't think there were any prospectors left these days," said Zia.

"Oh, there's a few of us. Real prospectors, I mean. Not the tourist folks who do a little panning in the summer. It ain't a bad way to make a little hard money. Price of gold the way it is you can pick up a hundred dollars in a day if you get the right stream. And there's always a chance that someday you'll hit that big one. All kinds of paperwork and regulations if you do, here on government land, but it could be worth it."

Harry had been looking for that big one ever since he'd started prospecting four years ago. He'd cut and sold firewood before that, living in a cabin he'd built on the outskirts of Pickettsville. What he earned from that enterprise augmented his thirty-year pension from the navy. When his wife had died he'd decided to prospect full-time. She'd disapproved of it when she'd been alive.

Zia now explained what she and the others were doing here.

"Bigfoot, eh?" Harry Yates knuckled some food away from the beard around his mouth. "Well, I'll tell you. I always figured I'd see that critter again sometime."

"Again?" Zia raised her head sharply.

"Yup. I saw it once, all right. Not too far from here, as a matter of fact—ten, fifteen miles maybe. I was comin' up a stream, lookin' for a good sandy bend where I might pan, and I saw somethin' on the far ridge, goin' upslope, disappearin' once in a while behind the trees, but then showin' itself again. It was big and furry; big enough to be a grizzly, which you don't hardly see at all these days. But bears don't walk on two feet like this thing was doin'. Short distances, maybe, but not steady, all the time. I didn't have binoculars, but my eyesight's still pretty good, if

155

I say so myself, and I could get an idea of its size even at that distance. I could swear the damned thing was eight, ten feet tall. I watched till it disappeared for good, and then I sat down and had a nip from my whiskey bottle just to be sure I wasn't dreamin'."

Dick smiled. "Maybe you had a nip *before* you saw the creature. Maybe several."

Harry shook his head stubbornly. "I ration my whiskey, careful. It runs out quick. Hardly any left in my pack now, as a matter of fact."

"Would you like a drink, Harry?"

"A drink? Well, now, I wouldn't want to put you folks out or anything—"

Dick laughed and found the Chivas Regal.

"Ahhh!" said Harry, smacking his lips. "First rate! Well, anyway," he continued, "I went over to where I'd seen this critter, to look for sign. Took me a spell to get there, workin' through the scrub. First thing I noticed was an awful stink in the air. Like skunk and the lion house at the zoo, mixed. The ground was too hard for tracks, except one place where there was a spring. That was where I saw the footprint. Looked human, but it must have been two foot long. I knew damned well then I hadn't seen a bear."

"Where was this, Harry?" asked Zia. "Here in this valley?"

"Over the ridge, as I remember. I'm not even sure I could find the exact spot again. *Might* have been this valley. Say, do you suppose I could have another drop of that whiskey? Gettin' kind of chilly now the sun's gone down."

"Help yourself," said Dick. "The bottle's yours."

"That's right nice of you, partner. Thank you kindly." Harry poured again. "Guess I might as well spend the night here. If that's okay with you folks. Got my own bedroll. I won't get in your way."

"We're glad to have you," Zia said. "In fact, if you want to tag along with us—"

"No, no, I wouldn't do that. I've got to find me some

156

color tomorrow. Been wastin' time long enough. I kind of like this valley for it. Can't say why. A man gets a feelin', sometimes, when it's there."

"Good luck," said Zia.

"Same to you foks. Though I always figured old bigfoot never will let himself get caught."

"Why is that, Harry?"

"I figure he's a giant Indian of some kind. There's all kinds of stories about wild men like that. Like those stone-age men in the Philippines. I was at Subic when they found 'em. I got around in the navy, I'll say that."

"So far," said Zia, "he seems to be animal rather than human."

Harry downed another drink. His eyes were getting bright with it. "Sure be funny," he said, "if bigfoot turned out to be neither one. If he was some kind of spirit, like the Indians say. Or you know what else? Something from another planet, here to take over the earth. He could have come here in a flying saucer."

Zia laughed.

"There's flying saucers around, too, you know," said Harry. "Saw six of 'em one night. Over by Ross Lake and the dam. I'd made camp by a stream in a canyon and I got up late one night to answer nature's call. Right over the mountaintops I suddenly saw these glowing balls of fire...."

Dick laughed aloud now, but listened as Harry finished his story. Greer sat where he was, cross-legged and a little apart from the others, scowling at Harry with disapproval. Pete Hollinger took it all in, shaking his head sadly to himself. Harry became more expansive as he kept pouring and drinking scotch. By the time he finished the bottle he was telling how he'd been chased by genuine white-sheeted ghosts in an abandoned mine.

Harry was gone in the morning, having quietly slipped away sometime before sunup. Dick frowned

157

and insisted that all check their knapsacks, but nothing was found to be missing.

"There you are," Dick said to Zia at breakfast. "All those eyewitness reports about bigfoot. They're always from somebody like Harry."

She looked at him thoughtfully. "Dick, you're not getting ready to apostatize, are you? Several things you've said lately—"

"Well, when you boil it right down, we haven't really made much progress, have we? Seems to me there's *still* a possibility we're chasing after something that isn't there."

"What about the prints in the snowbank? You saw them."

He shrugged. "I can't explain them, of course. But there could be some explanation nobody's thought of yet. All I'm saying is that we shouldn't be too disappointed if it somehow turns out we've been wasting our time after all."

"We haven't been," said Zia firmly. "We're going to find bigfoot. I know it. I feel it."

"Dick smiled. "That's not very scientific."

"No, it isn't," she said with a laugh. "but then even a scientist can't be scientific all the time."

"I should hope not," said Dick, running his eyes over her figure appreciatively. Joe had noticed him doing that on a number of occasions.

The following day, when once more their explorations had produced nothing of interest, they headed back to Base Camp II at the foot of the valley to replenish their supplies. A rainstorm had struck, and they pushed against tiny ball bearings of rain in a driving wind. Pete Hollinger, lagging behind the others, puffed and cursed as he fought to keep up the pace. Joe had thought that Pete might lose weight with all the exercise he was getting, but he was eating prodigiously and for all Joe knew he had even gained a little.

Once, as they'd watched a formation of Canada

geese skimming over a ridge, Pete had said, "That's what this country's for. The birds."

"Hang in there, Pete," said Joe. "It'll be worth it when you get your pictures of bigfoot."

"If I ever do. For my money, we should drop the whole exercise right now. I can still make a pretty good film. Those footprints in the snow are kind of dynamite in themselves. We can work in some reconstructed shots—something big and hairy going through the trees. You see it and you don't see it at the same time. I know how to shoot it that way. We could still come up with a small blockbuster."

"Pete, we don't want anything faked."

"Faked?" Pete pursed his lips and looked like a surprised infant. "I don't fake. I just tell things truer than they are, kid."

As they approached the subcamp now, all began to feel a sense of something wrong. The main tent had 'fallen in,' part of it had broken loose from its moorings and was flapping, torn, in the angry wind. Greer trotted on, ahead of the others. He was standing near the tent, looking grave, when they caught up with him.

"Been somebody here," he said.

"What's this now, Em?" Dick looked around. "Who's been here?"

"Over there," said Greer, nodding. "The supplies."

Some of the crates had been opened, their contents spilled on the ground. And then the crates and much of what they had contained had been burned. There were overturned five-gallon gasoline cans, evidently used to start the fire, near the charred rubble.

"What the hell!" said Dick, staring at all of it.

"Who would do a thing like this?" asked Zia. "Why?"

"Got an idea," said Greer. He led them just beyond the burned supplies to where a carved walking stick was thrust upright into the ground. It was made in rough resemblance to a totem pole, with the gro-

159

tesque representations of several animals and fanciful creatures carved into it. The uppermost figure was *Squapappek*—bigfoot—the principal totem of the Tillamish tribe. Joe had seen these canes, along with other trinkets, in the little tourist shops on the reservation.

Dick pulled the cane out of the ground and glared at it.

"Tom Quick," said Greer. "That uppity college Indian. Maybe some others with him, but, anyway, Tom. He left this here cane so's you'd know."

Joe nodded. "He hinted he might do something like this. I didn't really think he would."

"I can understand how he feels," said Zia.

"Understand, hell!" said Dick. "He won't get away with this!" He looked at Joe. "Grounds for arrest, wouldn't you say?"

Joe shrugged. "It'd be hard to prove he did it. Besides, where is he now?"

Greer peered into the rain in several directions. "Somewhere around, I figure."

"Does that mean we can expect more of this?" asked Dick.

"I wouldn't know." Greer spat. "Nobody ever knows what's next when it comes to Indians."

Pete Hollinger was getting his camera ready and taking readings with his light meter. "Dynamite!" he said. "Stick that damned cane back in the ground, will you?"

Dick reached in under his parka now and drew out the Smith & Wesson .44 Magnum he carried, holstered, there. Joe remembered when he'd ordered it, as part of the expedition's equipment. He remembered Dick's unexpectedly embarrassed smile when he'd said he couldn't resist it. He had no idea what he'd shoot, out on the trail, with a Model 29 Magnum, eight-and-three-eights-inch barrel, red ramp-front sight, micro-click rear sight, adjustable for windage and elevation, but he'd always wanted to pack one, and this seemed a good excuse to do it. He spun the cylinder and looked up at Greer. "You say you think that Indian's still around?"

"Could be."

"Think you could find him?"

Joe stepped forward and shook his head. "Sorry, Dick. Nothing like that. This isn't Dodge City."

Dick stared back at Joe for a moment and a film seemed to dissolve from his eyes. "Just a thought," he said finally. He shrugged, put the Magnum back in its holster, and buttoned the strap down over its stock again.

They were relieved to find the radio in the main tent still undamaged. Apparently Tom Quick had wished to deliver a warning rather than create any real hardship for them. There was enough gasoline left in the tank to start the generator, and Dick had the radio working in short order. He called the airport and left a message for Eddie Lorenzo to fly in new food stores as soon as the weather permitted.

The storm continued throughout the night, which they spent comfortably in the shelter of the camp. By morning the wind had died down and the rain had become an intermittent drizzle. On the radio, Eddie Lorenzo said the mountains were still socked in and he didn't want to risk flying out there right away. Rummaging in the stores, they found about a dozen sets of mountain rations still untouched. They decided to return to the place where they'd left off and resume their search.

Again that day there was no sign. Zia was impatient to push on to the head of the valley, where she thought chances might be better, but she reluctantly agreed with Greer that it was best to cover all possible ground and do it patiently and systematically.

They bivouacked again by the same stream, farther up the valley. Searches in several side canyons had been time-consuming, and because of

161

them they had progressed less than a mile northward all day. The drizzle had ceased, and the clouds had risen away from the land, but they were still low in the sky, dark, thick, and glowering.

Immediately after the evening meal—which was served earlier than it was usually—Zia wandered upstream and out of sight for her customary daily interlude of privacy. She washed her face and neck in the cold water; it was too chilly to strip and bathe properly. That was what she missed most out here—a good hot shower. Cleansing her body had always been to her an almost religious ritual, as it is with the Japanese.

The sun, far to the west, had dipped below the cloudline and was sending indirect light into the sky. It was an unreal glow; a light for the setting of a dream.

She wandered upslope toward the rim of the valley. There was no purpose to her steps; she merely wanted to walk alone. Odd that out here, on all this space, she'd felt crowded much of the time. It was because all of them necessarily stayed close to each other all day and, in a sense, hemmed each other in. With little chance for any two of them to pair off for very long, there had been no opportunity for her to resolve some of their relationships. Two in particular.

Dick Charterhouse. She was definitely attracted to him, and she had been trying to analyze this attraction, which probably shouldn't be done, except that she had always been compulsively analytical. He was certainly physically attractive—downright handsome, though she'd forgive him for that. At least he gave no sign of being at all vain about it. He was quite confident of himself. His air was that of a man who always knew better than anyone around him just what ought to be done to meet a given situation. He was well educated and certainly intelligent. Good-looking, smart, able, cultured, good company. And with a flaw of some kind somewhere—she couldn't put her finger on it. Maybe not an actual flaw; maybe just something that wouldn't sit right with her, personally.

None of which would have been significant if she had not experienced moments of actual desire for Dick Charterhouse, and if she had not known, from the way he looked at her from time to time, that he wanted her, too. Whether for a mere roll in the hay—*wham, bam, thank you, ma'am!*—or for something beyond that she didn't know, but his eye was upon her, that was clear enough. Her own attraction toward Dick had coalesced into something recognizable the night he'd fought that big blond logger in the tavern. She'd been startled to feel a primitive thrill over his victory. She might have given herself to him that night, if he'd come to her cabin. It was that strong, this urge that had come upon her.

And then, on the other hand, there was Joe McBay. That quiet, slightly beat-up mug of his; the sardonic sense of humor lurking under it. His abhorrence of self-pity whenever it started to creep up on him. The unexpected sensitivity under the professional rhinoceros hide. At times, when his nearness aroused her, she craved physical contact with him. That brought her back to her old problem—the risk she'd take in carrying a love affair to its normal, natural conclusion. There was a good, plain Anglo-Saxon word for what she meant. She couldn't quite bring herself to think it.

"You, Zia Marlowe," she murmured to herself, with a little self-mocking smile Joe might have been proud of, "are a mixed-up kid."

Her aimless steps had taken her toward the foot of the ridge. The cloud cover had been dissolving all this time; a frosted moonglow was seeping out over the land. She could see presently that she was coming upon an indentation in the ridge—an opening that might be the mouth of a canyon they hadn't yet explored.

163

She was not conscious of time. It flowed thickly, if it flowed at all.

Suddenly—or was it gradually?—she found herself approaching one wall of this offshoot canyon, heading for a curious mist that rose from the earth a short distance ahead. Next she saw a glistening dark pool among the rocks beneath the mist and knew she had found a hot spring. Greer had said there were lots of them scattered throughout these volcanic mountains.

She went to the edge of the pool, knelt, and tested the water with her hand. It was decidedly hot, but after a few moments she could keep her hand immersed in it.

Zia rose and stripped, dropping her clothes beside her. For a moment she shivered, naked, in the cold air. Then she sat at the side of the pool, put her legs into the water, waited until they became used to the sudden change of temperature, and finally slid her body in after them. Her feet found a shallow bottom. She could crouch where she was, with the water up to her neck. She kept herself perfectly still for many moments until her skin adjusted itself to the heat and the slight initial pain was gone. Now the warmth of the water penetrated, filling her with a sense of utter relaxation and well-being; a delightful state of existence she'd almost forgotten could sometimes be achieved.

When she could move more freely without burning her skin, she pushed herself here and there in the pool, exploring its irregular sides. There was a deep drop-off near the center she learned to avoid. There was a kind of shelf where she'd entered, and this was the best place to stay and soak in this somehow spiritual warmth. God, how she'd needed this! It was cleansing her very soul. Drive right in to the soulwash, folks; turn off your motor and do not use the brakes. Let the soulwash do it all.

Shadowy movement and the sound of a scuffled

step beyond the edge of the pool startled her.

She looked in that direction quickly, and with alarm.

Dick Charterhouse stepped out of the gloom, came to a halt, and smiled down at her.

"Oh, it's you!" she said, relieved.

"So this is where you got to. Zia, you shouldn't wander off like this. Really. We've all been out looking for you."

"I'm sorry," she said quickly. "I guess I didn't realize how much time had passed."

"Well," he said, laughing, "we'll forgive it this time."

"Get the others here, Dick. Do you have your walkie-talkie? We can all use a hot bath. It's really great. I could stay here forever."

"They can try it later," he said. "Besides, they're not close by anywhere. Joe took the other side of the valley and Em went upstream. Pete's in camp, minding the store." He drew his parka over his head and worried himself out of it.

"All right," said Zia. "Your turn. Do you mind being just a little conventional? Look at something else while I climb out and get dressed."

"Why do that? Stay where you are. Enjoy, enjoy."

Moments later Dick was naked and sliding himself into the pool. Zia, not wishing to be absurdly modest, kept her eyes upon him and tried to be indifferent. His body was lithe and smooth-muscled; he was done in Carrara marble, and even his proportions were by Michelangelo—seven heads to one body, if she remembered correctly. Sexual excitement rose within her, and she tried to suppress it.

He too was now neck-deep in the pool, and he came toward her slowly, stroking with his arms to help propel himself through the water. Now she could make out his expression more clearly. Actually, his face was plain and there wasn't a great deal of expression. Except in his eyes. They were steady upon her; they did not waver.

"No, Dick," she said quietly.

He halted an arm's length from her. "Why not?"

"All kinds of reasons. And I don't want to run down the list. Just no—that's all. For now, just no."

Dick laughed softly. "I've been waiting for this, Zia. I knew there'd be a time. I think you did, too."

"Dick, listen. I'm not—I'm not like anyone else. Will you just accept that? Sometime maybe I might be able to explain."

"I'll say you're not like anyone else!" His laughter rose. "Zia, Zia Marlowe—do you know how beautiful, how lovely you really are? I've known a lot of beautiful women, all over the world, but the day you walked into my office . . . those first few seconds when I saw you . . ."

"I'm sorry, Dick." She shook her head quickly. "I could say nice things about you, too—and mean them. But please take my word for it, now. There can't be anything between us. Not tonight."

After a moment's pause, Dick said, "I don't know what's got you all tied up in knots, Zia. But I know this much. They need untying." He moved toward her, reached out, and put his hand upon her shoulder.

She held herself motionless. "The answer is still no, Dick."

"It won't be for long." He lowered his hand down along her arm, caressing the skin.

"Don't—don't push it, Dick."

"Zia, we're doing an awful lot of talking about this. Talk's not really the thing."

He took the sides of her arms now and pulled her toward himself, firmly. He pressed her body to his. She felt its muscled firmness, felt her breasts crushing against his chest. His penis, hard and risen, the braided butt of a slaver's whip, was nestled upon her thigh.

"Do I have to fight you off, Dick? Do I have to do it that way?"

"You can try," he said, tightening his arms around her, breathing more quickly now in his excitement. "If that's what turns you on, you can try...."

Big Male strode across the grass-cushioned soil of the lower levels, his countenance in its usual surly and somewhat stupid cast, an instinct in slow fission deep in his craw providing the motive force that propelled him along. It was night. One hunted at night. One could hunt by day, too, but night was best. The tastier game was abroad at night, and could be taken more easily then. He could sense its presence at night, partly through the special adaptation of the rods in his retina, and partly through an extra sense which detected vibrations beyond the spectra of ordinary sound and sight.

He had passed many hidden living things in his progress through this canyon. Marmots in the rocks, rabbits in thickets, long-legged brown bats—a species that tended to avoid caves—in a tall dead tree. Big Male was after greater game tonight. A fat deer would be best. He would take it either by cornering it or running it down—deer in flight soon tired and faltered—and then he would twist its head and break its neck to silence it, and he would feast upon the juiciest part of the hindquarter, then carry the remains back to the Place of Safety, there to be stored with the other food in the ice caves. There was no conscious altruism in this sharing of his kill with the others. It was merely what he was impelled to do; it was the way of the Ones.

Had it not been for this instinct to return from the hunt, Big Male would have foraged along forever, wandering wherever his predatory senses led him. He much preferred the freedom of hunting alone to the restrictions and annoyances of life in the high gorge and the caves of the Ones. Skiny One, his mate, was always trying to control his behavior; always trying to make him into some docile creature quite

167

foreign to his nature. Younger ones were always annoying him with play, for which he had little time. Old One was always boring him with tales, half of which he couldn't understand. Old One needed to be put into his final sleep, and Big Male would have twisted his neck long ago if some queer instinct hadn't kept him from it. As for sexual diversion, well, the female of not many snows, she who came up with so many irritating, incomprehensible notions and observations, was pregnant now, and no longer sought to entice him. In any case, Skinny One kept too close an eye upon him to let him enjoy himself with any of the younger female Ones.

Yes, it was the hunt, the night hunt, far from the Place of Safety, that gave Big Male his greatest sense of fulfillment.

Suddenly his extra sense told him of the presence of something large, mammalian, and warm off to his left. There, against the wall of the canyon. *Two* creatures. Probably a male and his mate. There, at a place of hot water, such as one sometimes found in the wilderness.

He moved silently in that direction, his eyes probing the darkness. The shapes of the things he sought presently formed themselves in the optic centers of his brain. They were partly immersed in the hot spring. They were making vocal sounds ... and ... yes! These were the chattering sounds the Pink Skins always made!

Big Male felt a sharp thrust of disappointment. He had hoped to find game, not Pink Skins. There was a prohibition against eating the flesh of Pink Skins, as there was against eating the flesh of one's own kind. He knew no reason for it. He never sought reasons for all the rules that made up the way of the Ones.

And yet, like any of his kind, he was curious about the Pink Skins. The very facts that they should not be eaten and that they were generally to be avoided made them fascinating. He had often thought he might hunt down a Pink Skin and kill it sometime. There was no prohibition against that, as long as one didn't feast on such a kill afterward. But caution was advised in such an undertaking. The Pink Skins could kill at a distance with their firesticks and, according to Old One, were full of all kinds of other dangerous surprises.

An arrogant awareness of his own strength and power came over him abruptly, blanketing his sense of caution. He was Big Male, unafraid of any other creature in the mountains or the forest; he could vanquish the big silvertip bear if need be, though that would take a bit of time and a great deal of concentration.

He came forward all the way, toward the Pink Skins in the pool, knowing that in a moment they would be able to see him, and, with a defiant feeling that pleased him greatly, not caring whether or not they did.

Chapter Eleven

It was Dick who first saw the sasquatch, looming tall where it stood, scarcely ten yards from the edge of the pool. He had been forcing Zia backward, holding her tightly, attempting to thrust himself into her and wondering whether it would be possible in the hot water; she had begun to struggle, which had only excited him further, and his determination had risen into a kind of wonderful madness.

All of that now disintegrated instantly within him, in an abrupt implosion. He had glanced beyond the edge of the pool for no real reason. And there he had seen the tall, hairy creature, its legs slightly spread, its arms hooked loosely at its sides, quietly regarding them.

"Oh, my God," said J. Richard Charterhouse III.

Zia looked. She drew her breath in sharply and her eyes froze upon what they saw.

There was a long, long silence. Dick had released Zia and she had floated away from him; she was just beyond his immediate reach now. She stared in wonder, hardly believing that a moment she'd long dreamed of—her first sight of the creature—had come upon her this way, so abruptly, so commonly, so casually, so without a triumphant major chord with every voice in the orchestra sounding.

"There it is," she said, almost whispering. "It's real. It *does* exist."

"Hold absolutely still, Zia," said Dick. "No sudden moves. Don't move at all."

"Look at him!"—Still *sotto voce*. "He's magnificent!"

"He stinks a bit," said Dick.

There was a pungent ammonia-sulphur odor in the air. It was mammal exudation amplified, until it stung the nostrils.

"Probably a sex-attractant," said Zia. "Like glyptol in the gypsy moth—"

"For Christ's sake, Zia!" said Dick. "Not the goddam textbook! Not now!"

"Oh, Dick!" said Zia, not really hearing what he'd said, and with her eyes still fastened upon the sasquatch. "I knew it! I knew there'd be a sasquatch! I knew we'd find it!"

"Now, listen to me, Zia," said Dick, also without taking his eyes away from the creature. "Come down off that cloud and listen to me. There is no telling what this thing is going to do. We're in a very dangerous position, Zia; you've got to realize that. So, for God's sake, take it easy. Play it cool—"

"He's not dangerous. Most animals aren't if they aren't provoked."

"Some animals never read those textbooks of yours. Once and for all, Zia, take care! That's an order! For my sake, as well as yours."

"Squatch!" she called to the beast. "Hello, there, squatch!"

Big Male cocked his head to one side. The female Pink Skin seemed to be calling to him. He wondered if she were making an overture, as the now-pregnant young female had done so many times before. Had Old One ever said anything about copulation between the Ones and the Pink Skins? Big Male couldn't remember that he had.

Zia moved slowly toward the edge of the pool.

"Zia! No!" said Dick sharply.

"Be quiet. I know what I'm doing."

Dick weighed the dilemma in his mind. If he tried to restrain her, the beast might become alarmed at the sudden commotion and charge both of them. But if Zia alone moved toward him and he attacked, he would attack her alone. To be coldly logical about it, the least probable harm lay in letting her move toward it. He was used to weighing probabilities and coming to on-the-spot decisions in the wink of an eye. Like the time that homemade bomb had come through the window in Africa, and he'd thrown it out again to explode while everybody else was frozen with worry. They'd given him a commendation in a green leather binding for that one. They'd handed it to him in a secret ceremony, then taken it away to file it under a top-secret classification. You didn't get much chance to enjoy your honors in the spook business. He was glad sometimes that he'd been eased out and had gone over to private industry.

Except that he'd never dreamed he'd find himself balls-naked in a hot pool a hundred miles from nowhere with a dangerous beast glaring at him, pointblank. His Magnum, in his holster, lay with his clothes. He was sure he couldn't get to it in time.

Zia was climbing slowly out of the pool.

"Zia!" One more try to get her back....

She did not answer him. He saw the glistening line of her back, her golden skin steaming, the tight, round shape of her buttocks as she rose over the rock-edge of the pool. At any other time that would have driven him up the wall.

He looked at the sasquatch again. It had not left its place. Its head was waggling back and forth slowly now, from side to side. There was a quite human look of perplexity upon its flat-nosed beetle-browed face. Look here, God, Dick Charterhouse prayed, how about making the damned thing keep its temper? Is that too much to ask? I'd really appreciate it immensely. And I'd certainly owe you one.

Slowly—as slowly as the moon coursing the sky—Zia continued to approach the creature, and when she was only a few steps from it she just as

172

slowly raised her arm and extended her hand. She's hypnotized herself, Dick thought; there's no reasoning with her. The beast looked at her hand. It blinked slowly several times. Then its own hand, palm down, forefinger protruding, came up to meet Zia's. Zia's fingertip touched the fingertip of the sasquatch. The touch lasted only for an instant, and the creature suddenly withdrew its hand, as though he'd just remembered to be alarmed over this. He took one step back. He drew himself fully erect, expanded his chest, and beat upon it with the flats of his hands.

Zia was terrified in this moment. This was a hostile gesture, characteristically anthropoid, as were mock charges, and her only hope lay in the probability that the gesture was a pride-saving substitute for a real attack. She had the good sense to remain rock-still and not so much as switch her eyes back and forth.

The sasquatch stopped beating its chest. It scowled, for all the world like Emory Greer when there was blasphemy in the air. A rumbling, belching sound came out of the cavity of its short, thick neck and heavy jaws. It turned abruptly then, and walked away—walked, not ran—with what Zia could only think of as calm contempt for the puny humans it had just encountered.

It was gone in the darkness.

Dick scrambled quickly from the pool, grabbed Zia's parka where it had fallen—grabbed his Magnum, too—and rushed forward to wrap the garment around her shoulders. She donned it hastily, and then he slipped on his own parka. He took her into his arms and held her, while she trembled, put her head to his chest, and wondered why she did not weep.

He took the walkie-talkie set from the pouch pocket of his parka. He must remember to insist that Zia take hers along if she should go wandering off again.

"Joe! Em! This is Dick! Come in, Joe or Em!"

"Yeah, this is Joe," said the receiver. "Go ahead."

"I found Zia. She's okay. We found something else, too. You'll never believe this, Joe."

"Try me."

"A bigfoot, Joe! We just saw one up close! Zia touched it, for Christ's sake!"

"Did I hear you right? A bigfoot?"

"You and Em better get here right away. Got your guns with you?"

"Em has. He always has."

"On the double, then. Here—I'll try to zero you in to where we are."

Flashlight in hand, Greer searched the area near the hot-spring pool at great length, while Dick and Zia repeated their tale again and again to Joe and Pete Hollinger.

"I'll get the bar lights from camp tomorrow," said Pete excitedly. "We'll reenact it. Close shots of your reactions there in the pool. Christ, what a scene! Look, maybe we'd better get Eddie to fly in a fur suit of some kind. I know a costume shop in Hollywood where I can get one. We'll shoot it real soft focus and dim lighting. Just a suggestion of something out there, seen through the rocks—"

"Forget it," said Joe. "Can't you wait for the real thing?"

"Sure, if the real thing comes along, which maybe it still won't. Even if it does, this scene is still good. I can see it now. Zia, t and a, in the hot pool! Talk about production values!"

"Pete," said Joe, just what in hell *is* t and a?"

"Tits and ass," said Pete. "I thought everybody knew that."

Greer brought his flashlight and his scowl back to the pool. He hadn't found anything, just some bent weeds and a couple of rocks kicked over where it had walked. He studied Dick and Zia for a moment. "You really saw one, eh?"

"We swear it, Em," said Dick fervently.

"You sure it wasn't a bear?"

"Absolutely sure. Look. I had a few little doubts myself until tonight. Not anymore. Bigfoot exists, Em. He may be somewhere looking at us this very moment."

"Not likely," Greer said sourly. "Animals scoot as far as they can after they've bumped into a human. My guess is he went upslope from here. That's what most animals do when they skedaddle. They always figure the high ground is safer. Best we can do is keep that in mind and look for more sign in the morning when we can see better."

"All right," said Zia, nodding. "That seems as good a plan as any. Agreed, Dick?"

"Of course. It's the only option open to us at the moment. I suppose now we'd all better get a good night's sleep. If the adrenalin will permit it."

"First I'm going to have a hot bath," said Joe. "Pete? Em?"

"Dynamite!" said Pete.

Em glanced at Dick and Zia. "You two was there, in the pool, when you saw it, eh?"

"Yes," said Dick.

"Naked?"

"You don't take a bath in your parka, Em."

"Em," said Zia, smiling, "there wasn't anything you'd call wicked, if that's what's bothering you."

"Well, I'm glad to hear that," said Greer.

Joe frowned. He was glad to hear it too. So why was he frowning?

At earliest light they returned to the hot-spring pool and fanned out from it, searching the floor of the canyon and moving generally upslope to look for traces of the creature. At the end of an hour no one had found anything, and they regrouped and headed back toward the bivouac site. They'd decided now that Dick would return to Base Camp II and radio for the helicopter so that they could make an aerial search.

They were almost upon the bivouac when Greer

halted and frowned at something upstream and distant. Following his look, Joe saw the faint dark specks of birds wheeling in the sky. "Something dead up there?" he asked.

"Wouldn't be surprised," said Em. "Come on, let's go."

The distance was deceiving; it took them a good three-quarters of an hour to reach the spot. At first they saw a sleeping bag, lying rumpled a few yards from the stream. Coming nearer, they noticed a gold-panning dish and a small folding spade stuck into the ground. On the spade was a weatherworn broad-brimmed hat with an eagle feather in it.

"That there prospector," said Greer, nodding. He wandered off into the trees while Joe and the others inspected the remains of a campfire and an open blanketroll that lay neatly to one side with spare clothes, a messkit, and a pint whiskey bottle in it. About an ounce of whiskey remained in the bottom of the bottle.

Zia looked at Joe and smiled. "Well, now that we've seen a squatch we'd better talk to Harry Yates again. His tales might not be such tall ones after all."

"I'll have to get some shots of Harry when he comes back," said Pete. He had his camera in the shoulder rig he called a pod. "Joe, you go over and kick at the campfire, like you're checking it out, okay?"

"I wouldn't do that," said Joe. "I'd just look."

"These are *motion* pictures, kid. There has to be motion."

Joe shrugged and complied.

"When Harry shows," said Pete, "I'll have him do some panning. Closeup of gold in the pan. That's always good. I was a little worried at first, but now I think I can get enough cut-ins to stretch this thing out to ninety minutes, easy. They'll cut it for TV, of course, but it's nice to have it full-length for the theater market."

Greer reappeared from the glade. He looked somber. "Better come with me," he said.

He led them through the pale-barked aspens. The soil was dark and spongy underfoot, and there was a primitive smell, an odor of procreation, Joe thought, in the air all about.

Greer came to a halt at the carcass of Harry Yates' mule, lying on its side in a small clearing. The animal's eyes were milky in death; flies swarmed at its grinning mouth and still-moist nostrils. Its head was twisted too far to one side upon its neck. Its entire left hindquarter had been ripped away, the femur wrenched out of the pelvic socket, which was sickeningly exposed in a bloody nest of torn flesh.

Pete quickly pointed his camera at this, circling around it and taking footage in brief spurts.

"The sasquatch?" said Zia staring. "Is it *that* strong?"

Greer stared at her oddly for a moment, then beckoned, stepped off, and said, "Over this way, Miss Marlowe."

Harry Yates' body was crumpled at the base of a tree a short distance beyond the carcass of the mule. He was obviously dead. Joe nevertheless rushed forward to touch his neck and feel for a pulse. His head had been wrenched almost entirely around. His eyes, latex-dull, stared up into nothingness, and his mouth was spread, exposing his gapped and stained teeth in the grimace of a gargoyle.

Greer bent toward the ground a little beyond the body and picked up a rifle. He flipped its safety on, sniffed at the muzzle, then broke the chamber and looked at the cartridges. "One shot," he said. "He got one off at the critter."

"Bigfoot?" asked Joe. "You think bigfoot did this?"

"Can't see what else," said Greer.

"I knew that damned beast was dangerous!" said Dick.

"It's incredible!" said Zia. "The one we saw didn't attack."

"That don't mean nothin'," said Greer. "You never know with animals. You never know for sure. Way I see it, Harry got surprised while he was sleeping. The critter was maybe after that mule. He got in one shot, and then the critter got to *him.*"

"Poor Harry!" said Zia, looking again at his corpse and shuddering.

"We'll bury him," said Dick.

Greer suddenly stopped at another place in the clearing "Here's what I been lookin' for!"

The footprint, in a soft stretch of loam, was clearly delineated. It was the same kind of print Joe had seen in the snowbank: huge, humanlike, flatfooted, deeply imprinted by tremendous weight into the ground. Several other partial footprints led away from it in long strides.

"Perhaps the next time you see one, Zia," said Dick, "you won't be so eager to pet it."

"It must have been provoked," Zia said stubbornly. "The sight of the gun, I think. I've a feeling they know what guns are. Crows do, and they're not nearly as intelligent."

Greer had bent over to examine one of the other footprints. He picked up a fallen leaf, studied it, and said, "Looks like Harry didn't miss."

Joe looked at the slightly coagulated splotch of blood on the leaf. He frowned and said, "Funny we didn't hear Harry's shot."

Greer shrugged. "You don't hear, sometimes. In trees like this the sound can get lost. Besides. we must have been sleeping pretty deep when this happened."

"I'll want that leaf," said Zia, taking her knapsack from her shoulders so that she could get at its contents. "That blood goes on a slide. It'll be important—especially if we never catch up with the squatch."

"Well, it looks like we just might get to him now," said Greer. "He's dropping blood. I can follow it."

"Dynamite!" said Pete. "Lead the way!"

"As soon as we bury Harry," said Zia.

Pete showed blubbery surprise. "Are we gonna waste time on that? We've got a hot trail here—"

"We're going to bury Harry," Zia said firmly.

"Well, I guess that would make a pretty good scene at that. Grave scenes are always good."

It took them well over an hour to make a pit in the earth near the stream, then wrap Harry's body in the sleeping bag and lower it into the grave.

Greer intoned from his pocket Bible, "'Man that is born of woman hath but a short time to live, and full of misery. He cometh up and is cut down, like a flower; he—uh—fleeth as it were a shadow and never continueth in one stay. . . .'"

Joe threw the nearly emptied whiskey bottle on top of the sleeping bag before they filled the grave.

Emory Greer, ranging a little ahead of the others, was a hunting animal, coursing back and forth as he sought out the trail, his senses keen, his muscular frame loose and alert. He covered the ground with the grace of a loping cougar.

"Looky here," he said at an outcropping of rocks. He pointed to a yellow splotch in a patch of snow. "Stopped to take a piss here, that's what he did. 'Scuse my language, Miss Marlowe."

"I'll want a sample of that, too," said Zia, loosening her knapsack.

"Well, make it quick. He's putting distance between him and us all the time."

"He can't be very badly wounded then," said Joe.

"Hard to say," shrugged Greer. "That was a thirty-thirty Harry had. Wouldn't be more'n a mosquito bite to a critter that size. But no telling where he's hit. I knew someone brought down a bear with a twenty-two long once by gettin' it just right. Myself, I ain't takin' chances." He patted his rifle. It was a Steyr-Mannlicher bolt-action that accepted the massive, hard-hitting .460 Weatherby Magnum cartridge; Greer had persuaded Dick to procure it.

Zia looked up from her task of transferring a smudge of yellow snow by tongue depressor to one of the slides in her small case. "Em, I don't want you to shoot the sasquatch when you see it. Let's have an understanding on that right now."

"That so?" Greer looked annoyed. "How you gonna bring it in if I don't shoot it?"

"You know what we hope to do, Em. We've discussed it enought times. We'll use the dart gun."

"I got my doubts you'll drop him with that toy. You don't even know how much of a shot to give him."

"We'll find out. We'll use the dart gun."

"What do you think, Mr. Charterhouse?"

"Do it Zia's way," said Dick, as though bored with the question.

By midafternoon, the trail had led into a winding offshoot canyon farther up the valley. They had gained altitude and were approaching the timberline; the trees here were stunted and sparsely scattered, and there were small patches of snow wherever there was constant shadow. A cold rivulet ran down through the center of the canyon in a twisting course.

"We might just have him boxed in," said Greer, peering ahead.

The canyon seemed to stop at a back wall a short distance beyond them. Greer, still finding occasional traces of blood along the stream—a natural route for the creature to take—pushed on. A surprise awaited them at the apparent end of the canyon. It wasn't the end; it had only seemed to be because of two steep shoulders that came together here, narrowing the defile. The canyon doglegged and widened again past this narrow place. Presently they could see a high cliff ahead, and then a long, thin waterfall plunging down from a tunnel mouth hundreds of feet up the face of the cliff.

"This is what Fred Garvey mentioned!" said Joe.

"A waterfall out of a tunnel! The tunnel leads into a gorge up there! That's where he saw the sasquatches!"

Dick frowned at the cliff. "How the devil did he ever climb down? That's not an easy piece of rock."

Joe shrugged. "People do the damnedest things when they have to. We should have looked for this waterfall before, though I don't think it really shows up as a fall on the map. And the way this canyon squeezes in, it'd be hard to see from the air."

"Well, there it is," said Dick, still surveying the cliff thoughtfully. "And something of a problem, I'm afraid. *I* can take that cliff all right, but I'm not sure the rest of you can."

"If Fred Garvey could climb it, we can," said Zia.

"He had more luck than anybody ought to count on. Besides, he fell, didn't he? That's how he got those internal injuries."

"We've *got* to get up there," said Zia. "Now, while we've got this trail. If we go back and try to fly in it might be several days. All the sasquatches could be gone by then."

"Tell you what," said Dick. "I'll go up there by myself and take a look. If I find something we'll figure out how to get everybody up."

Zia shook her head. "I'm not going to stop now, Dick. Not now, when I'm this close."

"Hey, look, kids," said Pete Hollinger. "You're not talking about climbing that damned cliff, are you?"

"We have to, Pete," said Zia. "You can stay back, if you wish. I think we ought to take your camera, though."

"Nobody takes my camera! Look, I'm the photographer on this expedition! Hell—no offense meant—the rest of you wouldn't know what to do with the camera anyway."

Joe turned to Dick. "Isn't there some way you could help Pete up? I think the rest of us can make it if you can do that much."

181

There was agony now in Pete's expression. "Goddammit, I've got to do it! I'm scared as hell of heights, but I've got to! This is the dynamite chance! I can't boot it now!"

Dick surveyed the rockface again. "Well, maybe I could put some hardware in, and belay some line. I could find the footholds for Pete. If he could haul himself up on the rope in places—"

"I can do it!" said Pete. "I *will* do it!"

"Let's give it a whirl, then," said Dick.

He spent the next quarter hour giving Pete hasty instructions. "The thing is, Pete," he said, "when there's not much in the way of footholds or handholds you've got to keep moving. It's like riding a bicycle. Stop and you'll fall. We'll have a rope on you, of course, but ropes slip and break, and we still don't want you to fall."

"I'll make it," said Pete grimly.

Dick chose a route to the right of the waterfall, pointing out the exact path of the climb to everyone— a ledge they'd traverse when they reached it, a crevice in the rock up which they could chimney, a glassy stretch where they'd have to use the rope and the Jumar stirrups. "It's not really a tough climb," he said, "but any climb's dangerous if you're not experienced. Just play it cool and don't panic. Keep going. Don't look down. Above all, don't look down."

Dick himself switched loads and carried Pete's camera and his film supply. He hung his carabiners and jam nuts on the D-rings of his climbing harness, affixed the rope to each member by a bowline-like knot at proper intervals, then started first up the cliff-face. Pete was second on the rope, where Dick could keep a close eye upon him. He had cautioned everyone that only one climber was to move at a time, and whenever Pete was moving they were all to be belayed so that they could support him if he fell.

The first stretch of fifty or sixty feet was easier

than Pete had thought it would be. He breathed a bit hard with the strain of pulling his own weight upward with his flabby muscles, but Dick allowed him to take it slowly, and many minutes later, to Pete's surprise, he had made it to the first ledge, where he could actually stand free, flattened against the sloping rock. He faithfully obeyed Dick's admonition not to look down.

Terrified of heights he was, just as he'd said. He'd never been able to get close to windows in high buildings or the edges of rooftop observation platforms. When he'd been a kid the others had teased him over his refusal to try roller coasters or the parachute jump on the cable. He'd never gone out much with the other kids anyway. He'd been an only child with a mother who'd had to work after the standard divorce (standard in his suburb of L.A.), and he'd spent most of his time with his precious film projector and his books on motion pictures. He knew the cast of every major movie ever made, from the silents on. He knew the famous scenes—the shooting of Ben Lyon by his brother in *Wings;* the sudden revelation of Lon Chaney's horrible countenance in the first *Hunchback of Notre Dame;* the lyric opening of *Shane,* when Alan Ladd appeared between the antlers of the deer; the butt-shuffling stalk of the bandit upon Humphrey Bogart in *The Treasure of Sierra Madre;* he knew them and he knew how they had been made.

He knew his craft fully; he'd been a grip, a prop man, an extra, a film editor, and a gopher. But so far he'd never been closer than the fringes of success. There was always something to keep him from making dynamite. Backing withdrawn...leading actors quitting...the unions zinging everybody...the whole project canned by the executives for any of a hundred frivolous reasons. Murphy's Law was strictly enforced whenever Pete Hollinger undertook anything. The vehicles he *did* finish always bombed at the box office. He couldn't understand why. They were never all *that* bad. He worked very hard to make them good, changing the scripts when he had to to bring them closer to the proved ways, and giving them the action and suspense that was mandatory even if he had to drag it in by the scruff of the neck.

The bigfoot documentary would be different; he didn't see how it could fail. That thought sustained him as he went up the cliff, his terror tightly bottled deep within him.

He continued the climb as in a dream, with Dick Charterhouse directing his every step and with the others telling him he was doing fine, just fine. Once, with his toes resting on a narrow shelf, he thought he felt himself falling and grabbed in panic at the rope. "Steady, Pete!" Dick called down to him. "Get your left hand in that crack just over your shoulder. That's it. Now you've got it. Keep going, Pete!"

Somehow, somehow, he negotiated that passage and the others above it. Somehow he found himself at last on the platform at the mouth of the tunnel from which the waterfall emerged.

"You made it, old boy!" said Dick. "Congratulations!"

Pete looked down for the first time. The cliff plunged away from him in sickening perspective. A wave of dizziness came over him, and a gray mist began to form before his eyes. Dick grabbed him and pulled him back to safety as he fainted.

Chapter Twelve

It was Self who first saw Big Male returning from the hunt. She had been in her favorite nest of rocks, resting, contemplating the mysteries of her own mind. She had been slipping away for these lone meditations with increasing frequency lately; that was because they were beginning to shun her now that she'd acquired a young one in her belly without a proper mate. How they knew she was pregnant she couldn't understand; she hadn't really begun to bulge yet. The other females seemed to know most readily.

She heard a soft murmuring, now, as though someone were in pain; she stirred from her lounging position and looked over the tops of the rocks. There was Big Male, approaching the caves. Across one shoulder he carried the hindquarter of some huge animal. But he was not walking easily; he was, indeed, staggering from side to side.

He halted and swayed a little as he saw her. His eyes seemed unable to steady themselves upon her.

"I will carry the food," said Self, by means of grunts and gestures.

He allowed her to take the burden from his shoulder. She headed for the caves, and he stumbled along beside her. Big Male was not ordinarily communicative, but this time he seemed to wish to give an account of what had happened to him. Self had noticed this in others; when they were troubled they wanted to explain.

"Pink Skin," said Big Male. "Firesticks...great noise...I killed Pink Skin...twisted neck...thus!"

Everyone in the group gathered around as they reached the caves. They jabbered and shuffled back and forth, and Big Male, scowling, finding it difficult to stand upright, repeated several times all he'd said to Self. Old One directed Yellow Fur to carry the hindquarter up to the ice caves. Yellow Fur, who would rather have remained to hear the rest of Big Male's report, trudged off with it reluctantly.

Now Skinny One began to prance in front of Big Male and started to berate him. Anyone knew it was wise to stay away from the Pink Skins and their firesticks! Anyone except stupid Big Male, at any rate. He could have brought back much more food if he hadn't permitted himself to be wounded.

Finally, unable to put up with her nattering any longer, Big Male growled and swung his good arm in a vicious blow, just missing the side of her head. Startled, Skinny One scuttled away.

Self approached Big Male. He glanced at her, then away again. But he made no move to stave her off. She reached out and lightly touched the blood splotch on his shoulder. He flinched, but didn't pull entirely away. From examining the wound, Self imagined that a small, sharp stone hurled with incredible force had penetrated his skin, then, even more remarkably, had passed out the other side, where there was an even larger wound. He had lost much blood.

She took his good hand and pulled him toward her nest of rocks. He allowed her to do so, or perhaps in his daze he barely realized what she was doing. When he was stretched out, exhausted, in the rocks, Self hurried first to one of the caves, snatched a handful of moss away from one of the beds, then went to the stream and dipped the moss in icy water. She returned to Big Male and began to daub at his wound.

He flinched again, then grunted and blinked at her sleepily. She sponged the dried blood away and licked at the spot to clean it even more thoroughly. She made gentle, crooning sounds. Big Male answered

186

her by murmuring softly several times, then put his good hand lightly and caressingly upon her shoulders. It stayed there as he dropped off to sleep.

Emory Greer, probing the darkness ahead with his flashlight beam, led the way through the tunnellike fissure high in the escarpment, where the stream roared and echoed past them, on its way to its long fall into the canyon. The rock underfoot, beside the stream, was jagged and irregular; traversing it was difficult for everyone, and occasionally Greer had to halt, turn, and direct the beam of the flashlight toward them.

Joe, moving along behind Pete Hollinger, watched his silhouette closely and several times had to reach out to study him when he seemed about to slip and fall. They'd all been alarmed when he'd fainted, but he'd opened his eyes again within a few seconds and now seemed recovered.

The first indication that Zia had fallen was when they heard her cry out, and, in the next instant, a splashing that sounded above the roaring of the stream. Greer, in the lead, turned immediately to direct the beam of his flashlight back upon the others. Joe saw Zia at the edge of the stream, in plunging water up to her hips, clawing frantically at the rocks to keep from slipping farther down.

When they had pulled her back to the ledge again, she reached into the front pouch of her parka and said, "Oh, damn! The slides! I must have left the pocket open. That was stupid!"

"Don't worry about it now," said Joe. "Just get dry."

"But those slides—blood and urine samples—our only proof—"

"Forget it. The critter itself is up there ahead somewhere. Come on; wring yourself out so we can get going!"

The tunnel made several broad turns and at last

led to an exit on the inner wall of what seemed to be a high gorge. The mountains here, formed of buckled plates, volcanic deposits, and glacial scars, were so jumbled in the making that it was difficult to describe the features of the landscape, but Joe thought of the gorge they had entered as a huge gouge in a narrow plateau. Roughly vertical cliffs bordered this rock canyon on both sides; irregular slopes and shoulders buttressed these cliffs. Mountainsides swept upward above the cliffs, at times resting upon their edges. The floor of the canyon—if that broken surface could be called a floor—was strewn with ice patches, snowbanks, and boulders. The stream ran in a sharp cut near the center of the gorge, coming toward them out of a gray mist that thickened into opacity several hundred yards away.

It was colder here than it had been below. The wind whistled softly but threateningly, and incipient snow flurries darted about in the air, angry sentinel bees looking for something to sting.

"Storm gettin' ready," said Greer, contemplating this. "Not that I can say for sure—nobody can in these mountains. But it looks like it."

"Do you think it will keep us from going on?" asked Zia.

"Might. We'll keep an eye on it. If it starts to hit, we'd best find cover."

"Maybe we shouldn't have come this far," said Dick, frowning at the hostile vista ahead of them. "We're a long way from a lot of things we might very well need."

Joe shrugged. "Let's see what happens. If we made a wrong move, what the hell, we made a wrong move." He turned to Greer. "What do you think, Em? Push on some more, or stay here in the tunnel till the weather settles?"

"We can move on. There's shelter around if we need it. Plenty of overhangs in those cliffs; maybe some caves. But I got to say one thing. We're short on rations—plenty short. Everybody eats real small till we fetch some more."

Dick laughed and slapped Pete lightly on the shoulder blade. "You're going on a diet, Pete. It'll do you some good."

"You don't have to bring it up. I'm doing okay. I climbed that goddam cliff, didn't I?"

"Don't be oversensitive, Pete." Dick's laugh had trickled down into a smile.

"Who's oversensitive? I'm just a little fed up with your barbs all the time, that's all."

"What barbs? Come on, now, Pete."

"We can't all be big handsome overachievers," Pete grumbled sourly.

"I must say *that's* a bit gratuitous," said Dick. He stared at Pete evenly now, and without smiling. "You might take some of that lard off, Pete, and start doing a little achieving yourself. And you might get into the habit of appreciating favors while you're at it."

"What do you mean, favors?"

"I didn't have to bring you along, Pete. I could have gotten plenty of cameramen. Better ones, perhaps. I just thought you'd be thankful for the break, that's all."

"Take your sweet charity and shove it!" said Pete.

"Hey!" said Joe quietly. "Hey, you two. We're all on the same side, remember?"

"We better get movin'," said Greer.

In single file and close together, they pushed into the gorge, taking a course parallel to the stream, deviating from it only when rough terrain made miniature detours necessary. Greer kept searching the ground ahead with his eyes, finding several blood splotches, some quite clear in patches of snow, as they moved on. Occasionally they halted to examine sharply defined footprints. "We ain't far behind him now," said Greer. He unslung his rifle and checked its chamber. Zia took a cotton-padded box of tranquilizer darts from her knapsack, loaded several with

M99, drawing back the plunger after inserting the needle into the vial, and then armed each chamber with the tablet that would form expanding gas and force the plunger forward when the dart struck. She slipped a dart into the breech of the gun, tucking its streamer of red wool in after it, and finally inserted a CO_2 cartridge behind it.

"Better let me take that," said Dick. "I'm a pretty fair shot."

Zia nodded and handed the gun to him. "In the thigh or buttock, if you can. A lot of flesh to sink into is best."

"I know. I've seen it done in Africa."

"Is your camera ready?" she asked Pete.

"It's always ready," said Pete.

Presently Greer came to another halt. As they drew abreast of him he pointed to an irregularity in a long stretch of snow that swept down in a shallow grade from the wall of the gorge toward the center. Squinting, Joe thought at first that it might be another outcropping of rock. A moment later he grasped its shape more clearly in his mind's eye.

It was the canted wing of an airplane.

They made their way toward the wreck with great excitement. They had to flounder through deep snow for the last fifty yards. Then they were digging in the snow, clearing the doorway in the fuselage until Joe could squeeze his way into its interior. They searched the airplane, hoping to find rations, but were able to retrieve only a log book and a number of charts. Joe lifted a pair of baby shoes that had been hanging from the instrument panel. "Eleanor will want these, I guess." He stuffed them into the marsupial pocket of his parka.

Greer was still looking at the swirling gray air all around them. The flurries were dancing even more angrily now. "Okay, folks," he said. "Let's find a place to hole up in."

"How about the plane here?" asked Zia.

Greer shook his head. "It could be buried under." He stared now toward the cliff face across the gorge, then pointed in that direction. "Looks like a cave over there. Let's go."

They crossed the stream over a line of rocks, with Pete, at one point, almost slipping and falling into the icy water. A gentle ascent then brought them to the foot of the cliff. Some thirty feet above them was a cavemouth that formed a rough arch over a broad ledge; the cliff slanted outward slightly, creating further shelter.

"Can you get up there and drop a rope?" Greer asked Dick.

"Easy," Dick said.

Within minutes he had gained the ledge, belayed a line on jutting rock, and payed it out until it reached the floor of the gorge. They climbed to the level of the cave without difficulty, even Pete making it in fair time and looking quite proud of himself.

The cave was a huge chamber, the size of a good living room, that reached into the rock. A sharp turn on the rear formed a small alcove. "Neat," said Dick. "All the comforts of home."

It was cold in the cave, but there was neither the biting wind nor the icy wetness of the snow and sleet. They unpacked their knapsacks, unrolled the compact bundles of their goosedown sleeping bags, and laid them out on the floor. Breaking open a carton of mountain rations, they ate sparingly. The tiny propane flame of the Phoebus stove, as they cooked, provided a welcome spot of warmth.

"Keep your fingers crossed," said Zia. "Let's hope our sasquatch and his friends—if he has any—are still around in the morning."

"They should be," said Joe. "If Fred really saw a bunch of them, like he said."

"No reason to doubt his story now."

"We'll know better tomorrow," said Dick. "Right now we'd better be certain we're safe here. I think we should stand watches."

"Really?" Zia looked doubtful. "I don't think there's any danger."

"That's when it comes. When you don't think there is any."

"From the sasquatches?"

"Zia," said Dick, "let's not have another lecture on their behavior and what sweet and kind and cuddly creatures they really are. My guess is that they're good climbers and could get up here easily. But they're not all we have to watch out for. For all we know, that Indian, Tom Quick, is still following us. Maybe he's been watching us all the time. Maybe he's got his whole tribe out watching us. They might do anything they can to keep us from getting a sasquatch. The strongest motivation for chicanery, remember, is religious fanaticism—religious or ideological; they're in the same bag. Never underestimate it. They might quietly cut our throats while we're sleeping."

"Dick," said Zia, smiling, "you aren't having just a little touch of paranoia, are you?"

"Of course I am," said Dick. "I take little doses of it now and then to immunize myself against big paranoia if it should ever come along."

Everyone except Greer laughed, dissolving away the tension of the moment.

It was decided that there would be five two-hour watches throughout the night, the person on watch to sit, armed, at the mouth of the cave. It was dark outside now; the wind was keening in the darkness, steadily rising in pitch and volume.

Joe lit a small cigar; Pete Hollinger lit a filter cigarette.

"Tobacco ain't good for you," said Greer, scowling.

"So we know," said Joe. "So we all know."

"God give us these here bodies of ours, in his image, and we're supposed to take care of 'em. He just lends 'em to us for our stay on earth. We give 'em back when we enter unto the gates of Heaven."

Pete Hollinger looked at Greer with a smile that bordered on the sardonic. In some subtle way Pete had changed since he'd overcome his own fears enough to climb that cliff back at the waterfall. He had always been careful not to gainsay anyone over small matters; quick to change the subject if it seemed to be leading to disagreement. He'd formed this habit after a lifetime of seeking handouts. Other people had always held power over him, and basically he'd been afraid of them. Ever since the other kids used to tease him or beat him up because he was fat and slow. And bright. That was what they really couldn't forgive. Nobody likes a smart-ass. He'd learned to camouflage it. Suddenly now he didn't want to camouflage it any longer.

"Em," he said, "what happens when you go to Heaven?"

"What happens? Why, it's just all peaceful and everything."

"How do you spend your time?"

"I don't know. You just spend it."

"Doing absolutely nothing?"

"You praise God in all his glory, that's what you do," said Greer.

"Do you sing hymns? Play a harp?"

"I expect there's some of that."

"Can you play a harp, Em?"

"What? Of course not. I can't even carry a tune much. But I expect in Heaven I'll learn."

"Is that what you want to do more than anything? Learn to play a harp and carry a tune?"

"I don't know what you're talkin' about!" said Greer, angrily.

"Well, it seems to me," said Pete, "that anything a person really wants to do, he doesn't get to do at all in Heaven. Do they eat good food there? See any good shows? How about sex? None of that, I've heard. Just sort of sitting around doing nothing for eternity. Tell

193

me, Em, why are we supposed to look forward to *that?*"

"I'm goin' to forgive you your blasphemy," said Greer, glaring at Pete with murderous hate. "It's up to the Lord to punish you, and, mark my words, he's gonna do it!"

Pete laughed. "Whatever you say, Em." It had been like shooting fish in a barrel. He was going to enjoy his new assertiveness.

"We'd better discuss something else," said Dick. "I saw a menu in a navy wardroom once that said officers and gentlemen shouldn't discuss religion, politics, or ladies at the table."

"What else is there?" asked Zia.

"Damned if I know," said Dick.

Greer was still scowling. "You think you're makin' fun of me," he said, scowling at each of them in turn. "The Devil's makin' you say all this, to try me. He can be mighty slick. Like, the way he does with professors and such. This here evolution Miss Marlowe talks about. I ain't blamin' you, Miss Marlowe; you just been led wrong. But anybody who claims man is descended from the apes is blaspheming God, who made man special. Folks who think man is just another animal forget their glorious destiny and start *actin'* like animals. That's why we got all the trouble in the world today."

"In a way, you're right, Em," said Zia. "Right for what I suppose are the wrong reasons. But we'd better take the navy's advice and not get into it. I don't suppose anyone thought to bring a deck of cards, did they?"

"Cards?" said Greer.

Zia sighed. "I suppose they're wicked, too."

"We ought to be spendin' our time prayin'," said Em.

"We are," said Zia agreeably. "Whether we seem to be or not, we really are."

"I'll buy that," said Pete. "I'm praying," he said,

"that I'll get some good shots of those apes tomorrow. That the camera works and I don't do anything stupid, like leaving the lens cap on. I tell you, this is going to be dynamite! They'll be falling all over themselves trying to sign up Pete Hollinger after this!"

"Yes," said Zia. "We'll all get feathers in our caps, won't we? Joe will get to be sheriff. Dick will be at least a vice president. You'll be famous, too, Em; you'll have quite a platform for spreading the gospel, if that's what you want. I'll probably be turning down offers from universities. But the really great thing about all of this is that we'll be bringing some truth in and giving it to the world. Am I being grandiose? Very well, I'm being grandiose."

"On you it looks good," said Joe, grinning.

The wind howled through the night, and they took their watches and slept in turn. Zia, beside Joe in her sleeping bag, reached out and groped in the darkness until she found his hand. They rolled toward each other and pressed themselves together. Joe kissed her and gently stroked her hair and her cheek.

"I want you, too," she whispered. "As soon as it's the right time, the right place..."

"I'm beginning to doubt it ever will be."

"When we get back, Joe. I won't be bootstrapping anymore. I'll be free to take chances. Even if I should have your baby it won't interfere with anything. I almost think I'd like to, now."

He kissed her again, and after a while they slept, arms around each other. There was only the banshee wail of the wind. And the sound of Pete Hollinger's snoring.

It was quiet outside the cave when Joe awoke in the morning. Lowered cloud still hung in the gorge, but now it was infused with gray, pearly light. Dick Charterhouse, who had just finished the last watch, was lighting the Phoebus stove and had breakfast

195

rations—powdered egg, mainly—set aside for cooking. Pete Hollinger had his baby-blue eyes open and was smoking a morning cigarette, right there in his sleeping bag. Zia still slept. Emory Greer was hunkered against the wall of the cave, reading his pocket Bible.

Joe muttered good mornings and went to the mouth of the cave to stretch himself and look at the new day. The mist was thinning out. The floor of the gorge was as he remembered it: a rock strewn, sterile moonscape. It was a place no one would ever come to, because there wasn't anything here anyone could want. The sasquatches, fleeing the expansion of man, had been driven here. Like the Navahos and Apaches who had been pressed back into the worst of the land when the white man came west.

He stretched. He yawned. It felt good.

The low cloud at the far end of the gorge was dispersing. He could make out the massive shapes of the cliffs that marked the end of the canyon. Beyond them rose the pale bulk of what seemed to be a glacier. On either side of them loomed steep mountainsides, heavy with snow that clung to them too precariously, Joe thought.

Movement.

Joe became alert. Something had moved at the base of the cliffs that were the end of the canyon. Right there, below a pockmarking of a number of caves and indentations, formed like Swiss cheese when the volcanic rock had cooled.

He saw what he thought might be erect, manlike figures among the tumbled boulders at the foot of that distant precipice. He stepped back and said quietly, "Who's got the binoculars?"

"I have," said Dick. He found the glasses near his knapsack and handed them to Joe.

Joe focused them upon the cliff. A large sasquatch, walking idly, came into view. He still couldn't make out much detail, but he could see that it was, without the slightest doubt, a bigfoot.

"There they are," said Joe, and handed the glasses to Dick.

Excitement now broke over everyone. Questions, cries of wonder, milling about. Zia awoke and scrambled out of her sleeping bag. They took turns looking through the binoculars. Pete kept saying over and over again: "Dynamite!" Greer deepened his scowl, but only, Joe felt, to keep himself from showing the pleasure that was really inside him. Dick Charterhouse looked thoughtful, as though already planning what the next move might be for the sake of the greatest efficiency.

Moments later, Pete was pointing his camera at the sasquatches, levering its zoom lens down. He lowered the camera and shook his head. "Too far. They won't show up worth a damn."

"Try anyway," said Zia.

Pete shrugged and ran off a few seconds' worth of footage.

"Well," said Dick presently, "I don't like to spoil a great moment, but it seems to me we're not really any closer than we ever were."

"Then we'd better get closer," said Pete.

Zia frowned. "Which might not be easy. They may very well run off once they see us. Pete, are you *sure* you can't get pictures from here?"

"Take my word for it, will you, kid?"

"Sorry. I didn't mean to question your competence. Look, we've got to sneak up on them in some way. Do you think we can, Em?"

"*I* can. Not so sure about the rest of you. You got to do it real slow, and pick your cover."

"Perhaps we'd better brainstorm this a bit, and come up with a viable plan," said Dick. "We want to be sure we know exactly what we're doing, and that everybody knows everybody else's part. Sorry if I'm being elementary about this, but I think a few basic principles may be in order right now."

"We've got to take a chance," said Zia.

"On what?" asked Joe.

"On alarming them. If we stay here and do nothing we'll certainly accomplish zero. We'll just have to risk an approach. We know the sight of a gun might scare them off, so that rules out even the dart gun—at least for the moment. But if we can work our way through the rocks, up to perhaps a hundred yards from them, the rest of you can cover me while I show myself and try to get nearer. Once they get used to me, we can all show ourselves."

Dick frowned. "I can't let you do that, Zia. Too damned risky."

She shook her head firmly. "I can get close. I did back at the hot spring. I *know* these creatures. I'm the only one who *can* get close to them. At first, anyway. It's that simple."

"Which isn't simple at all. Zia, you could be killed, don't you realize that? How do you think I'd feel if I let you go ahead with this and then you got yourself killed? Sorry. I'm just going to have to veto your idea."

"You can't, Dick. It's my neck. I'll risk it the way I want."

Dick sighed deeply. "I was hoping I wouldn't have to put it this way. Zia, this is my expedition. I call the shots. We agreed on that, remember? You don't walk up to them alone, Zia. That's an order."

"And I'm afraid I'll have to disobey it." She looked at the others. "Does anyone else object?"

"It *would* make a hell of a shot," said Pete. "You walking right up to the damned things..."

Greer said, "You want to try it, that's your business."

Joe shook his head. "I'm with Dick. Too risky."

"Well, you and Dick are outvoted," said Zia.

Dick said angrily, "Who said this was a goddam democracy?"

"Now, listen to me, all of you," said Zia. "We've *got* to get close enough to at least one creature to tranquilize it eventually. Without that, and without the samples we'll take, we've wasted the whole expedition. All we'll have is another sighting, and as far as science is concerned the sasquatch still won't exist. Now, put aside all your macho gut reactions about protecting a mere slip of a girl, if that's how you feel. If I were a man, you'd let me go ahead. Honestly, now—admit it. But I have by far the best chance of getting to them—gaining their confidence, if you want to put it that way. And if I don't do this, we've blown it. We've blown the whole thing away."

"I still can't let you," said Dick.

Joe had been thinking. "Maybe Zia's got a point," he said slowly. "It's her way or nothing at all. There's a risk, sure. But we can cut it down a bit. Em's a fine shot, and he can watch her closely. Dick and I know how to handle a gun too. I'll take the dart gun; Em and Dick keep the rifles ready. If one of those things so much as looks at Zia the wrong way, we waste it."

"The answer is no," said Dick. "We'll try to get close enough to shoot one—period. One good carcass is all the proof we need."

"Sorry, Dick," said Zia. "You can't stop me from it."

"Can't I?" He stared at her quietly but threateningly.

"No, Dick," said Joe. "I don't think you can."

Dick turned slowly to face Joe. The two men measured each other's stares. Dick showed his dangerous smile. "I've been wondering when we'd tangle, Joe," he said.

"That's up to you," said Joe.

The moment hung.

"Well, maybe sometime," Dick said finally. "Sometime when it really counts. All right. I guess we have to go along with Zia. If anything happens to her, though, it's your responsibility, all of you. Not mine."

"To hell with all that," said Joe. "Let's just get it done."

Chapter Thirteen

"Let me speak to Sheriff Winfield, please."

"Whom shall I say is calling, sir?"

"Eddie Lorenzo."

"How do you spell that, sir?"

"Look, lady, just get me Zack, will you?"

"I have to write down the names, sir."

"Okay, okay. L-O-R-E-N-Z-O."

"Thank you, sir. I'll ring the sheriff."

Brrrt! Brrrt!

"Yeah. Winfield."

"Sheriff? This is Eddie Lorenzo."

"Who?"

"Out at the airport. Northern Lights Helicopter Service."

"Oh, sure. How are you, huh?"

"Fine, fine. Listen, sheriff, I'm a little worried about those bigfoot people."

"Worried, huh? What about?"

"They haven't called in for several days. Up to now they've been keeping close touch."

"Well, why don't you fly out and take a look, huh?"

"I did. Just got back. Nobody at the base camp. No sign of 'em anywhere. Now the weather's socked in again. I just wondered if you ought to alert mountain rescue."

"I need more to go on before I do that, Eddie. It costs money even to have MR stand by. Hell, the county's got to pay your chopper rental from the minute we notify you. Six hundred bucks a day. And the commissioners have been screaming about department expenses lately."

"Just the same, I don't like it. That's rough country out there."

"You don't have to tell me that, Eddie. You're from back East, aren't you?"

"How did you know?"

"The way you talk. Brooklyn, huh?"

"New Haven, Connecticut."

"Well, it's all the same. Look, Eddie, I was raised in these parts and I know it's rough country. But these people know what they're doing. They got Emory Greer along with them, huh? He's the best. If you don't mind putting up with all that Jesus stuff, he's the best."

"Sheriff, they went off from the base camp with just a few supplies. They picked up a bigfoot trail and decided to look close at the area. I was thinking that maybe—"

"Now, hold on a minute, Eddie. I don't know what kind of sign they raised, but it wasn't bigfoot, you can be sure of that."

"There were tracks, sheriff. I saw 'em."

"You, too, Eddie? This bigfoot business really brainwashes some folks. If you saw tracks they were bear or something. I've been round and round on this before. Besides, why call in mountain rescue when these people out there *are* mountain rescue? Greer's a volunteer. McBay's assigned to the team."

"I just thought I'd be on the safe side, sheriff."

"Well, I appreciate that, Eddie. But I wouldn't worry too much, huh? They'll get back okay. If you hear anything definite, let me know. I'll tell you what. If they really get lost, I'll go out *personally* and help look for 'em. How's that, huh?"

"It'll have to do, I guess."

"So long, Eddie. Have a nice day."

Tom Quick made his way up the winding offshoot canyon slowly, as, with some difficulty, he followed the trail of the five bigfoot hunters. A short distance

201

ahead, there was a steep cliff with a thin and silvery waterfall plunging from it, spurting out of an aperture near the top. There was no sign of the hunters in the canyon, and he wondered if they'd somehow managed to climb that cliff. He hoped not. He wasn't about to risk his neck trying to climb after them.

That probably would have surprised them, had they known. Doubtless they thought of him as a great outdoorsman. Stereotyping again. They were waiting for him to fold his arms and say, "Ugh!" He was a lousy outdoorsman. He'd had a hell of a time following them so far, and it was a miracle he hadn't starved or frozen to death by now. In fact, if he hadn't stolen some rations in the base camp to sustain him he would have turned back long ago. He'd done what the secret council of shamans had asked him to do; he'd harassed the bigfoot hunters by burning some of their stores and leaving that tourist cane so they'd know who'd done it; his responsibility had been discharged. He'd be perfectly within his moral rights to return, report on what he'd done, and then get back to all the tribal legal business still piled on his desk.

But something impelled him to follow the hunters a little longer. They might find bigfoot; they might try to bring a carcass back. And he might just run into an opportunity to prevent them from doing that.

The shamans wouldn't care if he went all the way, resorting to violence or even murder, but that was out of the question. Murder never solved anything and afterward ate away at a man's spirit. Both the Christianity he'd been raised with and the old tribal religion he'd revived pointed that out. It was all right to kill enemies in war, but not otherwise. Of course, with the white man going after the very soul of the Tillamish now, maybe it *was* war....

There were strange dichotomies in Tom's beliefs. One part of him knew very well that much of the lore he solemnly acknowledged was pure nonsense and that such powers as *stiquayu*, the wolf spirit, and *cubadad*, who traveled the world by walking (and was possibly also bigfoot), and *subetak*, who visited the land of the dead, existed only in the imagination. But without the spirits to act as symbols the entire fabric of the old religion would begin to fray and fall apart. The great truth behind it all was too vast, too starkly simple to be expressed except in terms of magic. Christianity was like that, too, and he might have stayed with the white man's religion if its lore and symbols, ethnically alien to him, hadn't always made him uncomfortable.

Tom had attended the white man's church as a child. He'd gone to the white man's schools, eaten the white man's food, worn the white man's clothes, and played the white man's games. He'd been a star quarterback at Pickettsville High. The Tillamish had never drifted too far away from the white man's civilization, as had some tribes in other parts of the country. They dwelt on fertile soil; they grew plentiful crops and they took a rich harvest from the sea. They waxed fat—a little too fat. Tom realized that when he studied Toynbee's theories in college. A civilization needed a balance of both prosperity and adversity in order to thrive. Too much of either started the process of decay. America—the white man's America—was beginning to feel the results of too much prosperity and comfort right now. There would be a day when the darker-skinned peoples of the earth, the hungry fighters, would emerge as dominant. Tom's own mongoloid strain would be among them. Yehtl, the raven spirit, willing and the cricks didn't rise.

He came now to the base of the cliff and surveyed the dizzying upsweep of black rock on either side of the silvery waterfall. After several moments of peering, he detected a small metal object wedged into a crack forty or fifty feet above him. It was one of those things mountain climbers used. They had climbed the rock, then, and were possibly in close pursuit of the wounded sasquatch now. He'd seen its footprints and its blood, and he'd found the grave of the old prospector it had killed. You didn't have to be a skilled woodsman to read all the obvious signs that showed what had happened.

Well, decided Tom, let them be. He'd be damned if he'd climb that cliff—and anyway, he'd now thought of a better idea to keep the hunters from bringing back a sasquatch. A more likely idea at any rate. With a little luck and the right timing, this way ought to succeed. All he could do was try.

Tom Quick turned and began to retrace his steps back toward the vicinity of the base camp.

Zia crawled forward across the rubble on the cold ground, working her way through the boulders and outcroppings that kept her hidden from the creatures at the base of the cliff. Her companions, according to the carefully worked-out plan, had ensconced themselves in other places of concealment behind her. Greer was off to one side, on his belly behind a slight hump of earth, his Steyr-Mannlicher resting in place, his finger on its trigger, his cheek to its stock. Dick Charterhouse, with their other weapon, the Browning autoloader, was in the trench of the stream. Joe, with the dart gun, and Pete Hollinger, with his camera, were in a clump of rocks between the two marksmen.

She could feel her heart larruping against her ribs. She thought the sound might even carry and alert the beasts. She didn't believe they'd charge if they were startled; she was most afraid that they'd take flight and be lost forever.

She peered through a slit between two rocks and saw the creatures for the first time at close range. Some were feeding, some were grooming each other, and some were simply sitting or leaning in place among the rocks in languid fashion. They might be getting ready to hibernate. No other primates were known to do this, but then bigfoot wasn't like other primates in most respects.

She was gratified to see that the creatures were much as she had deduced them to be. They were truly bipedal and gave no indication of using their forelimbs in locomotion. From the way they handled their food and picked for fleas they seemed to have the beginnings of opposable thumbs. The males had sagittal crests on their skulls for the attachment of strong jaw muscles; that meant that their diet had once consisted primarily of coarse vegetable matter, though they were probably omnivorous by now. As for their temperament, it struck Zia as phlegmatic, and even a bit solemn and surly. In their very movements they seemed to be saying that they wished only to be left alone.

Near one of their caves she suddenly saw and recognized the huge male who had approached Dick and herself at the hot-spring pool. There was a wound in his shoulder, and the fur around it was moist and glistening, as though the blood had been wiped or licked away. A young female was beside him, searching his fur. She heard rumblings and groanings and belchings from the various creatures along with occasional high-pitched crooning sounds.

Zia raised herself slowly. She came up a few inches, halted, remained still for another moment, then rose a little more. She bent one knee so that she'd be able to spring to her feet quickly if necessary.

It was an older creature—one with ragged, gray-streaked fur—who first saw Zia. He had been squatting not far from her, nibbling on what looked like sprigs of some kind of evergreen. She saw his eyes fall directly upon her. There was a remarkably human look in his eyes; indeed, in all their eyes. There was a soft, penetrating quality in them—an actual glow of intelligence that was probably an illusion, but struck her as real, nevertheless. The creature stared at her in obvious disbelief for a moment, then suddenly sprang to its feet and ran toward the caves, chattering and screaming.

The others—all of them seeing her now—began to chatter. Some followed the old one in his flight. A mother picked up her infant and carried it off, tight to her chest. Most of the beasts, however, stood in place and glared in Zia's direction.

Zia brought herself fully upright. She stood there, still as granite. The chattering died down a little. The beasts who had stood in place remained where they were, and she could see the puzzlement and uncertainty in their expressions.

And now one of the creatures took a few steps toward her. It was the young female who had been grooming the wounded sasquatch. Her steps were hesitant and cautious; it came to Zia that some of the chattering apparently directed toward her might represent warnings. Zia moved her hands a few inches away from her sides and opened them to show that they were empty. The young female came forward, a few steps beyond the nearest creature up to this moment, then halted and stood there, regarding Zia with a look of wonder and curiosity.

"Squatch!" Zia called gently. "Easy now. You can see I can't hurt you."

The sound of her voice brought on a new round of chattering. Some of the sasquatches thumped their feet upon the ground and made what looked like shuffling dance steps. The young female bent her head to one side in a clear expression of puzzlement.

Zia stilled herself again and waited. A few of the creatures sidled away from wherever they had been standing, but kept their eyes upon Zia. The female reached up and scratched the side of her head.

Suddenly all of the beasts were staring at a spot behind Zia. The alarmed chattering began again. Zia turned to see what had distracted them and saw Pete Hollinger, risen slightly from his nest of rocks, pointing his camera at the sasquatches. She turned to look at the sasquatches again, and as she did so they all suddenly broke from their places and rushed toward the caves. A few moments later there wasn't a beast in sight. She thought she could feel the staring of their eyes from the darknesses of the caves, but supposed she would naturally imagine that.

Clear enough what had happened. They'd thought the camera was some kind of gun. They knew guns—that was confirmed now, as far as Zia was concerned.

She waited many seconds, but still the sasquatches did not reappear.

She heard Dick's voice, calling softly to her from behind. "Zia! Get back here! Now—while you still can!"

She stepped backward slowly, her eyes still upon the caves. They stayed black and silent. Her foot scuffed a rock and for a moment she was off balance. She recovered herself. Finally she turned fully, and then, with constant backward glances, walked slowly toward the nest of rocks where Joe and Pete were stationed.

"I still can't believe it!" Zia said.

She was sitting cross-legged in the high cave. She and the others were eating what little of their rations they thought it prudent to consume for now.

"It's all too wonderful to believe!" Zia's eyes were shining.

"It's dynamite, all right," said Pete. "I only got a little footage, but my God, what dynamite!"

"We'll have to be careful. The camera frightens them. They think it's a gun."

"Come on, now, Zia," said Dick. "What do they know about guns? They look pretty stupid to me."

She shook her head. "They're not stupid. They're even closer to human than I thought they'd be. It's in their eyes. We'll know more, of course, when we get some blood samples tested. The protein sequence will

207

settle it once and for all. I suppose you know how that works."

"Haven't the faintest," said Dick impatiently. "Zia, you have a way of complicating all this—"

"But the protein sequence is definitive—the only absolutely sure way to determine the closeness of any species to man. Twenty amino acids, arranged in different sequences for different species. The number of differences shows the relationship. There are only two differences, for example, between man and gorilla—thirty-two between man and monkey. If this and the DNA and antibody tests work out, we might well find ourselves classifying the sasquatch as genus *Homo*."

"Are you tryin' to say again them things are human?" Greer brought his head up.

"Who cares what they are?" said Dick. "They're out there, big and ugly. And we haven't got what we came for yet."

"For once I have to agree with you," said Zia. "Let's review the bidding. Pete thinks he has a little film, but that's not enough. Pictures alone won't make a dent in the status quo. As corroborative evidence they're fine, but we *must* have biological samples. We've simply *got* to tranquilize a squatch and take them. The problem, of course, is getting close enough to do it."

"Glad you recognize the problem," said Dick dryly.

"We've got a start on it," said Zia. "They allowed me to get pretty close today. I think I can earn their confidence and get closer. Eventually I should be able to maneuver one of them to where we can get a dart into it."

"And how long do you think that will take?" asked Dick.

She shrugged. "Days. Weeks. I don't know."

"We can't hold out that long. We're all hungry as hell. Use your head, Zia."

"I thought Em might be able to slip away and

bring back some food. The longer we stay here the better, actually. I want to study the creatures' habits—learn everything I possibly can about them in their natural state."

"And I'd like to get some *really* dynamite footage," said Pete. "There's a high place off to the right—on top of the cliff—where I could shoot down and get everything. They wouldn't even know it. I think I could make it up there if Dick would give me a hand."

"Well, at least your suggestion makes some sense," said Dick. "As for zapping the damned things with darts, I say forget it. We know now we can get within rifle range. Why don't we simply shoot one and get it over with? All the biological samples you could want. Cut off its damned privates and bring them in, for all I care."

"I won't see one killed," said Zia, shaking her head stubbornly.

Dick shrugged with great exaggeration. "Okay, let's leave it at that for now." He turned to Pete. "Do you really want to go up there and take those pictures?"

"It's not exactly that I want to. It's that I *have* to."

"First thing in the morning, then," said Dick. "If the weather's right and the damned things are still around. And Em, you better be covering us. I'll try to climb up where they can't see us, but if they *should* spot us, we'll want protection."

"You'll get it," said Greer, grimly. "All I need is one good excuse to drop one. I *know* they're Satan's critters, now I've seen them. They don't belong here, on God's good earth."

The air was still and the sky was clear. Most of the mist had lifted from the gorge, and there was only a thin haze that softened the outlines of whatever was distant.

At a point down the canyon, where the cliff wall took a turn and could not be seen from the sasquatch caves, Dick Charterhouse clung to another ledge he'd found, hammered a jam nut into a crack, clipped a carabiner to the ring, and slipped the bight of his rope into its eye. He called down to Pete, who was a short distance below him. "You're belayed now. Pull yourself up to this level. And don't forget to sing out, 'Climbing!' the way I told you. That way I know, for sure."

"Oh, Jesus!" said Pete. "I don't know if I can take this much longer!"

"It was your goddam idea," said Dick. "Be a man now and stick with it."

Straining and grunting, Pete hauled himself along the rope, placing his feet precariously against the rock, gritting his teeth, sweating, wishing he'd never been born.

"Good!" said Dick, when Pete had made the ledge. "Just a little way to go now. Don't look down!"

Pete nodded and kept his eyes from lowering themselves, the way they wanted to. He looked at the camera secured in Dick's Chouinard pack. Dick had left him free of any impediments so he could climb more easily, but he still hated to let that camera out of his hands. Dammit, but life could be a pain in the ass. Seemed he was constantly doing things he didn't want to do, so he could do things he *did* want to do, but somehow he never seemed to get around to that second set of things. All his life that way. Running around frantically to work out deals, toadying up to bastards he despised, and the sum total of the caucus race was zilch. Up till now. The bigfoot thing would really do it at last. There'd be a house with a swimming pool in Bel Air or someplace. Broads in bikinis at the pool. New ones every day. A goddam Chinaman to keep house and cook. And for food, not just chop suey. French cooking—all those great sauces. Pasta with lots of olive oil and garlic. Kosher food—thick pastrami sandwiches on warm, fresh rye. American country breakfasts; sausages and hotcakes with plenty of butter and syrup. No more

Charlie Chaplin eating his shoe in the Klondike. Great scene that had been. They'd remember Pete Hollinger's scenes that way someday. And his would be true—the real thing. He didn't have to fake anymore. Well, maybe a *little* reconstructed footage for dramatic effect, but no real outright faking.

He kept filling his head with these thoughts so there'd be no room for the fear that was trying to push into it. He kept climbing.

Emory Greer was far below, in the gorge, behind a rise that also concealed him from the sasquatch caves. He sat on a rock with his rifle across his knees and kept his eyes on the climbers—small specks way up there now. When they made the crest and headed along the rim toward the end of the canyon, he would keep abreast of them, ready to shoot if any of the beasts spotted them and started to climb after them.

Back in the shelter cave, Zia Marlowe was stretched out on her stomach, watching the sasquatches through the binoculars. She had an open steno pad beside her and every once in a while she would jot down a note. She kept discussing her observations with Joe.

"Well, that's one mystery solved," she said. "How they feed. Nobody could ever figure out how this ecosystem, which is so low in protein, could sustain them. They've adapted to it. They still eat coarse pulp—bark, leaves, shoots, berries—but they supplement this with meat. They deep-freeze the meat, as the wolverines do. They've developed a sophisticated social system in order to do it. Individuals seem to go out on actual missions to procure food. Division of labor. Species like insects specialize, of course, but blindly, compulsively. The squatches seem to do this with forethought. They look more human to me all the time."

"Don't let Em hear you say that. It shakes his world."

"Of course it does. New discoveries shake everybody's world. If *Homo sapiens* has any real distinc-

211

tion from his animal cousins it's that he's been opening Pandora's box ever since he found the tools for it. The more he learns, the more of a mixed-up kid he becomes."

"Then why do you keep on learning?"

"I'm compelled to, as I am to survive and procreate. Don't ask me why. I just am."

"I can see one thing now," said Joe, laughing. "We'll have lots to talk about on long winter nights."

"I'd rather devote them," said Zia, with an answering laugh, "to that equally compelling urge for procreation...."

Pete Hollinger was almost to the top of the cliff now. Dick Charterhouse had already made it and was sitting at the edge up there, the rope belayed in proper fashion across his chest and under his thigh. Pete had a mere fifteen or twenty feet to go. Ironically, in this last tiny stretch, there seemed to be no holds—at least none he could discern. He couldn't imagine how Dick had made it.

"Come on!" Dick called down to him. "You can do it!"

"I can't find any place to hold on!"

"Try the bumps. Bring yourself up fast. Remember the guy on the bicycle!"

With one hand on the rope and the other feeling for a hold, Pete grimaced and pushed with his toes. He found a small ridge with his fingers—no more than a transverse lump on the surface of the rock. He squeezed, trying to get a grip on it. He drew a deep breath and gathered himself for an upward spring.

"Wait a minute!" called Dick. "You're not hooked on!"

Pete suddenly remembered that he'd slipped the double loop from the beaner on his belt in order to readjust it before resuming the climb. The realization came, to his horror, too late. He had already pushed himself upward. In the next instant he was swaying out and away from the rock; his own considerable weight was tugging to bring him down.

He panicked. He took his one hand from the rope and grabbed in desperation at the rockface.

"No!" yelled Dick.

Pete was in midair. He was slanted away from the rock, and only an instant passed as he hung there, free, but it stretched out in his mind and gut to an agonizing eternity.

Pete fell.

He screamed as he fell, and the sound of it diminished in a Doeppler effect as he plunged to the canyon floor. He struck with a thud and bounced sloppily.

Dick stared down from the edge of the cliff and said, "Holy mother of God!"

Dick felt stunned. He could not immediately accept the reality of what had just happened. No one ought to fall like that, so suddenly, so casually, so unnecessarily—especially not anyone under his expert direction. Pete had been a compulsive loser all along, of course, but he didn't deserve an abrupt and senseless end like this. At least, Dick told himself, it had been Pete's own fault. Greer, who was watching, would bear witness to that. The others wouldn't blame Dick. In a way, he was obeying a principle he'd always lived by in the spook business. CYA. Cover your ass. Always make sure of that before you did anything.

Dick stepped back from the edge of the cliff as Greer, below, rushed toward Pete's broken body. No chance at all that Pete was alive. Dick didn't suppose he'd be greatly mourned in many places; Joe and Zia had more or less tolerated him, and Greer, for some reason, had hated his guts. But too bad he'd fallen and died. It was a damned inconvenience.

His foot bumped the camera he'd laid aside upon reaching the top of the cliff. He stared at it for a moment, then stooped and picked it up. After several fumbling tries, he found the latch that opened the magazine. He swung the cover away and took reels from the spindles. Glancing down to see whether or not Greer could observe him, and seeing that he could not, Dick tore the film from the takeup reel and tossed it aside. The footage he'd destroyed was what Pete had taken of the sasquatches the day before.

He put the camera back together again. He secured it in his knapsack once more. He donned the knapsack, brought in the rope, coiled it over his shoulder, and finally lowered himself over the edge of the cliff to begin his descent.

"We'll have to bury Pete," said Zia.

"Already did," said Greer. "The ground was too hard to dig, but we got him covered up with rocks the best we could. It'll keep the coyotes away. For a while, anyhow."

"We should bring the helicopter in and get his body later," Zia said.

"Maybe we should turn back and do that right now," suggested Dick.

"We can't. We've got to finish what we started here. Pete would understand that, I think."

Within a few hours Pete, although not forgotten, was no longer the principal subject of their conversation. Zia brought them all back to the business at hand by discussing with Greer his projected sortie to procure food.

"What I figure I'll do," Greer said, "is try to get back to the base camp real quick. Let's hope the raccoons didn't get into the rations there. But if I run across any game before I get there, I'll take that instead. Whatever's quickest."

They watched Greer, who had slung the Browning instead of the Steyr-Mannlicher across his back—handier for smaller game, he said—as he walked down the valley with his swift moccasin steps until he disappeared.

That afternoon, and again the next day, Zia reapproached the caves of the sasquatches. She did as she had done before, crawling toward them slowly under cover, then showing herself. Dick suggested that she take a walkie-talkie with her, but she thought that too might alarm the beasts, especially if it gave off the sound of a voice, even accidentally.

The creatures were beginning to accept her presence now. Most of them dared amble closer toward her than they had before, pretending that they weren't particularly interested in her. They gave themselves away, however, with a series of stolen glances.

Zia spent long minutes watching them from her close vantage point. She sat on a rock, crossed her legs, folded her hands in her lap, and simply watched. Returning to the cave each time, she would make notes on what she had observed and deliver running comments on her findings.

"I think they're monogamous," she said. "There are definite male-female pairings. That's to be expected in a species where the young undergo a protracted maturing period. Witness the elephants. Witness *Homo sapiens*, for that matter."

"Whatever you say," said Dick. He sounded bored. He paced the floor of the cave a great deal and suggested several times that they wrap this thing up and get it over with.

"It can't be much longer now," Zia said. "Just a few more times to get them a little more used to me. Then I know I can get one to follow me."

They were recognizing individuals among the sasquatches now, and they had begun to give them names. The fussy, older beast, who was always in a state of alarm, was Foxy Grandpa; the surly male, who seemed to be recovering from his wound, was Macho, and the young female who followed him around all the time was Sassy—short for sasquatch. There was a skinny older female who was obviously something of a shrew; they dubbed her Kate. The yellow-haired, somewhat vain male became George Armstrong Custer.

"Sasquatch naming," said Zia, "is a high art that well may rank with cat naming."

215

On the third day after he had left, Greer finally returned. It was evening and almost dark when they spotted him coming up the gorge, almost to their cave by now. He swiftly climbed the rope Dick had rigged to hang permanently, and, gaining the upper level, he took the bulging knapsack from his back and dropped it on the floor.

"Meat," he said. "Found some game and figured it was quickest and best. I even butchered it up for you. Deer. Nice fat doe."

Dick roasted chunks of it on the Phoebus stove, smearing each small cut with salt, pepper, and marjoram. They tore into it hungrily.

"Em," said Dick, "we certainly appreciate this, but it won't last long, I'm afraid. We've got to get out of here. Tomorrow, I'd say."

"All right," said Zia. "I'll try to get a squatch to follow me first thing in the morning so you can tranquilize it."

They kept up their watches throughout the night, with each watch lengthened slightly now that Pete Hollinger was gone, and all slept well enough in spite of the cold and the hardness of the cave floor. After a breakfast of the venison Greer had brought, they were eager to approach the caves of the sasquatches once more. For the last time, all fervently hoped.

Zia walked casually toward the beasts, who had apparently been up and about since earliest dawn. The humans had learned by now that the bigfeet would tolerate the sight of Zia's companions as long as they kept a greater distance and did not show their guns. Once when Dick had accidentally brought his rifle into view they had become greatly agitated.

She made a somewhat bolder approach this morning, coming closer to the caves than ever before. A few of the sasquatches stared at her a little longer than they did ordinarily, but soon returned to the game of assiduously ignoring her.

Zia was looking for the young female she'd named Sassy. This one had come closer to her than any of the others, and twice, as she'd turned to leave, had followed her for several steps. She'd be easiest, Zia thought, to entice into dart-gun range—she hoped as little as twenty yards. Not seeing Sassy at first, Zia thought she might be in one of the caves or even absent from the area. Altogether she'd counted sixteen beasts in the troop, but noticed that frequently one or two of them would go off somewhere, perhaps on foraging trips.

Finding herself deeper than ever before in the territory of the sasquatches, Zia felt a sense of danger she hadn't expected. Several of the beasts were now actually behind her and could easily cut off her escape if she needed escape.

Suddenly she saw Sassy. The young female had just emerged from a clump of boulders not unlike the nest that concealed Joe, Dick, and Greer some distance down the canyon. Sassy had probably gone into the rocks to relieve herself, Zia surmised. She'd noted that the creatures tended to seek a little distance and even some privacy for their natural functions.

Zia now strode through the midst of the other sasquatches in order to get to Sassy, feeling a little like Farragut braving the mines in Mobile Bay. She passed George Armstrong Custer almost close enough to reach out and touch his tawny fur; he scowled at her slightly, but shuffled off to one side and went off about his business. Kate, the scrawny female, made chattering, complaining sounds as Zia walked by her, bared her teeth slightly, but also gave way.

Sassy, ahead, appeared to have noticed Zia now. She halted, cocked her head, then slowly came toward Zia, closing the gap between them. Zia continued forward at the same pace.

Moments later Zia and Sassy halted simultaneously, a little more than an arm's length apart. Sassy's eyes were bright and alert; there was neither fear nor hostility in them. They radiated, instead, an intense curiosity.

Zia moved her hand slowly toward the chest-high

pocket of her parka. Sassy's eyes followed her hand closely. From the pocket, Zia took the remains of a small chocolate bar she'd saved. She brought it to her mouth, pretended to bite and chew, then broke off a small piece and extended it toward Sassy.

Sassy cocked her head, first to one side, then the other. She lifted her hand, held it hesitantly in midair for a moment, then brought it forward and took the morsel from Zia's fingers. She inspected it closely, smelled it, and suddenly put it into her mouth. Her face relaxed in an expression of pleasure and satisfaction.

"Like it?" Zia asked. "Good. Now. Come on, Sassy. This way." With the rest of the chocolate bar held toward the creature, Zia backed away a few steps. Sassy followed. Zia gave her another portion. Next, Zia turned and walked several steps away, looking back at Sassy as she moved on. Sassy narrowed the gap between them and, seconds later, was walking almost abreast of Zia. She was making soft, murmuring sounds. Zia was sure she was asking for more of the chocolate. And quite politely, too. Zia halted. She slowly raised her free hand, reached out, and took the creature's hand in her own. Sassy made no move to pull it away, then returned the light grip of Zia's fingers.

Her bloodstream in a torrent of excitement, Zia gently pulled Sassy along with her. Sassy came quite willingly. Zia could almost sense her thoughts. This was some kind of new game, the object of which would be revealed presently.

It was a moment of triumph for Zia. It was a moment she'd worked for over a period of many years, even when she hadn't known precisely what form her ultimate triumph would take. She had achieved a relationship—a friendship, perhaps— with a creature still uncatalogued by science, a species that would undoubtedly turn out to be closer to man than any other primate, and perhaps be classified as the only other nonextinct species in the genus, *Homo.*

She was filled with great fondness for the creature walking beside her. She wished only that she didn't stink so much, like all the sasquatches, but that was a minor flaw, and besides, she'd almost become used to the acrid, musky odor. Humans stank a bit, Zia reflected, in their natural state; they merely covered it up when they were civilized as part of their compulsion to rearrange everything, even themselves.

She felt like a Judas goat now, leading Sassy to the poisoned dart that would take away her consciousness briefly and allow them to rob bits of her flesh and blood. "You see what this superior intelligence of mine leads to?" she said to Sassy. "It makes me devious, and a bit of a bastard."

Sassy murmured appreciatively.

Still holding Sassy's hand, Zia turned away from the caves and began to walk toward the stand of rocks where her companions were concealed.

Macho, the big male, was suddenly in front of them. He'd scuttled into this position so quickly and abruptly that Zia hadn't noticed his move. His feet were spread and his huge arms were hooked loosely at his sides. His massive brows were kneading a great scowl into shape over his deepset, bloodshot eyes.

Sassy chattered at Macho. Macho, still barring the way, chattered back. They were clearly in mutual contention. Sassy dropped Zia's hand and stepped forward, as though to push Macho aside, and, at this, Macho swung his arm and cuffed her with great force on the side of the head. Sassy stumbled to one side, slightly dazed.

Fear gripped Zia now and held her rigid. Macho reached forward, grabbed her by the torso, and swung her upward, like a loose sack, over his shoulder. He ran with her. He seemed to be heading for the clump of rocks from which Sassy had originally emerged. Zia began to kick and struggle. Macho only gripped her more tightly, and she felt the crushing pain. The sound that Zia uttered now was something between a gasp and a scream. It came out of her involuntarily, in a sense squeezed out of her by Macho's painful grip. She struck at him awkwardly with her fists, and at this he merely snarled in annoyance.

Somewhere, in the midst of this kaleidoscope of fearful impressions, Zia gathered that the other sasquatches were staring at Macho dully and with little more than passing interest as he ran forward with his burden. Zia could not see Sassy now; she doubted that she could count on her for an attempted rescue.

And then Macho was bounding into the nest of rocks, clearing the barrier with an easy leap. Zia was jolted as he landed. He threw her to the ground. She screamed again and rolled to one side in an attempt to scramble away.

Macho cuffed her on the side of the head with a great swinging blow. She saw flashing lights. She was somewhere between consciousness and blackness. The terrible image of the fearsome creature bending over her, and now thrusting himself toward her, was rocking and spinning in her diminished sight.

He was tearing at her clothes. He was ripping and clawing the fabric away with his incredible strength. He had already split the front of her parka in two, tossing shreds of it aside. He was clawing at her shirt and trousers now, tearing bits away in fierce, fumbling agitation.

It can't be, thought Zia. No, really, it can't be. It was plain enough what the beast meant to do—at least there seemed no other explanation for its actions. She still could not quite absorb the reality of it. Her mind was not working fully, anyway. She was dazed by the blow Macho had delivered . . . in a dream state . . . yes, that was it . . . a dream . . . a nightmare. There was the dual awareness of a dream: you know it's not real, but somehow that doesn't melt away the terror.

220

Unconsciousness seemed poised like a great breaking wave ready to fall upon her, and now she wished it would. She wondered if Macho would injure her seriously when he penetrated her. She wanted to laugh wildly. laugh and cry, together. She was truly crazed with the terror that permeated every cell, every molecule of the complex arrangement of proteins and amino acids that was Zia Marlowe. And don't forget the ectoplasm. The soul, or whatever it is. That was slipping away from her, too....

Chapter Fourteen

When Joe McBay saw the animal lift Zia to its shoulder and begin to run with her, he rose immediately from his crouc...ing position in the rocks and brought the dart gun to his shoulder, pointing it in that direction. In the portion of a second this reflex action required, he remembered that it wasn't a regular weapon and that the range was too great. He squeezed the trigger anyway. The weapon popped, and he never saw where or how far the dart had gone.

Emory Greer, with his heavy Steyr-Mannlicher already in aiming position, held his fire. As always when he was about to shoot, Greer had become a cold and emotionless aiming machine—an instrument for tracking the gun. Even with this awesome urgency before him, he waited for the moment when his shot would be effective instead of wildly thrown. Right now there were too many other animals and too many scattered rocks between himself and the running target. Even when the target did flicker into his sights, Zia's body was too close to any area where the sasquatch might be shot effectively. This had been clear to him from the moment the beast had lifted her. It was the legs he wanted to get. Most anywhere in the legs.

He could anticipate the precise effect of his shot without running all the specs through his mind— he'd done that part of it long ago. The .460 Magnum slug, hurtling at sixteen hundred feet per second when it had traveled two hundred yards, would strike the animal's flesh with an energy of nearly three thousand foot-pounds; it would smash whatever bone it touched, and its shock effect would shatter all nearby bones whether it touched them or not.

Greer loved the moment of firing a gun. The deadlier the weapon, the greater his love. Em was at peace at this moment.

Dick Charterhouse had also risen out of concealment. Upon seeing Zia attacked, he'd said, "Oh, Christ!"—as much in disgust as in alarm. He too had pointed his rifle, desperately trying to line up a shot. He'd been against this insane idea of Zia's, getting so close to the creatures, from the first. That gave him bonus points in the game called I-Told-You-So. He usually came out ahead in that game. Zia's own game with the sasquatches had been rigged against her from the beginning. She hadn't listened when he'd tried to tell her so. Now she was about to be canceled out. He'd do his damnedest to prevent that, of course, but the way things were working out at the moment, he wasn't too optimistic.

All three men had thus shown themselves, and the sasquatches had seen them rise from the rock cluster. As each beast detected their presences, it diverted its attention from Big Male and the Pink Skin female to this sudden new threat, and became greatly agitated. The beasts began to shuffle and stamp, chattering and whistling—a sound that was also much like whinnying—in alarm. Milling about, they became additional obstacles between the riflemen and the specific target they sought. *Pink Skins with firesticks. The magic objects that could kill at a distance.* Some of the beasts had seen firesticks before. Some had even listened to their terrible thunder. Those who hadn't had been warned about them by Old One countless times.

Several males charged toward the men in the rocks, rushing forward a few steps, then halting suddenly and scrambling back again. They seemed

223

to understand that the firesticks had a range of effectiveness, and that at a certain distance you were relatively safe from their deadly magic. They charged, broke off their charges, then thumped at their chests and howled angrily in their high-pitched voices.

Joe McBay was not in control of himself—and didn't give a damn that he wasn't. He was filled with a sense of horror that left no space for any other emotion, let alone rational thought. He had quite hopelessly fired the dart gun, knowing it wouldn't have the slighest effect. All that he could focus his mind upon now was that Zia was in deadly peril and that somehow he had to get her out of it. He rushed forward, across the rough terrain, and toward the jumble of boulders into which the sasquatch carrying Zia was now disappearing. He held onto the dart gun, supposing in some vague way that it might be used as a club if necessary.

A sasquatch who limped a bit detached itself from the group and charged Joe at an angle to his course. Dick saw this, sighted his rifle upon the beast, and pulled the trigger. The report of the gun sent echoes rollicking back and forth between the walls of the gorge. The gun kicked at Dick's shoulder and its muzzle jerked upward as it recoiled. A spurt of dust flew up from the sasquatch's leathery chest; the beast halted, tried to clutch at the spot, then staggered back and howled.

At the sound of the shot, the other animals scrambled for cover, throwing themselves behind boulders or little humps of terrain. Several of the females fled toward the caves. Dick put his front sight on the back of a running creature and squeezed. The beast stumbled, but kept running.

Greer had not yet fired. He was aiming toward the rock nest into which the ugly brute carrying Zia had leaped. If the damn thing showed itself, even in one of those cracks, and even for only a flashing second, Greer would get him. Except that Joe McBay was

224

now putting himself between Greer and the rocks. The damn fool! What did he think he'd accomplish, getting that near, and with only that empty pop gun in his hand? The woman—in danger she'd brought upon herself—had made Joe lose his senses. That was what women did to men.

And the Lord God caused a deep sleep to fall upon Adam, and he slept: and he took one of his ribs, and closed up the flesh instead thereof; and the rib, which the Lord God had taken from a man, made he a woman.

Some things the Lord God had done sure seemed to be mistakes, and all you could do was remember that He had some purpose in mind which was beyond you.

Joe McBay came leaping into the small, hidden place ringed by the jagged boulders. Zia was sprawled on the slanted rock; the big male primate was on top of her, covering most of her body with his own, snarling with excitement as he tried to rip her clothes away.

The beast turned its head and saw Joe.

In this moment, the absurdity of what he'd done came to Joe. All right, he was here—but what in hell could he do? Slam himself upon the beast and start giving him left jabs and right hooks or something?

The beast came to its feet. It howled at Joe, drawing its lips back from its teeth. They were large, yellowish teeth; the canines were pointed and prominent.

Zia, on the rock, stirred, coming out of her daze.

"Run!" said Joe. "Get the hell out of here!"

The sasquatch was less than ten feet away, and for some reason Joe couldn't understand, and maybe didn't care to understand, it wasn't attacking. It was glaring at him, shaking its head, snorting and growling, while saliva shone on its bared incisors. It struck its chest with the flats of its hands.

Zia staggered to her feet. Her eyes were somewhat milky. She lurched forward, almost losing her balance, then threw herself across the rocks, scrambling forward again until her scrambling became running steps.

Suddenly it came to Joe why the beast had not thrown itself upon him. It was the dart gun he carried. The creatures knew that guns were dangerous—how or why Joe couldn't guess—and this one had no way of realizing that the weapon in Joe's hand, already discharged, was now little more than an empty piece of pipe. That Joe had kept it in his hand was now, as it turned out, more luck than anyone could hope for, but that wouldn't keep him from accepting it gladly. To confirm his suspicion, he brought the weapon into firing position against his shoulder. The sasquatch shook its head and drew back a step. This big male was the same creature who had attacked Harry Yates, the prospector; he must have been this close to Harry before he had charged, and he must be recalling now that when he'd charged he'd been shot in the shoulder; meeting this situation a second time, he had become more prudent. Some kind of pride kept him from fleeing altogether, some kind of caution kept him from closing the attack, and he stood there now, caught between plus and minus.

Joe backed away slowly. He managed to roll himself awkwardly over the rocks with his eyes still upon the sasquatch, and with the empty dart gun held in a position he hoped the beast would continue to regard as threatening. When he was out in the open again, the sasquatch followed hesitantly. From his grimacing, Joe could guess that he was wondering about that weaponlike thing the human carried and already beginning to suspect that it might be harmless.

Other bigfeet were now scattered about in front of the caves, all seeking at least partial cover, their attention upon the men with aimed guns farther down the canyon. Zia was half running, half stumbling across the broken terrain; Dick was moving forward cautiously to meet her, his gun readied, his glance moving from beast to beast, looking for the slightest indication of attack. There were beasts he might have shot, but it was best to save the shots in his magazine for any direct attack upon Zia.

Still in his original position, Emory Greer kept the Steyr-Mannlicher steady upon his cheek. The big animal who had attacked Zia—demon of Satan that he really was—had emerged again from the rocks, and just the edge of him showed beyond Joe McBay's running figure, which was blocking Greer's line of sight. If Joe would come just a little more forward now, and if that bigfooted demon would angle over just a little more to the left...

There! A clear shot. Right smack in the middle of the ugly brute's head, with the sight raised just a tad to take care of the trajectory. And a firm, careful squeeze—don't hurry it—and his eyes open and steady against the flinch.

The gun went off. The big male looked surprised and staggered back. Greer could not see immediately whether or not he'd hit him dead center. Maybe he had—but maybe that sloping, armor-plated forehead had deflected even the five hundred grains of that soft-pointed Magnum slug. The sasquatch swayed in place. Greer saw no mark upon its head and suddenly realized what must have happened. His aim had been a cat's hair off—even he couldn't drop one in dead center *every* time—and he'd creased the evil, foul-smelling sonofabitch. The terrible force of the massive bullet had rocked the brain in its skull, dazing the beast. Greer shot again, and this time he saw the spurt of bone and brain as the bullet struck just above the creature's eye. The big male toppled stiffly and, hitting the ground, twitched its leg several times before it was completely still.

Zia was now almost upon Dick and about to throw herself into his arms. Greer saw another sasquatch, over to the left, who had risen to expose itself momentarily. He caught it in the side of the gut with a snap shot. It grabbed its belly and howled and began to spin in circles. A moment later, miraculously, it stared at Greer and then, still screaming, charged toward him. God, but these beasts were tough! Harder to kill than grizzly, and maybe elephant, too! Greer put another shot into the charging beast's chest, and this time it managed a dozen leaping steps before it tumbled flat on its face.

Four shots. Magazine empty. Greer reached quickly into his parka for another load.

"Em! Let's get out of here!" called Dick. He was holding Zia, who was trembling uncontrollably. "We can't shoot them all!"

Joe, still carrying the dart gun, came abreast of them. They grouped themselves more closely together. And then they began to move away, slowly at first, turning their heads with every step to watch the sasquatches, presently at a faster walk, and finally at a stumbling, broken trot. The beasts followed, matching their pace, keeping themselves almost three hundred yards off. Greer was surprised at how they seemed to sense effective range. He could maybe hit one at three hundred yards, but it would take some doing.

They hurried down the canyon, crossing it at an angle. They sought the high cave that had become their own territory, their sanctuary, in this hellish canyon that at times seemed to Zia—who was having wild, irrelevant thoughts in her state of fright and exhaustion—a parallel plane of existence, reached through a flaw in the continuum....

There was no time for Self to grieve over the loss of the mate she had recently taken away from Skinny One. Big Male had been put into his final sleep by the firesticks of the Pink Skins, and his carcass lay where it had fallen. There would be no dance in the moonlight, no whistling night song, and no removal of the body, at least not for now.

The members of the group had more urgent

228

business. The Pink Skin interlopers now had to be destroyed.

Self found her own protected place behind a sharp embankment where the stream had cut its meandering scar in the floor of the gorge. It was not completely clear to her why she, and all the others, were now impelled to post themselves in places of concealment along a kind of arc before the cave of the Pink Skins, all keeping some distance away where the magic of the firesticks could not reach. Yellow Fur, by grunts and gestures, had directed that this be done. He had become the dominant male, now that Big Male was dead, and she was not sure why this was suddenly understood and agreed upon by all. Yellow Fur's leadership would probably be challenged before long, but that wouldn't happen until this immediate crisis had been resolved.

Yellow Fur had taken a position by an outcropping in the center of the arc. He was crouched there now, peering toward the high cave where the dim moving figures of the Pink Skins could be seen now and then. Self was not sure that Yellow Fur would be able to hold onto his leadership as Big Male had. Yellow Fur was too easily distracted from serious purpose and too fond of his own comfort or pleasure. He groomed himself as often as he allowed someone else to groom him and on more than one occasion Self had watched him masturbating when he thought he wasn't being observed. But there had to be a leader, and for now he'd do.

What annoyed Self most about the entire turn of events was that she had apparently been wrong about the Pink Skins. She hadn't believed there had been any harm in them, and indeed at first it had seemed that way. The smallest Pink Skin—Little Female—had stayed close to them for long periods without the slightest threatening gesture. The other Pink Skins had hung back, out of sight, evidently lacking Little Female's courage. And then, unaccountably, the Pink Skins had attacked, using their firesticks. It was as though this had been their purpose all along. The attack had somehow been precipitated by Big Male's foolish decision to attempt copulation, of all things, with the Little Female. Deviant behavior, to say the least! Self did not condone this, but she still couldn't understand why such a relatively insignificant act had so greatly angered the Pink Skins and caused them to use their firesticks. Maybe there was no connection. Maybe the Pink Skins were like Big Male—full of just plain foolish impulses they sometimes couldn't control.

There were four Pink Skins in the cave. (Using the new grunt she had invented, Self was now able to count to four; the others still couldn't grasp her concept.) They still had their firesticks, and it wouldn't be wise to approach them too closely. It was impossible for the moment to twist their necks and kill them. But if they could not leave their cave they would soon be without food and become so weak that possibly they'd be no longer able to wreak their magic. Or, in time, they'd simply die. All that was needed to bring this about was to stand guard, for the Pink Skins were also exhibiting caution in the matter of direct attack. The Ones would stay in place, day and night, individuals breaking off occasionally to fetch food or perform natural functions, and they would be alert for any opportunity to attack, but if such an opportunity failed to come along, they would simply wait. The intruders would die and the high canyon would be at peace again....

"They're still out there," said Emory Greer, peering at the floor of the canyon in the first gray light of morning. "They got us boxed in, that's for sure."

It had been a fearful night for everyone; they had stood double watches, using the flashlight to probe the darkness below the cave at intervals, and seeing the shadowy figures of the sasquatches, who dared to come closer at night from time to time. Greer had twice shot at the lurking beasts, but, unable to see them clearly, had apparently missed. Everyone had tried to sleep in turn, but no one had been able to do more than doze off occasionally.

Greer was flat on his belly at the mouth of the cave. The others were squatting behind him, partaking sparingly of what little meat was left.

"I'm damned if this tastes like venison," Dick said.

"Fat doe," said Greer, his eyes still on the canyon. "They taste different."

Dick began to look at him suspiciously. "Em—you didn't—I mean—good God, Em, is this really deer meat?"

Greer's glance was heavy with annoyance. "What else did you expect it to be?"

"For a moment I thought—well—there was Pete's body out there—"

"This here's just what I said it is," said Greer angrily. "But now that you mention it we just might have to do somethin' like you thought."

"Em!" said Zia. "What are you saying?"

"You know what I'm sayin'. Some things you got to do, like it or not, that's all. And you know what? What I'm talkin' about wouldn't be no sin. The Bible don't say nothin' against it, anyplace. I'm not sayin' I'd *like* anything like that, but it wouldn't be no sin."

"Forget that terrible idea, Em!" said Zia. "Let's concentrate on ways and means to get out of here."

"Been thinkin' about that, too," said Greer.

"I daresay we all have," said Dick.

"We could take our chances," said Greer, "and just start walkin' out. Shoot any critters that try to get near us. But there's too many of 'em. We'd kill some, but the others would get to us. Either that, or they'd figure a way to sneak up on us—specially when it got dark. They'd stalk us all the way back; I got no doubt of that."

"All right, Em," said Dick, impatiently. "You've summed up the situation very well. What we want to know is what in hell we can do about it."

231

"Ain't a thing we *can* do, except hold out. Somebody's bound to come lookin' for us sooner or later. I'm surprised that heeliocopter ain't showed up by now. But to hold out, we've got to eat. We'll be so weak in a few days they'll be able to get to us. Water's no problem with all these rain puddles, but some kind of food is what we need pretty quick."

"Now, wait a minute, Em." The first shadow of approaching horror was lowering itself over Dick's face. "This isn't going to be the old Donner party bit, is it? Or those people who went down in the Andes—"

Greer made a snorting sound that might have been his version of a laugh. "I was thinkin' of that bigfoot I dropped. Its carcass is still up there—I can see it with the glasses. The critters are afraid of guns, and, by showin' a gun. I could maybe work my way up there. I could slice off a few hunks of that big buck ape."

"Eat a sasquatch?" Zia was aghast.

"They're meat, ain't they?" said Greer. "Sorry we can't rustle up no prime ribs of beef."

"I think," said Dick, nodding slowly, "that Em's got a pretty good idea here."

Zia sighed sadly, bitterly. "We hunted them down just because they were there. Now we have to kill them and feed upon them. Man, the predator."

Dick ignored her and said to Greer: "Do you really think you could get to that carcass?"

"Way to do it," said Greer, thinking it out as he spoke, "would be to work up the canyon real slow, along the cliff, so's I'd have one flank covered. Meantime, you'll be up here, coverin' me with a gun. The range won't be too far till I get up there. If either you or me drops one before I get there, so much the better. That's the carcass I'll use for meat."

Joe interrupted. "Em, maybe *you* should cover from the cave. You're the best shot. Dick or I could go up there."

"This here gettin' meat is my job," said Em.

"I can cover him from here," said Dick. "I know how to use a gun. Let's not get bogged down in a lot of

232

talk now. Let's get started while we can."

They spent several minutes surveying the canyon floor with the binoculars, picking out a route along the base of the cliff, selecting a course that would keep Greer in sight at all times so that Dick could cover him. They swung the binoculars toward the siege line of the sasquatches more than two hundred yards out and caught occasional glimpses of movement as some of the beasts stirred and showed themselves partially from their places of concealment. Finally, Dick dropped the rope from the cave again, and Greer, with the Steyr-Mannlicher slung on his back and his hunting knife secure in its scabbard at his belt, lowered himself to the floor of the gorge.

Glancing constantly toward his left, where the sasquatches were, Emory Greer moved carefully along the base of the cliff, his steps feline and delicate, his huge, slab-muscled body taut and alert, his every nerve and sinew under his total control.

In his mind he was asking God to make him stop being afraid. His companions didn't know it, of course—it just wouldn't do to let them see it—but he *was* afraid. He knew he could keep the critters away from him if everything went as planned, but he also knew that they, as demons of Satan, would be under the Devil's direction and might find some sneaky way to get to him. God was directing him, Emory Greer, and the Devil was directing those creatures, so the fight was really between God and Satan again.

There was comfort in knowing this to be the nature of things. Before he'd joined the Pillar of God Church, and had been born again, he'd had no such comfort. He'd gone through life restless, discontented, always afraid, though his fear had been with him so long he didn't even recognize it for what it was. He had bespoiled his God-given body with drink and tobacco and had consorted with harlots just like any other man. He had at first resisted the blandishments of the P.G. who called upon him one day and gave him those tracts to read. He'd never been much for reading, anyway. But he'd opened them idly and had found himself suddenly caught by some of the words. Kingdom of Heaven...everlasting life. Before he knew it the words were leaping out at him, great shining missiles of truth.

He'd gone to the church, and had found himself spellbound by the voice of the Reverend Ernest Osterman, up there in front. He could never remember exactly what he said, except that it always seemed to answer everything. Folks came up with all kinds of illnesses—deafness, arthritis, cancers the regular doctors couldn't touch. Osterman, short and plump, a big white flower always in the lapel of his natty suit, would call upon the Lord, bang them lightly on the forehead, making them swoon momentarily, and, by God, they would walk away whole. Greer also had been impelled to come forward and be touched. In that moment he had been born again. Hallelujah, praise the Lord.

Dahlia went to church with him obediently, and once in a while she even sallied forth to ring doorbells and pass out tracts. He knew her heart wasn't really in it, though. She was still too weak in the face of temptation—like that awful sin she'd entered into with Pete Hollinger. He was still trying to forgive it, like he was supposed to. It wasn't easy. He was still trying to keep himself from being glad that Pete had fallen and died.

Movement over to the left brought him out of these thoughts. Near the stream, a bigfoot had suddenly risen to show itself. He aimed at it, hoping he wouldn't have to waste any of the four shots in his magazine just yet. Altogether, he hadn't brought too many cartridges for either of the guns: they were getting low on ammunition.

There was the crack of a rifle from the cave. The creature ducked out of sight again. Dick hadn't hit it—not at that distance—but at least he was up there, covering.

Some of Greer's fear dropped away. The way the animals were keeping their distance, it seemed pretty sure now that the Lord had decided to preserve him. It was just like in the psalm. He was walking through the Valley of Death and fearing no evil for the Lord was comforting him. He was even preparing a table for him—that bigfoot carcass up there—in the presence of his enemies. Why, this here was a prophecy come true!

His head was spinning with this revelation when he reached the carcass of the big buck male. It was as though he'd taken strong drink. There'd be a tale to tell and a testimony to make in church when he returned. He'd done the Lord's work in slaying the demons of Satan, and the Lord had showed him how every step of the way. Let that snippety little professor, with all her wicked ideas about evolution and such, try to answer *that* one!

He bent over the body of the animal. He put his gun on the ground where he could grab it again, quick and easy, drew his hunting knife, and started a cut along the heavy ham of the dead sasquatch.

The Lord was speaking to him. He couldn't hear the words, exactly, but there was a great, floating hollow voice coming out of the firmament. It was telling him what he must do. The others had been brought here that they might die; that God's kingdom would be shed of their wickedness. Unless they would surrender themselves to God. He, Emory Greer, would be the instrument of surrender. He'd bring back the meat, hold it before them, and make them beg like dogs for it! Except ye shall be saved, ye shall not feast. That wasn't from the Bible, but it sounded like it ought to be. He'd make them believe. He'd bend them to his will. He'd grab them with his great, slab-muscled arms and shake the wickedness out of them. He'd strike them with all his might, bruising their flesh and breaking their bones. He'd let them know the pain he'd always known in a hostile world. For everyone was his enemy and always had been. And now that he was born again he could attack his enemies and even slay them if need be! As an act of love, reveling in the pain he inflicted upon them for their own good and God's greater glory!

Greer did not see the sasquatch that emerged from behind a nearby boulder until it was already loping swiftly and silently toward him. When he did see it, he snatched up his gun in a swift reflex action.

He pointed the gun, and the great, growing shadow of the beast loomed into it. The dirty-yellow one, blond as the whore of Babylon it was. He'd worked his way here under cover, like a damned Apache Indian, and Greer hadn't spotted him. The Devil had maybe even made him invisible as he'd approached....

Greer fired pointblank into the mass of destruction that was hurtling toward him. Monster of evil...eight feet high...of giant breadth...a snarling, slavering, incredibly evil ogre's countenance that was a mockery of God-created man. The bullets did not stop it. It was upon him. It tore the gun from his hands and tossed it far aside. Greer reached for the throat of the beast. It crushed into him. Its overpowering stink enveloped him like a poisonous cloud. Its falling weight—by God, it was already dying!—bore him backward to the ground. Its hands clamped themselves to the sides of his head. It twisted his head in a quick, snapping motion.

Greer had often thought that in the moment before he died—which was bound to come upon him as it was to all men sooner or later—he would glimpse Heaven, where he was surely slated to go. He *did* see something, by God! A kind of pink cloud and a lot of swirling, endless blue. He heard harps playing and angels singing. Real sweet-like. He wished he wasn't so tone deaf and could appreciate it more....

Chapter Fifteen

In the telescopic sight of the Browning, the figures of Emory Greer and the tawny sasquatch that had attacked him were insect shapes dancing unsteadily around the crosshairs. Dick Charterhouse squeezed off every shot in the magazine, knowing even as he fired that he was not finding the target.

Zia stared, sickened and horrified, through the binoculars.

Joe squinted at the distant scene, seeing it imperfectly, but, also in horror, understanding fully what was happening.

When it was done, and when they realized, through a gelatine of shock, that there was no undoing of it, they stared at each other dumbly.

"Oh, my God, poor Em!" whispered Zia.

Dick scowled as he lowered the rifle. "What in the hell are we going to do *now?*"

They stirred about, looked into each other's eyes vaguely, and tried to unclog their senses. Time rode along on a blurred line; Joe did not know how much later it was when Dick spoke again. Minutes—maybe more. It didn't make any goddam difference how much time had passed. Somehow, right now, nothing made any goddam difference.

"Now, look," said Dick. "We've *got* to get out of here!"

Zia didn't seem to hear. "First Pete, now Em," she said. "Is it going to be all of us, one by one?"

"Forget it, Zia. They're dead. Erased, kaput, gone. Now let's concentrate on our own little bucket of worms."

Joe nodded. "Em went a pretty long way before that thing got to him. The sight of a gun still keeps them off. Maybe I could be luckier. Maybe I could make it down the canyon. Get to that waterfall and go for help. I don't think we could all slip past them, but one man might make it."

"I don't think you *would* make it," said Zia. "They're too much in command, here in their own environment. They not only have the hunting instincts of animals, but they also *think*, as we do, in terms of cause and effect. They'd find a way to get to you. They'd *invent* a way. They have the beginnings of this human characteristic."

"Will you please stop writing the textbook on the sasquatches for us?" Dick said angrily. "*Homo sonsabitches*, that's what they are to me. I went along with all this nonsense of yours about not killing one, and now look what's happened!"

"Drop it, Dick," said Joe sharply. "Don't blame Zia. We all got ourselves into this."

"Yes, you did, didn't you? You didn't listen to me, and this is the result!"

"Why didn't you just go ahead and shoot one, then, when you had the chance?"

"I was trying to get along with all of you—against my better judgment. Don't forget that I came through and sold this thing to Cadbury when you couldn't find anyone else even to believe the goddam things existed. I saw that they *did*. Simple logic. You gather intelligence and you believe what it tells you, even if it doesn't fit your preconceived notions. That tooth alone had to belong to a species nobody knew about—the best goddamn forensic pathologist in the world confirmed it."

"Wait a minute," said Joe. "What pathologist?"

"All right, you might as well know. You wouldn't let go of the tooth, but I had to know for sure. I got it, and—"

"You slugged me, there in my own pad?"

"No, that was some creep I hired. I put it back, though, after I was finished with it. Look, don't get your balls in an uproar over it now. You got the expedition out of it, didn't you? Anyway, I sent it to the lab we used to use in Washington. Rush job—personal favor. I made sure before I decided. I always make damned sure of everything."

"What's your point? What does all this prove—how sharp you are? Is that what you want to hear us say?"

"I don't give a damn what you say. I'm thinking—putting it all together. There has to be an answer. There always is. You get all the data, look at it in the right way, and there's an answer."

"What Joe suggested might be the only answer," said Zia. "One of us going for help."

Dick moved to the edge of the cave mouth, balanced himself there, and looked upward for a moment. He turned to face them again. "Maybe the way out of here," he said slowly, "is right up the face of this cliff."

Joe also stared upward. "We'd never make a climb like that."

"You two wouldn't," said Dick.

"But you could?"

"It'd be rough. But I know what to do."

"Are you sure?" Joe looked at the way the cliff slanted outward above them; he scanned its dark, vitreous surface, which seemed to offer few footholds.

"The odds aren't as good as I like them to be, if that's what you mean," said Dick. "But I might have to take them. This begins to look like the only game in town."

They discussed Dick's plan eagerly and looked for flaws in it. Would he be able to find his way back to camp even if he did reach the top? He thought so. If not the camp, someplace else where he could summon help. What if the sasquatches tried to climb after him? In that case Joe would shoot the sonsabitches. Dick would leave the rifle behind; he wouldn't carry its extra weight on a climb like this. For his own protection, later, he had his Smith & Wesson Magnum revolver anyway. Something had told him it would come in handy.

The mist of the morning had lifted by now; the gray cloud ceiling had risen high, as though to make a domed stadium for Dick's spectacular effort. He slipped into his climbing harness, with his ice ax and carabiners hanging from it. His various oddly shaped jam nuts were in the pouch pocket of his parka, along with a few conventional pitons. The perlon rope, shortened to solo length, hung in a coil from his shoulder.

"Should I say good luck?" asked Zia. "Or is it bad luck to say good luck?"

Dick smiled. "You can say what we used to say in the organization. From the old OSS operations in France in World War II. What one of Napoleon's generals said. The word of Cambronne."

"Merde," said Zia.

"That's it," said Dick. *"Merde."*

"What's that mean?" asked Joe.

"Don't tell him." Dick laughed. "It'll be our secret."

"Get back soon," said Zia. "Get back all in one piece and soon."

"Of course. As soon as I can."

The badinage between Dick and Zia was trivial enough, and Joe was well aware of this; he therefore thought it stupid and unreasonable of himself to feel a twinge of jealousy over this shared secret of theirs, whatever it was; over the fact that they had some common knowledge in a field of information that smacked of sophistication, and possibly even some kind of snobbery. The implication was that of course they knew the word of Cambronne; didn't everybody? Everybody smart and stylish, anyway; everybody with a good store of what might be called trivia for the well educated. It put Dick and Zia into the same class—and to hell with this base canard that America in this day and age was a classless society.

All societies developed classes—probably even the society of those sasquatches out there. It put Dick and Zia closer together, and that was what he'd hoped would not happen. Call it jealousy, call it bruised ego, call it a great leaping inferiority complex on his part. Call it anything—he was stuck with it.

Because of the jealous twinge, he turned a momentary scowl upon Dick. Because of the scowl, he looked at him very closely. And because of that he saw—

What was it?

It was something in Dick's eyes when he said he'd be back as soon as he could. It was an almost imperceptible shifting of the orbs—a jiggling like the dance of a distant star seen by telescope through the unsteady molecules of the atmosphere. It was something he seemed to detect not by sight alone. Another sense was at work here, thought Joe; one he did not quite understand. One he'd probably deny having if anyone began to describe it.

Dick was either lying or snowjobbing. Whatever the technicality of it, he was saying one thing and meaning another. Joe had talked to enough criminal suspects who were concealing information to recognize the subtle indicators. When you developed this sense you didn't need a polygraph. Like the polygraph, your sense wasn't admissible as evidence, but it was there, for your own guidance.

So if Dick was saying he'd be back soon—and the machine of Joe's sense was flashing "Tilt!"—it meant that Dick, for some reason, *wasn't* coming back soon.

Having gone this far in his thinking, Joe reined in upon himself. Now he was being more than stupid; he was being unnecessarily emotional. Face it, Joe, he told himself. You never have liked the way the guy looks at Zia, so you're trying to find something bad in him. Really *reaching* for it.

Dick swung himself out of the cave and onto a precarious starting foothold in a thin diagonal crack a few feet beyond the entrance. In a flowing motion, he curved himself upward to a fingerhold upon a protuberance Joe hadn't even seen till now.

The computer tapes of Joe's subconscious were whirring.

Joe said, "You *are* coming back, right?" He wasn't completely sure why he said it. "Either that, or sending someone here. That's what you're going to do, isn't it?"

Glancing back only briefly as he moved upward another few inches, Dick said, "What the hell kind of question is that?"

"It's one I don't think you're answering," said Joe.

"Shut up!" said Dick. "I've got to keep my mind on this!"

He had come to a stretch with a rougher surface. He quickened the pace of his climbing, moving lithely and fluidly, propelling himself at each step from footholds Joe still failed to see. He knew his stuff, you had to give him that. He'd seemed to be saying, tacitly, on several occasions, that he was the greatest goddam rock climber in the world. He just might be.

He was higher above them—beyond the reach of their normal voices now. He was completely encapsuled in his task; he was as alone up there, now, as though he'd been a million light-years removed from them. He would pause now and then to find a hold, and presently continue with his climb, floating upward, making a liar out of poor old Isaac Newton.

Joe kept alternating his glance between the climber and the sasquatches out in the gorge. One lifted its head momentarily over a rock; Joe hefted the rifle, and the creature ducked back into concealment again. So far, so good.

"What was that all about?" asked Zia.

"What was what all about?"

"What you said to Dick. About his coming back."

Joe frowned. "I don't know. Maybe I'm thinking crazy. Maybe this lack of nourishment has made a couple of brain cells go haywire."

242

"Why on earth wouldn't he come back?"

"That's the key question."

"Joe, this is no time for Zen koans, if that's what you're up to."

"The sound of one hand clapping?" That made him feel better. Now *he* was sharing one of these little intellectual snobberies with Zia. He peered at the climber, sixty or seventy feet above them. Dick had found a temporary resting place and was hammering a jam nut into a fissure; a rope affixed to this would give him a start toward the next fingerhold.

The computer tapes kept whirring.

Joe began as though musing. "Everything seemed awfully easy from the beginning," he said. "The way you got Cadbury's backing almost immediately. Good for their image, they said. Somehow it didn't ring true, even then. And then the tooth disappearing the way it did. Dick admitting just now he'd had it stolen. As though he knew only one way to get the information he wanted. The cloak-and-dagger way. Do you see what I mean?"

"No."

"Okay, take it from another angle. He'd said he was impressed by your presentation. He seemed already sold on the idea that bigfoot existed. But he had to confirm without a doubt. He had to get that tooth secretly analyzed by an expert he had confidence in."

"Understandable," said Zia, shrugging.

"But how was he seeing bigfoot, provided the thing existed? As something that ought to be found—or as something that ought not to be found?"

"Now you *are* getting Zenful," she said.

"Think back, Zia. There were times when Dick almost seemed to be sabotaging the expedition. At first he didn't want to see the tracks Eddie had found. Didn't want to land there; since when was he such a stickler for regulations? He didn't want all of us to climb the waterfall. Said at first he'd go himself and take a look. He kept saying we ought to simply shoot a sasquatch, but, with plenty of opportunity, he never went ahead and did it. As though he didn't *want* the quick, simple evidence that would have been. He tried to keep you from approaching the creatures. He kept talking about turning back—bringing in the chopper, which would have scared them away. He couldn't overplay his hand, of course, but if there was a seemingly reasonable objection, he made it."

"Are you saying he didn't want us to bring a sasquatch in?"

"I'm still trying to figure out what I'm saying."

"Joe, Dick had as much of a stake in this as any of us."

"But what kind of a stake?"

"Joe, please. You're looking for trouble where there isn't any. I used to ride a horse like that. A perfectly clear day with everything quiet, and he'd be looking from side to side, hoping a rabbit would pop out of the brush and scare him so he could shy and throw his rider."

"I hope," said Joe, "I honestly hope I'm wrong as hell."

They watched in silence as Dick, now a speck on the cliff face above them, continued his climb. For brief intervals he would be hidden by an outthrust of rock, but then he would appear again, still moving steadily toward the crest.

The sun, behind a fraying blanket of cloud, was higher in the sky now. They could see its diffused pale-yellow disc almost overhead. Across the gorge, the heavy snowbank that rose from the top of the cliff took on a beige-tinted glow in the increasing light. Joe hadn't liked the look of that snowbank from the beginning; he'd been greatly relieved when the concussion from the shots they'd fired hadn't jarred loose an avalanche. Maybe Zia was right; maybe he just kept looking for trouble that wasn't there.

Far above them now, Dick reached the top and disappeared. There should have been a joyous pealing of bells. There was only the gray silence of the canyon.

"Thank God!" said Zia.

Joe nodded. "Mind if I join you in that?"

"I didn't know you indulged," she said.

"I didn't, either," said Joe.

Chapter Sixteen

Shreds of cloud swirled in the wind outside the cave. Snow flurries danced through the canyon. Wraiths were out there, thought Joe, searching for them. Evil spirits out of Emory Greer's catalogue of the grotesque, or Tom Quick's list of the supernatural, or out of someone else's arcane netherworld he hadn't heard of yet. They all existed because the mind of man created them. And, having created such evil, man looked upon it in surprise and immediately blamed his God or his gods for it. Who, me? I didn't do it. The Greater Powers did. They made *me*, and then they made all these troublesome things just to bug me. Why? I don't know why. Must be some kind of game they play.

Joe sighed. Crazy thoughts. Was this part of the slow disintegration? Did the mind start wasting away, just like the body? Somewhere he'd heard the mind remained clear to the end. It just went to show you; you couldn't believe everything you heard.

"How long have we been here now?" asked Zia.

"Since the world began," said Joe.

He sat with his back against the wall of the cave. He stayed near the mouth of the cave with the rifle across his knees, at an angle, so that the sasquatches would be able to see it if they looked. The beasts had to be looking; they were surely watching constantly. By day he glimpsed them occasionally. They were showing themselves more often, more boldly now. At night he heard them grunting and snuffling about just below the cave. With Zia, he shared the night watches, alternating two hours at a time through the long darkness. Occasionally they'd stab the darkness with the flashlight beam, but the batteries were weakening now and soon they'd be deprived of even this puny weapon against the forces of evil.

He had fully expected the sasquatches to climb and attack by now, but for some reason they had not. Zia said they saw the simple truth of the situation. Why bother themselves to kill their trapped quarry when time would do it for them?

He glanced at Zia. Her face was haggard. He knew his own was too. He saw it each morning when he heated water on the Phoebus stove and shaved in the small signal mirror. It was something to do to keep from falling apart. Zia kept herself busy too; she'd used the little sewing kit to repair her torn clothes, and each day she took a whore's bath, as they'd called it in the army, dipping a rag in a pot of water and dabbing here and there.

And, Christ, he was hungry! It had been a sharp ache at first. Now it was a dull ache. He kept tasting his own bile.

Somehow, he had to keep talking. About anything. Even nonsense would do.

"You're wrong about me," he said to Zia.

"In what way?"

"I don't look for trouble, like that horse of yours. I look at the bright side."

"You do?"

"Sure. For example, here we are in this mess. And I keep thinking: well, I *wanted* to be alone with you, and now it's happening."

"Are you trying to cheer me up?"

"I'm trying to cheer myself up. And doing a lousy job of it, too."

"You're doing fine," said Zia. "What are you like at a real breakfast table, Joe?"

"Grouchy," he said. "Isn't everybody?"

Okay, the bright side. They still found each other

good company. They hadn't, for a moment, lacked something to talk about. They rubbed these little jokes on each other like balm for their mutual despair.

"I miss Pete," said Zia. "I miss Em. They both used to irritate me, but now I miss them." She sighed. "I miss everybody in the world."

Outside, after a while, the wind stopped blowing in gusts and became a constant hoarse whisper from the south and west. A thick layer of cloud, pushed along by the wind, kept rolling across the sky. Joe watched it for some minutes. "Even if we could get out of here," he said, "we'd have this crazy weather. And the rocks and cliffs and snowbanks and all the ridges—world's biggest obstacle course. We'd have to travel light. Maybe even leave the knapsacks behind."

"I'll take it," said Zia. "I'll take anything if it gets us out of here."

"Wait a minute," said Joe.

"What for?"

"What did I just say?"

"Something about walking out of here."

"Knapsacks," said Joe. "I was thinking about the knapsacks."

"What about them?"

"Pete's. Em's. Dick's. They left them here. Dick all but stripped himself to make that climb."

"Of course!" Zia lifted her head. "Maybe something in them. Something edible, let's hope. Why didn't we think of that before?"

Joe rummaged excitedly in the first of the Chouinard packs. It had been Emory Greer's. He found several pairs of clean wool socks and Greer's pocket Bible. But no food. Pete's knapsack was next. There was a reducing glass for viewing a scene and a small packet of lewd photos. And then, in Dick's pack, he found what he'd hoped for. In triumph he withdrew a plastic envelope of dried beef sticks. *Perky Jerky*, said the label; *The New Taste Treat!*

They forced themselves to chew slowly.

Joe poked through the rest of the pack's inedible contents. He found a crumpled newspaper clipping, evidently stuffed into the pouch at one time and then forgotten. He opened it, flattened it, and began to read. He was not looking for anything significant, he was merely satisfying another, lesser hunger. The old cowboys, in their bunkhouses, with nothing else to read through the long winters, had turned to the cans on the shelves and memorized their labels, reciting them to each other, as a litany.

He read:

SOLONS SEEK RULING
ON LUMBERING RIGHTS

The House Environmental Resources Committee began hearings today on proposed legislation to designate the Kayatuk Wilderness in Washington State as a "dedicated area," closed to lumbering and mineral rights.

Under the present Wilderness Act, Public Law 88-577, lumber and mineral resources may be harvested from such areas, even though they are ordinarily closed to all mechanical equipment or construction.

Environmentalists, led by motion picture star Roger Kingston, have called for a halt to all logging operations, which, they say, contravene the purpose of the act to preserve a vast, pristine wilderness.

Kingston, president of the People's Union for Resources and the Environment, will be the first to testify today. PURE last year blocked construction of the Painted River Dam, which would have killed off the crowned otter, a rare species listed as endangered.

PURE claims that the Kayatuk hosts numerous endangered species, citing among them the legendary "bigfoot," a huge, apelike creature rumored to inhabit the Northwest.

Lobbyists for the National Forest Products Association are scheduled to present their side of the controversy in upcoming sessions.

Wallace P. Kegelmeyer, president of Cadbury, Inc., and a spokesman for the industry, issued a statement to the press at a news conference yesterday.

"To close the wilderness to logging," he said, "would be to virtually cut off the nation's supply of lumber—a resource as important as oil or iron, and rapidly becoming just as expensive."

The proposed Kayatuk restrictions are considered "pilot legislation" for possible further closures of other wilderness areas throughout the country.

Joe showed the clipping to Zia.

"Yes. I knew about this," she said.

"I'm wondering," said Joe. "I'm wondering if it doesn't explain a few things."

"Such as?"

"Cadbury agreeing to finance the expedition so quickly. Dick Charterhouse throwing all the little obstacles in."

"Joe, you're not going to get on that kick again, are you?"

"Okay, call me a suspicious cop. Call it built-in paranoia—an occupational disease. But listen. Dick is naturally devious. He's conditioned himself to operate that way. Like those professional bunco artists who can't buy a stick of gum; they have to invent an elaborate scam to get it free."

"I don't know, Joe—"

"Let me go on with this. I'm working it out for myself, too. Let's look at it from Dick's viewpoint. You come along with the best proof yet that bigfoot's somewhere in the Kayatuk. Chances are excellent you'll find the creature, if not with Cadbury's backing, then in some other way. If you do, it makes a big splash, out there. More than a snail darter or the crowned otter. A near-cousin of man people can really identify with. That does it, as far as the legislation is concerned. Kayatuk and maybe all the other wildernesses are closed up, tighter than drums."

"In that case, Cadbury would hardly help find the creature."

"You forget Dick's devious ways, Zia; his compulsively devious ways. Here's where it starts to twist and turn. You're going to find bigfoot, anyway—at the very least you're going to create an even stronger general belief in the creature's existence. So the thing for Cadbury to do is put somebody in control to make sure you *don't* bring the creature back with you!"

"I follow you," said Zia, frowning, "but I don't think I like where we're going."

"Stay with me. Okay, backing the expedition costs Cadbury fifty big ones or thereabouts. A drop in the bucket, considering the millions involved. Dick's got to pretend to be with us—he can't afford to show his hand. He goes through all the proper motions, many of them genuine, so that we can't have the slightest suspicion as to his real purpose. But all the while he's doing whatever he can get away with to make us draw a blank. Some of the angles he thinks out in advance, some he ad-libs. The more I think about this, the more everything begins to fall into place."

"It's still hard to believe—"

"So is bigfoot, till you start to put the evidence together. Now we start to see answers to some of those questions that were quietly bugging me all along. Why did Dick insist on Pete Hollinger as cameraman? He knew Pete was a loser; if Pete himself didn't blow it, Dick could dominate and control him. Why did he keep suggesting, in effect, that we break off the search? Because he had to be sure we came back empty-handed. And then he would have surprised us by denying we ever saw the creatures. It would have been his word against ours. The best part of the plan—from his viewpoint—was that bigfoot would have seemed more like a myth

251

than ever before. If an elaborate expedition and an expert such as yourself had failed to uncover the creature, then *surely* it couldn't exist!"

"I don't know." Zia's frown was going through a number of variations. "It seems to hold together when you say it, but when I think about it—well, I don't know."

"One more bit of evidence." Joe looked at the gray sky and the hostile floor of the canyon spread out before them. A bigfoot stirred its bulk behind a distant rock. "Dick hasn't come back yet, and he hasn't sent anyone. He's had time to make it out and get help by now."

Her eyes widened. "He wouldn't!" she said. "He wouldn't just—just leave us here to die!"

"You wouldn't," said Joe. "I wouldn't. Most people wouldn't. Dick Charterhouse would."

Zia was still struggling with the belief that was trying to press itself upon her. "I almost liked Dick," she said. "I almost liked him too much."

"So I noticed," said Joe.

"If what you say is true, we're—we're stuck here. Shall I say it plain? Yes, I think I will. We're dead, Joe. We're as good as dead."

"Not yet we're not."

"But what can we do? Go down there and run the gamut of those creatures? Maybe that would be best. Maybe that would get it over with, and we wouldn't be sitting here, dying slowly."

"Did I once tell you I was a philosopher without a philosophy?" asked Joe. "Well, I think I've got one now. We're all going to die sometime, and mostly we don't think about it because it would just make us flip our lids. Well, right now we still know that same, inescapable fact. The only difference is that we see it coming a little sooner than we thought. But there's a little time left. Let's use it. Let's go on living the way everybody does. Bravely. That's an exhilarating thing, and its own reward."

Zia studied Joe for a long moment, and then said quietly, "Joe, make love to me."

He raised his head. "Here? Now?"

"All right, it isn't the honeymoon suite. No soft lights and sweet music. Not even a hot shower afterward. But make love to me, Joe. Give me your baby if you can. I want to do this before I die. And I'm glad it's you, Joe. I'm glad it's you...."

In the bubble of the helicopter, Eddie Lorenzo kept scanning the broken landscape below. The jaunty tips of his mustaches swung like sensory antennae.

"Nothing but rocks and snowbanks here, Zack," he said.

Sheriff Winfield nodded. "If anybody *was* down there, in country like that, they'd be long gone by now, huh?"

"I'm afraid so," said Eddie.

They'd seen nothing alive since those bighorn sheep they'd spotted, high on another ridge, some twenty minutes ago. They had landed at the second base camp and found it deserted, with no signs to show them which way the bigfoot hunters had gone. The gusting winds had made the landing difficult, and had also kept Eddie from flying as close to the peaks and ridges as he would have wished. He'd had to fight the whirlybird a bit to make it behave ever since they'd entered the airspace over the mountains. He was feeling the beginnings of fatigue from the nervous strain of that kind of flying.

Zack Winfield wore a quilted vest with a collar that came up around his shock of stiff white hair, rather like the cowl of a lifejacket. His weathered face was expressionless as he searched the ground below, but his eyes were cold and bright. If there was anything at all down there, he figured he'd spot it. He still knew what to look for in the mountains, even though he spent most of his time behind a desk and within the confinement of four walls these days.

Eddie looked at the fuel gauge. "We'd better head back pretty soon."

"If we got to, we got to," said Winfield, shrugging. "I wish to hell people would let somebody know where they're going when they disappear like this."

"They should have used the chopper," said Eddie, nodding. "But they decided it would scare bigfoot off. I kind of doubted that, but, what the hell, it was their party, not mine."

"Swing over toward that big slope of snow," said Winfield, nodding at the white mountainside where it plunged down to the lip of the high gorge they were crossing.

"I don't want to get too close," said Eddie. "These damned gusts come out of nowhere."

"Well, do what you can, huh?"

The helicopter curved toward the flank of the mountain. Its peak was high above them, almost lost to sight. Puffs of powdered mist detached themselves from the slope in several places and drifted off to disperse in the air. One long stretch of snow seemed to quiver for a moment, as though about to break loose. The *whump-whump-whumping* of the chopper blades bounced against the mountain.

"This is close enough," said Eddie.

"Okay," said Winfield. "To hell with it for today. I don't think we're gonna find 'em anyway. Could be they're gone for good. A lot of people never get found again in this country."

"Maybe the bigfeet got them," said Eddie.

"Bigfeet!" Winfield snorted. "Come on, Eddie. Let's go home."

Joe and Zia, at the mouth of their cave, and close to the edge waved frantically at the helicopter across the canyon. It was silhouetted against the white flank of the mountain, which, by contrast, made it seem only more tiny and distant. It had swooped downward briefly, though not below the level of the tops of the cliffs. Now it was rising again, climbing away from the gorge at a shallow angle.

"Hey! Over here! Over here, goddammit!" Joe shouted with all the voice he could find. He knew that was useless, knew that they couldn't possibly hear, but he shouted anyway. The helicopter had been too far away, ever since it had appeared, for anyone inside to see them clearly even if he had looked their way, which probably he had not. In desperation, Joe fired the rifle into the air. The helicopter kept its course.

"Come back!" Zia whispered. "Please! Come back!"

It was crossing the glacier at the head of the canyon now and still rising. The side of the mountain trembled, and the snow rippled like skin on flexing muscle. A cold white smoke of powdered snow suddenly rose from it, upward and outward. The massive snowbank twitched and heaved. A great long chunk of snow broke loose and began to slide. It carried more snow along with it as it plunged downward. There was a rumbling sound, and then the rumbling sound became a roar. It was like a speeding freight train in the night. It was a harsh, angry sound that cauterized the air of the canyon.

Joe and Zia stared in icy shock as they watched the avalanche gather momentum. Huge masses of snow began to pour into the gorge. Tons of white stuff, tumbling down like liquid filmed in slow motion; it began to fill the jagged gash of the gorge below the mountain.

The sasquatches, in their places of concealment, had remained motionless as the helicopter passed by, but now they suddenly broke from the rocks and began to run before the great moving walls of snow that were trying to overtake them. Joe saw one creature throw itself forward in a diving motion before the line of white oblivion dropped over it.

"Oh, no!" said Zia, staring. "Oh, no!"

Joe put his arm about her and pressed her shoulder.

The roaring sound died away, falling in upon itself like the settling snow. White smoke rose from the canyon floor. High on the mountainside several minor avalanches stirred, as though to join the big slide that had left them behind.

The sky was still. The canyon was settling into its new silence. Joe and Zia looked at each other, and then outward again, unable to speak, or, perhaps, finding nothing in their minds that needed to be said.

Chapter Seventeen

The terrain, here in this lower valley, began to look familiar to Dick Charterhouse. Of course, all the valleys looked much like one another in these mountains—and there were so many, so endless many of them—but it was his feeling as much as his conviction that this was the watershed where he'd almost made it with Zia in the hot-spring pool, and where Harry Yates, the prospector, had died. If so, he was on the home stretch.

He'd entered this valley at a place near its farthest end, surmounting a sharp ridge of sawtoothed rock to get to it, and sliding down an almost vertical incline of rubble and scrub timber to the shallow V of its floor. The V was beginning to broaden as the valley widened and as it descended gently and almost imperceptibly to a lower altitude.

It was green here—greener than anywhere he'd been for the past few days. He'd walked through Hell, and he still could hardly believe his luck in making it. Well, yes, he *could* believe it—it hadn't been entirely luck. As much as anything it had been his consummate skill and his rock-jawed determination that had pulled him through. He knew all there was to know about wilderness survival, after all. He knew how to survive in the mountains, in the jungle, in the air, and under the sea, and even in the environment of civilization, where the dangers were more subtle but no less threatening. He'd been born with a magnificent body and a superior mind, and he'd trained them to survive, anywhere.

After leaving Joe and Zia in the cave, and gaining the summit of the cliff above them, he had started out over a rough plateau of rock and ice in jumbled profusion. He'd thought at first of circling toward the place where the waterfall emerged from its tunnel, but ridges that would have exhausted him had he tried to climb them barred his way in that direction. Using his pocket compass, he had embarked upon an even more circuitous route. He'd worked out the true compass points mentally, cranking in the twenty-two degrees easterly variation in this part of the world, and hoping that metallic deposits in the rock were not adding significantly to the deviation. He'd checked his directions against the sun when he could see it from time to time.

He traveled light and he traveled fast. He'd carefully weighed the advantages of any gear he might bring along against the weight and bulk of such gear as an impediment to his difficult climb. He had almost left the Smith & Wesson Magnum behind, but had decided at the last moment that this was the one piece of equipment he couldn't do without. He wasn't thinking of protection; he was thinking of food. If he could keep himself nourished, he could push on through this wilderness indefinitely.

Well, all right, there *had* been a bit of luck, now that he thought it over. The sudden local squall had come upon him, assaulting him with rain that was like steel BB shot. He'd sought shelter in a natural lean-to of slanting rocks, and there, to his great and joyful surprise, he'd found the half-eaten carcass of a bighorn lamb. Some hunting animal—a cougar, for a guess—had dragged it there, and, after eating its fill, had left the remainder, probably intending to return. He'd hacked at the raw flesh with his hunting knife (that, too, had been necessary equipment), and crammed it into his mouth, disciplining himself not to eat too much too quickly at first. The squall had mounted in fury, and he'd had the good sense to stay where he was rather than go out into it. It had trapped him there all through the freezing night and for much of the next day. He had waited patiently.

There had been another delay at the bottom of a deep ravine. Crossing a broad patch of volcanic rock, he'd fallen through a sinkhole into one of the sewer-like tubes found in lava formations. The walls of the sinkhole had been sheer and glassy, and at first he'd been unable to climb out again. He wished, at that moment, that he had not discarded his ice ax, rope, and climbing hardware after reaching the top of the cliff; he'd made a bad decision there because he'd acted too hastily, but even J. Richard Charterhouse III couldn't hit the nail on the head a thousand times out of a thousand. Nine hundred and ninety nine, perhaps, but not a thousand.

He had patiently collected loose rock in the tube, chipping some of it away with his hunting knife, and, by the end of the day, he'd been able to build a pile of rock to stand upon. Reaching upward, he'd found the first handhang, raised himself into the sinkhole and chimneyed up the rest of the way.

He followed an erratic course to the long valley, but kept his bearings all the way. The meat he'd brought along from the bighorn lamb sustained him. He came upon a rabbit and shot it. The Magnum slug, smashing through the creature, didn't leave much, but what there was at least afforded a change of diet. He nibbled upon juniper buds and the shoots of sweet alpine grasses. This was how the bigfeet ate.

The valley was looking more familiar every minute. If it *was* the right place, that offshoot canyon with the hot-spring pool would be, maybe, half a day ahead of him. He'd look forward to a bath there. Too bad he'd been interrupted there before he'd scored with Zia Marlowe. Cute kid, Zia. He'd remember her. You forgot most of the women you actually had, and, for some reason, always remembered the ones you didn't quite make it with. That was probably because the ones you didn't make it with were fewer in number.

A thousand feet above him a falcon crossed the sky. At least it looked like a falcon, the way it coursed swiftly along on its pointed wings. He'd looked into falconry once—that sheik in the oil and desert country he'd operated in had been quite a nut on it—and he knew the difference between the broad-winged accipiters and the true falcons. He hadn't thought there were many falcons left in the world.

He pushed on, down the valley, feeling better and stronger with each passing moment.

Self stirred in the great whiteness that had closed over her. She was alive! How could that be? It was surely death that had descended upon all of them only a moment ago. The mountain had fallen, as Old One had said it might sometime, and that had seemed another of his foolish tales, and no one had believed him. Or had he said this? Had *he* said it, or was it something Self had once thought of on her own? She couldn't quite remember now. The snow all around her was pressing upon her mind, too, making it as immobile as the rest of her.

She tried to move and found that she could, a little. Her arms made progress through the packed snow. She wriggled desperately and tried to claw upward through the heavy stuff. Her lungs ached, and she realized that she was not breathing. She struggled frantically now, and more of the snow gave way. There was the beginning of light above her. Her hand broke through the snow and emerged into the air above its surface. With a final desperate heave, she thrust herself upward, and then, with her head free, gasped mightily, gulping in a series of welcome breaths.

When both her head and shoulders were free, she saw and understood what had happened, and why she had not died. She had been in front of an outcropping that formed a shallow overhang where the pursuing wall of snow had reached her, and this had kept it from slamming down upon her directly. And so, she *had* survived; there was life ahead still to be lived; she must now go about the business of accepting it.

Emerging fully from the snow now, and pulling herself farther upward on the edge of the overhang, Self looked all about and saw that the thick white cover of the snow was everywhere. Wisps of fine powder were still rising from it, and wind gusts were darting in to snatch these wisps and carry them away. None of the others were in sight. She'd glimpsed them fleeing from the avalanche, as she herself had done, and she'd seen some of them disappear under that rolling wall of white. She alone was alive, then, at least as far as she could determine in this moment.

She sought to move across the surface of the snow now, and found that she floundered in its depth, making little progress. She halted and looked for firmer ground somewhere. There was none of it between herself and the caves at the head of the canyon. In fact, most of the caves—those at ground level, at any rate—had disappeared behind the snow that had piled itself into the gorge. It was almost as though this were a new place; as though, here, the Place of Safety had never existed.

She continued to flop and stumble forward, toward the cliff wall that ran the length of the gorge. There she should be able to climb above the snow and make her way to the top. From the top, she would strike out and go...

Where?

Well, somewhere. It was only certain that she must leave the gorge. The gorge was no more. The others were no more. There was no one now to groom her or be groomed in turn; no one to bring food from the outside world; no one to communicate by grunts and gestures and give accounts, or listen to accounts, of what had been done. There was no male to penetrate

261

her and give her the joyous pain. There would be no more dancing in the moonlight.

She was on her own. She must find food first. She was not hungry at this moment, but in time she would be. She must strengthen herself with food for the long journey. The long journey where? She did not know exactly, but somewhere, across many mountains, there were others of her kind. And she had to find others in order to survive; to be able to bring forth the young one within her when it grew big enough to emerge. This was the most important of all the things she must do now: bring forth that young one.

Looking off to one side, she suddenly saw the tiny figures of the Pink Skins coming toward her.

She had almost forgotten about the Pink Skins who had been in the cave and who, in time, would die if they were to remain there. There had been four of them at first. One had left the cave and had been killed by Yellow Fur, who himself had been slain by the firestick. A second had climbed the cliff away from the cave. He had not been pursued; it made no difference whether he starved to death in the cave or simply removed his presence, for either of these produced the desired result, which was for the troublesome Pink Skins to be gone. And so two were already gone, and that left—how many? She couldn't handle the subtraction. She counted the Pink Skins approaching her and thus discovered empirically that the remainder was two.

One thing was suddenly plain to her. She was not afraid of these two Pink Skins coming toward her now. They were close enough to identify. One was Small Female, the other was Male-with-Broken-Face. He carried a firestick, but it was slung across his back and not pointed at her. Her feeling went even further than the absence of fear. She *wished* to have them come near. She needed someone else in order to survive now, and the Pink Skins—though puny and much too garrulous—were enough like the Ones to fill that need. Clearly, these two were not hostile. That was evident in the way in which they came toward her; in the very way in which they held themselves. They were not proper creatures, like the Ones, but for the time being, Self decided, they would do.

Joe and Zia, who had been stumbling with great difficulty through the deep snow, came to a halt several yards away from the sasquatch who stood before them. It still amazed Zia that the creature had stayed in place, evidently waiting for them.

"Sassy!" said Zia. "Good girl! Easy, Sassy. We won't hurt you. Really we won't."

"Don't make that a promise," said Joe cautiously.

"She won't attack," said Zia. "Keep the gun on your back. Stay perfectly still."

"I hate to say this, Zia, but we'd better kill her."

"No." Zia shook her head. Quickly, firmly, with finality.

"If we'd brought the dart gun we could just drop her and take those samples. Now the only way is to kill her."

"I can't let you do that, Joe. I just can't."

The sasquatch made murmuring sounds. Zia raised her hand. The sasquatch imitated the gesture. Their fingers touched. Zia tried to take the creature's hand, but Sassy hastily drew it back again.

"All right," said Joe. "You touched her again. Now let me kill her. God knows it'll make me sick, but we have to get our evidence and move out of here. It's a long, rough walk ahead. I hope we make it."

"We will. And so will she."

"What do you mean, so will she?"

"She'll follow, Joe. I know she will. There are darts at the camp. We can inject her by hand there, and take the samples. She *may* even gain enough confidence in us to let us take them without tranquilizing her."

"It won't work," said Joe.

"It will. I'll make it work. Anyway, I won't let you kill her. Rather than that, I'll lose her."

Joe sighed deeply. "Lose her—lose everything you've worked for. Well, what the hell. You can't win 'em all."

Dick Charterhouse found everything in place at Base Camp II. The helicopter had landed here recently, he noticed by examining the ground, but whoever had visited had disturbed little of the equipment or supplies. There was food, and there was even a bottle of Chivas Regal. He drank and felt refreshed. He'd bathed thoroughly in the hot-spring pool up the valley, and he was beginning to be himself again.

Now it was time to radio in, summon the helicopter, and leave the wilderness. He'd start the generator, switch on the rig, and begin calling. But not quite yet. First he had to work out a precise plan in his mind. He had to construct his story, examine it carefully for inconsistencies, then graft it upon his memory so firmly that it would seem real, even to him.

He sat in the main tent and sipped scotch slowly. The tactical objective, first. This was to convince everyone that bigfoot never had been found and, indeed, did *not* exist. That, as he'd carefully explained to Wallace P. Kegelmeyer, would almost assure the demise of any legislation to close the Kayatuk to logging on the frivolous grounds of protecting an endangered species. It would be a double-barreled shot at the opposition. Once he proved that bigfoot didn't exist, that fag-commie movie actor (*probably* a fag; *probably* a commie) would be discredited for bringing up such foolishness in the first place. With his popular leadership withdrawn, the environmentalists would lose most of their clout.

It was a good thing he'd been able to make Kegelmeyer see how this thing would go. The man was almost in awe of Dick's background. He read spy stories all the time. To entertain him, Dick made up tales about his own career. He told of shooting it out in dark alleys with sinister foreign agents when actually he'd been at a desk most of the time digging into open sources for data with which to compile folders. That was one of the weird things about the OTR, and the CIA, too, for that matter. They insisted you take all that cloak-and-dagger training—everything from parachute jumping to brewing the right poisons—and then sat you at a desk and made you put folders together or write reports. The closest you ever got to derring-do was recruiting foreign nationals to do the actual dirty work.

The legend, then. Spy buffs called it the cover story; in the business it was known as "the legend." It would consist of a series of patches designed to cover his ass. Asscover One: Joe and Zia *might* make it out of the wilderness. He'd have to deny leaving them behind deliberately; he'd have to claim that they'd become separated from each other and that he'd truly thought them lost and possibly perished. Asscover Two: by an even longer chance, they *might* bring back some evidence of the creature's existence. Stonewall this one; get some scientist who would cooperate to cast doubt on the blood tests or urine tests or whatever they came up with. Relieve them of the stuff before it was tested, if possible. They wouldn't know how to protect it securely. Asscover Three: The worst eventuality would be for them to be found, by the searching helicopter perhaps, and for a sasquatch then actually to be shot and brought in. In that case, his mission would have failed, but he'd plead blackout and amnesia under the rigors of his walk out of the wilderness, and even they wouldn't realize he'd left them behind deliberately, and his ass would still be covered. He'd be, in fact, something of a hero—the codiscoverer of the sasquatch—and even Cadbury wouldn't come off too badly. They could still make pious promises about protecting the precious creature while they continued their logging, and, since they'd now be regarded as such public benefactors, they'd be believed.

He had it knocked no matter what happened. And

he loved the devious way in which he'd worked it all out. It had the richness and complexity of a symphony.

Glancing through the fly of the tent now, he saw figures approaching down the long slope of the valley. There seemed to be three of them. He grabbed binoculars. Good Christ, there was Zia—and Joe next to her!

The worst had happened. They'd made it out of the gorge.

But who was the third figure, the very tall figure slogging along wearily beside them?

He swung the binoculars a fraction of a degree. He saw the sasquatch and he did not believe it. He, who had seen everything and was therefore prepared to believe anything, did not believe what he saw this time. Not for a long, hanging moment in which his heart went *lub-lump!* at least three times....

Joe and Zia, with Base Camp II in sight now, quickened their steps. They were weary, but not as weak or exhausted as they might have been without Sassy. In fact, as Zia observed several times, and in several different paraphrasings, they might not have been walking anywhere without her.

She had tagged behind as they moved forward, down the snow-filled gorge. She had followed even more closely in the tunnel, and then she'd climbed down the rockface beside them, to where the long, slender waterfall splashed into its icy pool in the lower canyon. And there, in the greener slopes of that canyon, she'd led them to edible buds and roots in the timber stands, at first sharing with them what she herself had gathered, and afterward looking proud, Zia swore, when they learned to find these things on their own.

She had found grubworms under rooted logs and they, following her example, had eaten these. They'd grimaced, but had eaten nevertheless. Nearer the great valley, she'd uncovered a nest of hibernating marmots, catching the torpid creatures easily before they could scuttle away. Zia noticed that she found a branch, stripped it of its twigs, and pointed it with her teeth to use as a probe for the marmots. "See? Toolmaking!" she'd cried, in a tone of voice Joe would have reserved for an announcement of the discovery of perpetual motion. She shared the marmots with them. Joe and Zia tore them apart and ate the still-warm, bloody flesh.

Sassy allowed them to touch her now, and frequently reached out and touched them. When they rested, she sought to groom Zia's hair; Zia allowed her to do this and then, when Sassy turned her back, she groomed Sassy in turn. Sassy now recognized the name they had given her. She understood such directions as "Come here," or "Go over there," or even "Look that way." They had picked up the meaning of several of Sassy's grunts and gestures. She could tell them, in her language, to be careful, to hurry themselves or to go more slowly, and even to be still when she wished to probe the surrounding area with her senses.

They all rested periodically to refresh themselves, halting to sit and stretch for a few minutes approximately every hour. During one of the early halts, Joe unslung the Browning autoloader from his back. Sassy shied at this, and he laid it down more slowly, while Zia spoke to Sassy in a reassuring voice. Sassy seemed less alarmed the next time he unslung the gun. Finally, a number of rests later, she sidled up to the weapon, reached out and touched it, then looked up at Joe and Zia with a querying expression that clearly said: "How does one work the magic of this thing, anyway?"

Joe marveled at her accomplishments. "She'd knock 'em dead at Disneyland," he said.

"I'll assume you're not serious," said Zia.

"I'm not. But it's a tempting idea."

"She goes free when we've got the samples. I hope we agree on that."

267

"She goes free," Joe said. "Though I *would* love to do the purple-cow bit with her. Stand her in front of somebody like Zack Winfield and say, 'There!'"

"That would be the ultimate moment!" said Zia, laughing.

Joe laughed with her.

Sassy stared at both of them for another moment, and then made sounds they swore were those of her own kind of laughter....

And now, as they began to mount the knoll on which the base camp stood, they were surprised to see someone emerge from the main tent. They were doubly surprised when they recognized J. Richard Charterhouse III.

He stood there quite calmly and watched them approach. He might have been watching them arrive in a limousine, thought Joe, up a long driveway to the porte cochere of his New England estate—or would it be Virginia? That wasn't a rumpled and dirty parka he wore—it was a fine Shetland jacket in understated harmony with his Paisley cravat and dove-gray flannel slacks. So nice to see you; so happy you could come.

Joe marched up to him, stared for a moment, and then, biting off the words as he paid them out, he said, "You son of a bitch."

"Hello, Joe. Hello, Zia," said Dick Charterhouse blandly.

Sassy halted a few steps behind them and looked at Dick quizzically, dipping her head from side to side.

Zia looked at Dick. "Let me say it, too," she said. "You sonofabitch."

"In a moment," said Dick, in his best pleasant voice, "I'm going to prove to both of you that you have no reason to be upset. That, in fact, things may have worked out to your advantage."

"Don't bother, you bastard," said Joe. "Don't even try to explain. We've guessed most of it, anyway."

"Really? What do you think you've guessed?"

"Your job was to keep us from bringing a sasquatch in. For those lousy timber rights or whatever they are. Well, you blew it, Dick."

Dick smiled. "But it's a bit early to make that assessment. I haven't finished with the job yet. At any rate, I'm glad you don't need a lot of explanations. This makes what I have to say a lot easier."

"You're not fooling us any longer, Dick. You're running scared now. You know it and we know it."

He went on as though he hadn't heard. "You know how big a stake Cadbury, Incorporated, has in this, I presume. Millions, even billions. You can understand why it will be very good for both of you if you cooperate. Money, jobs, clout—all kinds of goodies."

"What does cooperate mean?"

Dick glanced at Sassy. "There never was a sasquatch. After this one disappears, you realize you never saw any. Tracks will be all right—Eddie Lorenzo's seen them, so we're stuck with the tracks. But they didn't manage to convince the old guard before. The main thing is: no sasquatch, no pictures, no biological samples. You'll do better without all of this than you would have done with it. It's that simple."

"Did you really think we'd go for that?" said Joe.

"Of course. I wouldn't have brought it up otherwise."

"Well, now that you've brought it up, put it back down again. Let's talk about the charges I'm going to make, Dick. Leaving us to starve. Maybe attempted homicide. Malicious negligence at the very least. Five years. Nobody's ever gotten the maximum out of it before, but you will."

"There's something tacky about the next step," said Dick, still smiling. "I'd really hoped to avoid it. No choice now, I'm afraid." He took the long-barreled Magnum revolver from its holster under the parka and pointed it at them.

"What are you going to do? Shoot?" asked Joe, contemptuously. "Where will that get you?"

269

"Off the hook, I'd say. Oh, it'll be messy. Cleaning up and putting the bodies where they won't be found. Hard work, actually. But sometimes these nasty little chores have to be done. Know who always wins, Joe? The guy who's willing to do those nasty little chores."

"Murder. A nasty little chore," said Joe.

"Use any word you like for it, Joe. What I'm doing is right in the long run, you know. Two people die, but two hundred million get a resource that's badly needed to keep the nation strong. To keep the Visigoths with their hammers and sickles from slaughtering all of us as they pillage in the streets someday."

"Oh, Christ!" said Joe, in disgust. "Now, all of a sudden, you're a goddam patriot."

"In my perhaps insouciant way," said Dick, "I always was. But down to the nuts and bolts of this thing. What you do first, Joe, is very carefully and slowly take that rifle off your back and toss it toward me. A little to one side of me, if you don't mind. And very gently, Joe. No fancy maneuvers. My reaction time is a twentieth of a second. I've had it measured."

"Now, listen, Dick—"

"No, you listen. And get rid of that rifle. Now."

Joe slid the Browning over his head and off his shoulder. Thoughts of striking back tumbled like a string of Chinese acrobats through his mind. Swing the rifle at Dick. Throw it at him—distract him. Duck and rush forward, under the line of pistol fire. Get his finger on the trigger and fire the rifle. He thumbed the safety catch off with this in mind, but, watching Dick's eyes, realized that he could make none of these moves before Dick fired. He tossed the rifle to the ground.

"Thank you," said Dick. "Now, Zia, will you step forward, please? Come right here, in front of me."

"Like hell I will!" said Zia.

"I will shoot you in the leg if you don't," he said pleasantly. "It will be very painful."

Staring at Dick in disbelief, Zia moved toward

him. His cobalt eyes, flickering back and forth between Zia and Joe, were sending a clear enough message: whatever Joe was thinking of, don't try it.

Dick's free hand dipped into the pocket of his parka. He moved swiftly; Joe had barely the time to notice the tranquilizing dart with its red streamer of yarn. Dick took one step forward and, before Zia could react, jammed the dart into her thigh. She cried, "Oh, no!" and, scrambling back and away from Dick, pulled it out again.

And that *was* the moment. The one instant in which Joe might move and beat that advertised reaction time. He doubted that Dick had had it measured; it sounded like razzle-dazzle, like psychological warfare on Dick's part. Like fantasy. The man was all fantasy. Except that he translated his fantasy into real and dangerous acts. Simultaneously, now, Joe recognized the instant and used it.

Joe threw himself forward. He struck Dick in the lower torso, below the pointed gun. The gun went off with a great blast, somewhere over Joe's head. The report was ten times louder than Joe had expected it to be. He wondered if he'd been shot. He'd heard you usually didn't feel it right away. He swung his head and shoulder upward, deflecting the gun.

And then Joe knew that he had not been shot, as he'd feared. He had brought himself upright, and he had clamped his fingers on Dick's right wrist, and he was bending the big Smith & Wesson Magnum away. Dick was glaring at him; their eyes were almost in physical collision. They were rocking and jerking and swaying, each seeking to take the other off balance or break through the other's guard—

Zia felt nothing yet. She stared in dumb horror at her thigh, where the dart had penetrated. There was a spot of pain there from the bite of the needle. What had the dosage been? Enough to drop a sasquatch? That would be enough to kill a human. The antidote! she thought. The stuff came in two vials. The antidote nullified the effect of an overdose—that was why she'd chosen the M99 instead of phenocyclidine or succinylcholinechloride. If Dick had found the dart and the chemical in the main tent, the antidote ought to be in there, too. She started running toward the tent.

Dick, clamped his even white teeth together. Joe could hear his breath, and feel the heat of it. Dick could not force the revolver inward.

Joe anticipated the knee before it came up, with great force, toward his groin; he swung his pelvis back and away and shoved and, as Dick staggered back, lowered his head and butted Dick under the chin. The sound of the contact jarred painfully through Joe's own skull. Dick brought his feet back into line, shifted his center of gravity, and recovered his balance. Joe bent Dick's wrist back. The big revolver fell to the ground.

Zia reached the tent. A buzzing numbness was coming over her now. She threw herself forward toward the opened wooden box at the rear of the tent. The stenciled lettering on it said: *Finletter & Collier Pharmaceuticals*. She plunged her hand into the box and fumbled at its contents. She withdrew a vial, but could not see it clearly. The M99, or its antidote? She couldn't tell. Everything was becoming fuzzy.

Zia fell, and unconsciousness swept over her, quite languidly, and almost pleasantly.

Dick and Joe had broken apart. Now, lightly crouched, they faced each other. They moved in little arcs, first one way, then the other. Their stares were pasted on each other's eyes.

"Okay, Joe. Now we find out," said Dick.

He'd said it to distract Joe, of course, and Joe tried to ignore it, but it still started a train of thought in Joe's mind. Dick was right. Now they'd find out. It had been written, all along, that they would clash. They were...cat and dog...leopard and baboon...mongoose and snake...triceratops and tyrannosaurus rex. They were Macedonian and Persian, Roman and Goth, Gaul and Prussian,

Hatfield and McCoy. Ten million years ago each of their scrawny ramapithecine ancestors had fought this same battle on a dusty yellow plain.

They struck at each other, dodged, ducked, feinted, and struck again. They clashed together, heaved and struggled, then broke apart once more. It became a stilted ballet, like the sword duels in a kabuki play. Employing a karate blow, Dick bent and spun, then kicked at Joe's face, his leg shooting upward as it straightened itself in a line along which the *ki* could flow. In one of the bodily clashes, Joe got his thumb into the soft flesh under the angle of Dick's jaw and pushed upward until Dick gagged with pain. Each man tried to knee the other. Once Dick clapped his palms upon Joe's ears. It was the blow developed by the monk Pan Hui, of the northern Shaolin Temple school. Joe didn't know that. He only knew that his ears were numb, and he wondered if the drums had been broken.

Both men were bloody now. There was a gash across Dick's forehead and an open raw-flesh cut under Joe's eye. Several times each man tried to get near the fallen revolver in order to pick it up, but each time the other man anticipated this action and prevented it. Their swirling movements had now taken them away from the weapon, to a position lower on the knoll, where they maneuvered for the advantage of slightly higher ground, each man gaining it momentarily, then losing it in turn.

Joe was not sure when the terrible suspicion that Dick was going to win began to eat at his innards. It started with little nips, and presently was taking great, rapacious bites. Dick's blows were finding their marks a little more often than Joe's; striking a little harder than his own. Joe was backing away more; Dick was coming forward increasingly in their circling dance. Dick was an expert in dirty fighting. The dirtier the better. He'd spent much of his adult lifetime learning it and practicing what he'd learned. Joe was playing another man's game.

An old-fashioned right hook caught Joe on the side of the jaw, and he was dazed by it. He tried to strike back, but his counterpunch spent itself in empty air as Dick slipped his head to one side. Dick brought his knee up and caught Joe in the testicles, squarely this time. The pain was excruciating. Joe doubled over with it. That brought his head down, and Dick pummeled it viciously with a volley of blows from each side. The world, for Joe, began to spin. He tried to keep the strength in his extremities, but it was seeping away. His knees wobbled. He could not lift his arms high enough. Queerly, there was no pain. There were jolting shocks, but no actual pain along with them.

The ground came up and struck Joe in the forehead. He was sprawled upon the earth, with its black smell of procreation; he was supported by his elbows and knees, and Dick was kicking him with great force, first in one side, then the other. Now there was pain. It was spreading all through his gut.

He tried to raise himself and push himself to one side. He toppled instead and rolled over on his back. He threw his crossed arms up in front of his face. Dick jumped on Joe's chest. Joe thought he heard a rib crunch.

A final kick caught Joe on the side of the head. His brain, a mass of gelatin, smashed from one wall of his skull to the other. What came over him then was not absolute unconsciousness, but it might as well have been. He was immersed in gray sludge. He could not will any part of him to move. He could not so much as make his little finger twitch.

Inside the tent, Zia Marlowe was staggering to her feet. The strange buzzing sound was diminishing in her head, and her sight was clearing again. She did not know why she was recovering: she had not been able to find the antidote before she'd dropped. Perhaps Dick had not administered a lethal dose; perhaps he'd merely wished to render her uncon-

274

scious for a while to give himself a free hand with Joe. Perhaps, in snatching the dart out of her thigh so quickly, she'd kept the full dose from being injected. She couldn't think about it now. She couldn't think about much of anything.

She lurched out of the tent. Dick Charterhouse was a short distance downslope, standing over Joe's fallen figure, swaying a little. He was bloody and tattered, and his eyes gleamed wildly. His lacquered air of sophistication was gone now, and you could see him for what he was. He was insane, quite insane.

Zia saw the revolver lying on the ground. She snatched it up quickly.

Dick turned slowly to look at Zia. He blinked his eyes several times to bring them into focus. His chest was heaving. He forced himself to breathe even more deeply, gulping oxygen to nourish his senses. He saw the gun in Zia's hand.

"Give me that damned thing, Zia," he said.

She shook her head and kept the gun pointed at him.

"Give it to me!" he snapped.

"I think I'll be able to kill you," said Zia. "Yes, I think I will."

Dick shook his head. "You can't do it. You haven't got what it takes. Neither did Joe." He took an experimental step toward her. "All right, Zia, let's be reasonable. Let's be civilized about this. Obviously, you're in control. You win, Zia—I have to admit that. But you might find it difficult to stay in control till someone gets here. So let's work out an arrangement, Zia—"

And he kept walking toward her.

The hell of it was, thought Zia, that she knew what he was up to. He wasn't even being terribly subtle about it this time. He'd count upon her being unable to kill him, and he'd walk right up to her, take the gun away, then kill *her*, as he'd meant to do in the first place. Why could she not shoot him now—*now*, while it was still possible? Why did she hesitate when she knew he was hoping for that? Maybe she could do what he'd threatened to do: shoot him in the leg.

Startled by the sound of the shot when Broken-Faced Male had charged the other one, Self had scuttled away in panic. But curiosity drew her back to the vicinity of the knoll again to watch the battle.

She had seen males of her own kind battle before, but they never took their fury beyond a certain point. They would battle over females, or for supremacy in the troop, but they never meant to kill each other. That wasn't in the rules. They knew exactly when to exercise restraint and when, somewhere along the line, one had triumphed and the other had lost. The rules called for the winner to beat his chest and the loser to growl a bit as he slunk off to save his pride and show that he hadn't been *entirely* beaten.

The Pink Skins seemed to have no rules. The two men seemed determined to kill each other. She wished Broken Face to win, of course. He was her friend. She'd helped to feed him in the wilderness, and he had been gentle with her, long ago demonstrating that he meant her no harm.

They were fighting, these two males, over the female, of course. Since there was no troop around for either of them to dominate, there could be no other reason for their conflict. If Self liked the male with the broken face, she in a sense loved Little Female. Little Female had given her that strange brown food that tasted, in part, like wild honey. Little Female had touched her and groomed her and made soft noises at her, as Giver-of-Milk once had done. Oddly, Little Female had not stayed to watch the fight; she'd wandered into the curious soft cave, remaining there while the battle took place, and emerging again only when the fighting had stopped.

Now Broken Face had fallen and Blue-Eyed Male was turning away from his vanquished rival. Indeed, Broken Face seemed to be rather seriously injured.

He had certainly bled a lot—but then so had Blue Eye.

The little Pink Skin female was standing there, pointing a curious object at Blue Eye. He was walking toward her slowly, as though he feared this object. It bore a vague resemblance to a firestick. Come to think of it, it had to be a firestick of some kind. It had spoken with thunder before, just like a firestick.

It was suddenly clear to Self that Blue Eye meant to attack Little Female. And, if what he'd done to Broken Face was any example, he meant to attack her viciously and wreak terrible harm upon her.

Her first impulse was to charge Blue Eye and twist his head. Puny, like any Pink Skin, he'd hardly be able to fight her off. But Blue Eye—who seemed dangerously clever—might have some kind of magic in reserve. She'd already seen that an object other than a firestick could make that thundering sound.

Her eye fell upon the firestick which Broken Face had earlier tossed to the ground. It was still there, quite a few steps from where Blue Eye was closing in on Little Female. The idea of using the firestick came upon her in a great inspirational burst of light. She'd watched the Pink Skins use their firesticks.

She moved swiftly toward the fallen rifle and boldly lifted it from the ground. Here was the wider end, and this went against the body, near the crook of the shoulder. You pointed the narrower end at whatever you wished to kill by the magic thunder. You slipped your finger into the little ring on the underside, and rested it upon the twig that was contained there.

Dick, sensing the movement behind him, turned toward the sasquatch. His eyes widened in utter amazement.

When the firestick spoke something slammed into his chest and hurled him backward.

There was a moment of consciousness left. During it he did not, as tradition sometimes depicted it, see

277

his entire life flash before his eyes. He remembered how, in his moodier moments, he'd supposed he might die in violence sometime. A risk of his profession, after all. And he'd always imagined that if he ever did die that way it would be because he had encountered, as an enemy, someone brighter and more skillful and a hell of a lot meaner than himself. Since there weren't many people around like that, it reduced the odds considerably. That had always comforted him.

But this! To be slain by a dim-witted ape, coarse and ugly, offensively odoriferous, and not even human!

It just wasn't fair.

But nothing ever was, really. That was one of the beliefs J. Richard Charterhouse III had always lived by.

He fell and died.

Chapter Eighteen

Tom Quick watched the fight and saw the death of Dick Charterhouse through a pair of binoculars as he lay prone, high on a nearby ridge. He kept his lean, deeply lined face expressionless throughout the entire affair.

Here, just below the crest of the ridge, so that he would not readily be seen in silhouette from the valley, he had built himself a shelter that was part dugout, part lean-to. Here he had been living, waiting for the hunters to return to their base camp.

He had enjoyed building the shelter. It had been years since he'd worked with his hands. He'd taken the birch poles from the dark loam of the earth, sawn them with his folding camp saw, and trimmed them with his hunting knife; he'd added evergreen boughs, and he'd dug with his foxhole spade (nine bucks in the army-surplus store in Pickettsville), and then he'd fastened things together with twine he'd stolen from the base camp. Altogether, he thought, he'd done a job his great-grandfather, Catches Killer Whale, might have been proud of. His great-father had lived in a day when the Tillamish still had their Indian names.

Tom had visited the camp below from time to time to dip into its food stores, and, to supplement his diet; he'd caught trout in the streams with the little fishing kit he'd remembered to pack along. He'd made a whipnoose snare, hoping to catch a rabbit, but it hadn't worked too well. Maybe that was because of the peanut butter he'd used for bait. Peanut butter was great in mouse traps; it should have worked for rabbit. Anyway, the important thing was that he'd gone back to the woods and had become one with the great sky and the towering mountains. He felt spiritually cleansed.

What happened below surprised Tom now—as it must have surprised those who took part in it. The last thing he had expected to see when the hunters returned was a real live sasquatch tagging along with them. He had never seen a sasquatch, and, although he certainly believed there *were* sasquatches, he'd found it difficult now and then to sustain that belief. If it hadn't been a key element in the tribal lore—the religion he and all the Tillamish so badly needed—he might have called upon his rational side (that part of him so well educated in the white man's schools) and let that belief slip a bit.

Before he saw the sasquatch, Tom Quick had had a plan. The hunters, he supposed, would return with something like biological samples or perhaps even the decapitated head of the creature. His plan had been to relieve them of this evidence. He realized that this plan would require expert stealth on his part, or, if worst came to worst, downright threats of violence. He was prepared to rob them of the evidence at the point of a gun, if necessary. He knew he had little talent for either stealth or robbery, but rather than do nothing whatsoever, he had to make the attempt. Now it looked as though he might not be able to shortstop them after all. A puzzling turn of events indeed, down there. Only three of them had come back. The two missing hunters would be the fat movie fellow from Hollywood and Emory Greer. He could understand how the mountains might get the movie man, but he was surprised about Greer. Well, whatever had happened was in the scheme of things. *Kekahwan*, the spirit of the mountain, was both capricious and unforgiving; one should understand that before one even entered his hunting grounds.

Meanwhile, the real live sasquatch down there gave everything a new twist. He wondered how McBay and the girl had ever persuaded it to come along. They'd try to take it back to Pickettsville now, he supposed, and it would undoubtedly end up in a cage somewhere for grubby little kids with their fat mamas and mean-eyed papas to gape at. It would look out sadly through the bars and long for the freedom of the wilderness. They would, in effect, confine the sasquatch to a reservation and keep it there. The boundaries of the Tillamish reservation would then close in upon the tribe—either actually or metaphorically—and the long, slow death of his people would begin.

Tom watched Joe McBay and Dick Charterhouse battle each other. He saw Joe McBay fall. Then he saw the sasquatch pick up the gun and shoot Dick Charterhouse.

He watched as Zia Marlowe brought cold water from the stream and as she bathed his wounds. Presently she helped him to rise, put his arm around her shoulders, and supported him as he stumbled into the main tent. That was where they were now. The sasquatch was outside the tent. It was poking about idly on the knoll, perhaps looking for field mice or anything else edible in the weeds. Why it remained there Tom did not know. Joe and Zia had worked some kind of magic of their own upon it. They were probably radioing for a helicopter to come in and fetch them now; most likely they would then tranquilize the sasquatch and have the helicopter bring it in by means of a rescue stretcher on the skids.

Tom would have to work fast.

He picked up his gun—a Winchester lever-action carbine that dated back almost to the time of his great grandfather, Catches Killer Whale—and trotted downslope toward the camp.

Joe, stretched out on a folding cot in the main tent, ached in every muscle, every bone. The cuts on his

281

face smarted. Zia had daubed them with antiseptic cream, and she'd put sponges and tape where they seemed to be needed. With her help, he'd gone over all his body and found no broken bones—not even that rib he'd thought he'd heard crack—and that seemed to him a small and welcome miracle. The lacerations on his face would leave scars, and he would look more beat-up than ever. Zia had said that therefore she would love him more than ever.

She had called the airport on the radio. Eddie Lorenzo would be there as quickly as possible—weather permitting, of course. And what was this big surprise they were being so mysterious about? Zia told him to wait—and hang onto his britches.

"How do you feel now?" she asked Joe.

"Lousy. Sad and rotten and hating myself."

"Hating yourself?"

Joe sighed. "I couldn't take him. He was too good for me."

"For God's sake, get off that macho kick," said Zia. "I love you even if you're not the toughest guy in the world."

"Bully for you."

"We've got to stick together, that's all."

"Yes. I'm looking forward to that, anyway."

"Till we're both silver-haired and in rocking chairs. Just like the storybooks say."

"I wouldn't mind," said Joe.

"How about your plans for yourself, Joe? Specifically, I mean. You'll run for sheriff now, I suppose."

"I'm still not sure. Maybe you'll move on to some big university. Maybe I'll tag along and enter the ratrace again. I've been thinking. Leaving, the way I did, was running away. They need tough, ugly sonsabitches like myself to work on all those problems. Anyway, it shouldn't be hard now to make a new start. Not for the codiscoverer of *Homo Kegelmeyeriensis*."

"Not that," said Zia, smiling. "Anything but that!"

"What are you going to do with Sassy, anyway?"

"Do you think you can make it to your feet, Joe? I need a hand. We've got to take those samples, and some photos, and then let Sassy go when the chopper gets here. We'll let Eddie Lorenzo see her, or whoever comes with him. The more witnesses the better. I hope there won't be too much fuss over Dick's body, by the way."

"They won't believe how he died right away. But eventually they'll have to. They'll have to believe everything we jam right down their throats this time." He tried to raise himself from the cot. A surge of dizziness came over him. "Oh, Jesus," he said, and fell back again.

"It's all right, Joe," said Zia. "I think I can handle it alone."

"Maybe Eddie can give you a hand when he gets here."

"I'm sure he would. But that helicopter still might scare Sassy off. I've got to put her to sleep and get those samples before it gets here." She found a dart in the small crate and began to load it. She said, with the sense of a sigh, "I wish we could take Sassy with us. I've grown fond of her."

She was putting together her slides and thumbing the blade out of the handle of her field scalpel when they heard the sound of a shot outside.

It was followed by a second shot, and then another.

Disregarding his dizziness and pain, Joe swung himself upright on the cot. He stumbled out of the tent after Zia.

Tom Quick was standing near the knoll. He had a rifle to his shoulder, and he was pumping shots after Sassy, who was loping away, up the valley, with great running strides.

Zia threw herself at Tom, knocked the rifle to one side and said, "No! For God's sake, no!"

Tom turned and looked at her evenly. "It's all right, Miss Marlowe. I'm not even trying to hit the creature."

"Then what the hell *are* you doing?" Zia almost screamed it.

Tom glanced at the disappearing figure of the sasquatch. In a moment it would be out of sight behind a stand of timber. He put the rifle butt upon the ground and half-leaned on the weapon. "Just scaring it off, that's all."

Zia was aghast—pale with her fury. "You crazy goddam fool! It won't be back! You've scared it off for good!"

"That's what I sincerely hope, Miss Marlowe," said Tom.

Chet Anders, his fat pinky extended, and his fake-diamond ring glittering upon it, lifted his bourbon and branch water to his lips, tasted it, and said, appreciatively, "Ahhh!" He sat in his favorite booth in the Loggers' Lounge of the Pioneer Hotel, and Sheriff Zack Winfield, with his own bourbon and branch water, sat across from him.

"Well, what is it this time, Chet?" asked Winfield. "What is it, huh? Nothing serious, I hope. I thought things were going along pretty good."

"Oh they are, Zack. They are. You can't miss in the election now. That was a smart move, assigning young McBay to the expedition. Most people are convinced they found the damned critter this time, and they figure you had a hand in it all along. You've come up out of the manure pile smelling like a rose."

"I *still* wonder if they really saw those bigfeet. I *still* got this itchy feeling there's something to the whole story we don't know about yet."

Chet just shrugged. "I'd just drop it if I were you. The boat's on a pretty even keel now, so don't rock it. And, speaking of rocking the boat, that reminds me. You've been pretty rough on some of the little card games and things we have around the county lately."

"Little card games and things? Chet, you ought to see it. Roulette wheels. Crap tables. Bets on horses and football games. I swear, sometimes I think the Mafia's moving in on us, huh?"

"Oh, I wouldn't say it's that bad. There are outside interests, to be sure. Pickettsville's growing, and there's beginning to be a lot of money here. Naturally some outside people are going to be interested. In fact, I have some clients who are starting operations of one kind or another here. I've told them I'll use whatever small influence I might have to see that they're not interfered with."

Winfield's cold eye became suspicious. "Are you askin' me to lay off? Is that it, huh?"

"Zack," said Chet, with a dimpled smile, "you do whatever your conscience tells you to do. It's just that I'd appreciate any cooperation. I wouldn't like to pressure you into anything. I'd never spread it around, for example, that you have, on occasion, indulged in hanky-panky with some of those massage girls. I don't want our relationship to be anything like that. Just cooperation and mutual trust, Zack, that's all I ask for."

"I get it," said Winfield.

"Glad you understand. Let's face it, Zack, we all have obligations."

Winfield was frowning. He took out his corncob pipe and began to fill it from his tobacco pouch. "Is it gonna be like this from now on, Chet?"

"Relax, Zack," said Chet Anders. "Everything's going to be just fine."

Eddie Lorenzo, dressed and freshly shaved, the tips of his great mustaches newly waxed, came to the breakfast table, which was in a family room just off the ample kitchen of the cottage in the birch grove near the airport. Eleanor and young Denny were already there. Denny was eating something called Crunchies, with sliced bananas on top.

"Hi, Uncle Ed!" said Denny. "Are you going flying again today?"

"Yeah. Sure am, Denny. Taking some machinery out to the islands."

"When are you going to take me up in the helicopter, Uncle Ed?"

"Soon, Denny, soon. That's a promise." Eddie looked fondly at Eleanor, who was now pouring his coffee. She smiled back at him. He looked at Denny again. "You might as well stop calling me Uncle Ed. After tomorrow, anyway. Your mother and I would like you to be there for the ceremony. In that nice new suit of yours—and don't forget to scrub inside your ears."

"Will it be like going to church? I hate going to church."

"It'll be short and sweet, Denny. Joe McBay'll be best man. You like Uncle Joe, don't you?"

"Maybe I'll be a cop when I grow up. Or maybe a pilot. Maybe I could be both a cop and a pilot. Hey, Uncle Ed, if I'm not supposed to call you Uncle Ed, what am I supposed to call you?"

"Dad," said Eddie Lorenzo. "Okay?"

"Okay, Dad," said Denny. He attacked his Crunchies with the bananas on top of them, and concentrated quietly on the task.

In the Los Angeles hotel room, Zia awoke in the dark of the morning and reached over and touched Joe, who lay beside her.

"Hi," he said sleepily, coming awake.

It had been a busy day. There had been that TV talk show, and Joe's interview with that aluminum company about the security director they needed, and her own session with the president of the university.

"I'm hungry," she said.

"At this time of night?"

"I have this crazy desire for lox and cream cheese on a bagel and a glass of Cabernet Sauvignon."

He switched on the light and stared at her. "Hey!" he said. "Hey! You're not—"

"I don't know. I'd better have a rabbit test. If I am, Joe, you—well, you don't mind, do you?"

He smiled and leaned over her and kissed her tenderly for an answer.

Self followed the crest of a high ridge in the deepening gloom. In the darkness her silhouette would not be seen. She was drawn northward for some reason. She did not head directly northward at all times, but followed a twisting, turning route wherever pasage was afforded, bringing herself a little farther north with each leg of the journey.

Somewhere up there, deeper into the mountains, in country the Pink Skins seldom visited, there was another troop that had fled even farther from the slow advance of the predators. She couldn't remember whether Old One had told her this or whether it was something she simply knew. It seemed to her at times that something like sound, except that it was not sound, came out of the air and vibrated within her, telling her of the presence of these others, revealing the direction she must take in order to find them.

Find them she would; she was confident of that. With luck she'd make it before the Time of Snow really settled in. And having found her new Place of Safety, she'd drowse through the heavy winter, and then, in the spring, when the icicles dripped, and the streams ran high, and the edelweiss and heather appeared on the alpine slopes, she'd bring her young one into the world and become its Giver-of-Milk.

The members of the new troop would not know she'd grown the young one in her belly without a permanent mate. They would not shun her. She'd tell how she'd left her former territory when the snow fell from the mountain, burying all the others. They'd listen in wonder. They would probably have, among them, another Old One who would solemnly confirm that such things could happen.

The moon appeared, lifting its head over a sawtooth line of peaks, slowly, as though to see what the night held before gliding into it. It was fat and full now. The sky was blue-black and stars glittered against it all the way down to the horizon. The air was cold and clean.

Self stopped at a flat place along the ridge and turned toward the moon. She began to shuffle slowly, in time with the beating of her heart. A keening song rose in her throat, softly at first, and then in a great crescendo, rising to the sky. It was as clear as the waters of spring; it was as reedy-sweet as the lonely cry of the loon. It was a song of triumph and love, and of the exquisite joy of living.